LITTLE BIRD'S LULLABY

Kameo Monson

Little Bird's Lullaby

For more information about this title or other fictional works by Kameo Monson, please contact her directly at: kmonson.author@gmail.com or visit her website at KameoMonson.com

Cover Design by Wynter Book Cover Designs

Editing by Craig D. Barton

ISBN: 978-1-7325802-8-2

For Anne and her Grampa Russ

Pink Ducks or Kronosaurus?

Jen watched the brown recliner rock violently as her oldest daughter, Sydney, flung herself into it and tossed a small pile of clothing and hygiene supplies onto the floor.

"A linty toothbrush," Jen teased. "I don't think flossing works like that."

Rolling her eyes, Sydney huffed. "Why do we have to pack together?"

"Because we share supplies." Blake carried two framed backpacks into the family room and winked at their daughter.

Leaning against the couch, Jen held out her arms, and he handed her the moss-green pack. "Thanks, babe."

"The girls' packs are out there. But I can't find the one I got for Max," he said, setting his pack on the floor.

"Check by his bike," Jen said. "He's been using it for his survival supplies."

"You mean water bottles and action figures," Sydney chimed in.

"Both are imperative for survival." Blake tugged Sydney's braid and pulled a face, earning him a giggle on his way back to the garage.

Eighteen years of marriage, three children, and enough adventures for a lifetime of memories and Jen still hadn't tired of him. Smiling, she set a rolled pair of socks on his pile. She'd listened to him talk about taking the kids on a grand adventure, *the best of all, West Clear Creek*, for seven years. After hiking a portion of the wilderness area with his brother, Evan, the trip had been Blake's ultimate goal. But until Max could carry a small pack by himself, Jen wouldn't hear of it. What Blake expected the kids to do and what they could do didn't always line up.

It made sense. He'd grown up exploring the woods behind his childhood home. And with a stubborn personality, he always did what others said he couldn't. It was all he knew. It was why she loved him. But taking three young kids backpacking in a remote canyon and camping for four days hadn't screamed fun to her— not when Max had been barely out of diapers. Now that he was ten, it seemed feasible. She hoped.

Placing a small frying pan on top of the cooking-supplies pile, Jen glanced at Sydney. "Go get some pants, please."

"Dad said we'd be swimming and playing in the water the whole time."

"We'll be in plenty of water. Icy cold water that leaves you freezing once the sun sets."

As Sydney left the room, Jen's second child, Tessa, quietly straightened her pile. "She doesn't want to leave Braden. Do we need coats?"

"No, sweetheart," Jen answered. "Pants and your sleeping bag should be plenty. Did you get a second set of shoes?"

Tessa picked up one of her nylon-strapped sandals and waved it in the air. "I'll want my tennis shoes first, right?"

"That's what I'm planning on."

2

According to Blake, water shoes were a necessity. With no set trail and several water crossings, tennis shoes and hiking boots were more of a burden.

Jen smiled and shook her head as she remembered the night he'd told her why they needed to take the trip within the next year. He was adamant that the canyon was gaining too much popularity and that if they didn't go soon, the crowds would destroy the beauty found between the sandstone walls. His excitement had shone in his eyes, and despite her nerves, she couldn't tell him no.

"Mo-om!"

The pounding of her son's feet brought Jen's attention around to Max.

"I can't find my blue swimming suit."

"It's in your drawer."

"I looked there."

"Did you look in the other one?"

"Oh."

As her son ran back down the hallway, Jen started dividing supply piles.

A towel for each girl—along with three bags of homemade trail mix and a stove with a small propane canister. She opened the four-pack of waterproof flashlights, adding one to each family member's pile. Blake had his favorite hooked to his pack. As she dug into a plastic shopping bag and brought out six plastic pool tubes, Max dashed back into the room.

"I fou—I get the one with ducks!"

"It's pink," Sydney said from behind him as she threw some sweats on her clothing pile.

Max narrowed his eyes. "So. I like ducks."

Sydney's gaze tightened as she looked at Jen with desperation. She'd helped pick out the swimming tubes that they would use to float their packs across the creek, and she had chosen the pink tube with ducks for herself.

"What about this one, Max?" Jen held up a slightly smaller float with aquatic dinosaurs on it.

He shook his head. "Syd can use that one. I want the ducks."

The laundry room door squeaked as Blake walked in from the garage and set three smaller packs on the floor. "Jen, is that a Kronosaurus? That's my favorite dinosaur."

"It is?" Max eyed him.

"Sure. Do you have that in a bigger size, babe? My pack'll sink to the bottom on that one."

Max stared between the ducks and the dinosaurs.

"Besides, the gators won't be scared of the ducks." Blake picked up the pink float. "They look too much like dinner."

Their son's eyes widened. "We're gonna see alligators?"

"Blake." Jen scowled at her husband. "No, Max. There are no alligators in Arizona, remember?"

"Oh yeah, but I changed my mind. I want the dinosaurs. Kronosauruses have big teeth like alligators, except bigger. They're cool, right Dad?"

Blake took the float from Jen and handed it to Max, grinning. "Right."

Jen slapped a blue ring with cartoon swimming suits on it into Blake's hand. He glanced down, and Jen laughed as he swallowed a grimace.

"It's all they had left." She shrugged and handed a matching float to Tessa.

Blake made eye contact with each of their children, then sat down on the floor and held up five whistles that hung from bright-orange, quick-release paracord. "Do not blow these in the house or the car." He chucked a space blanket at each of them. "Who has the first aid kit?"

"Oh, Sydney—" Jen started.

Sydney slumped deeper into her chair. "What good will a pile of Band-Aids do in a canyon with a running creek?"

"Maybe not much, but the moleskin works great for blisters." Blake tapped his finger on his knee and pointed at the door leading to the garage.

Sydney clambered out of the recliner.

"Perk up, Syd. This is a family vacation. You'll love it. Green trees, refreshing ice water, trout straight from the creek. Wait until you see it. Besides, you and Tess will be the only teenage girls there. Who knows how many boys, I mean people, we might run into?" Blake winked at Jen.

"Don't make things worse." Jen gave him a friendly glare to enforce her words.

"What? Me?" He waved a hand. "Once we're back, she'll titter to all her friends about the fun she had cliff jumping."

"Cliff jumping?" Max's head popped up, and he stared at Blake. "I want to jump from fifty feet high. And I'll splash down like *spussh*."

Jen poked Max in the side and directed him to his pack and pile, then turned to her middle child. "Tess, can you divide the waterproof bags between us? Give Dad the extra one."

Grabbing the pile of assorted bags, Tessa began laying them on the piles. At least Jen had one even-keeled child. Over the past several months, Sydney had become a moody sixteen-year-old who wanted nothing to do with her family, especially her mother. Grumpiness accompanied Sydney everywhere but with her friends. And Max's energy kept Jen on her toes—probably a good thing for this particular trip. Tessa, however, was always there, happy and willing to help.

5

Sydney skulked back into the room and dropped the first aid kit at Jen's feet, then slumped back into the recliner until Blake pointed at her pack and pile. "Time to put it together."

Jen watched as her three children picked up various items and stuffed, prodded, or shoved them into waterproof bags. Sydney huffed as she put her sandals at the top of her pack and leaned back in her seat. "Can I go now? Braden will be here soon."

"Hold on." Blake waved her forward. "Let's check your pack."

Standing up, Sydney picked up her pack and handed it to Blake. "Looks pretty good, Syd."

He clapped his hand on her shoulder, and Jen watched the corner of Sydney's mouth turn upward before it quickly dropped back down. How Jen wished their oldest daughter smiled at her like that.

"Can I go now?" Sydney asked.

Jen flicked up her finger. "I don't—"

Blake interrupted her, obviously not realizing her intent. "Be home by ten. We leave before sunrise tomorrow morning."

The doorbell rang as Sydney darted down the hall to her bedroom.

"She said soon, but—" Blake grinned as his brother, Evan, walked into the room, no one having answered the door. "Intruder," he gruffed.

"Hey." Evan ruffled Max's hair as he walked past. "Just wanted to come by and see how all the packing's going. Wish Michelle were up to a trip like this."

"Eh." Blake waved his brother's comment off. "One day. Your kids are young."

"Sure." Evan ducked his head, his jaw tightening, then glanced back at Blake. "So, you'll be back on Saturday?"

"By five. If we get lost, you're our backup." Blake eyed his brother, seriousness darkening his eyes.

"You plan on getting lost?"

"No, but we still plan for the worst. You know that."

"Right," Evan cleared his throat. "Five o'clock, then I call search and rescue."

"It's basically an impossibility, but yeah." Blake clamped his hand on his brother's shoulder. "Come on, I've got to show you the trencher I got for Lazy Beetle."

Blake had been so excited about his company's new trencher that Jen was surprised Evan hadn't seen it yet. Turning her attention away from the brothers, she lifted Tessa's pack and helped adjust it.

A few minutes later, Blake came in alone. "I saw Sydney leave as I finished up with Ev," he said to Jen.

She smiled tightly as she leaned her pack against the entryway wall next to Sydney's and the others'. Sydney being gone wasn't right, but there was nothing Jen could do about that now.

Blake's eyes narrowed as he studied her. "Do we like this boy?"

"You've met him. He's respectful to every adult he meets and is every girl's heartthrob."

"No then."

Jen shrugged. She didn't really know Braden, but something about the way he treated Sydney seemed off. Crouched down, she fiddled with the ties of her pack and listened to the conversation that had picked up around her. As Blake talked with Max, a warmth thawed her cold chest.

"Dad," Max said, gazing up at his father. "If my sleeping bag gets too heavy for you, I'll take it."

"You will?" Blake ruffled Max's hair. "Thanks, bud. I'll remember that."

"Max, head to bed," Jen said. "We'll be there in a minute."

Watching her son clomp down the hall, Jen stood up and fell into Blake's arms. "You sure about this? What if something happens?"

"Like what?"

"A bear or mountain lion attack." She shrugged. "I don't know—" She waved her thought off with a shake of her head. It was nerves. Nothing more.

"It's gonna be great." Blake pulled her closer. "You'll see." He kissed the top of her head, and the even thrum of his heart calmed her tired uneasiness.

"I think *you're* going to be great. Especially when you end up carrying an extra pack and swimming each icy pool twice."

A few minutes before ten—as Jen shut off the kitchen light— the front door squeaked open. Jen peered around the corner and listened as Sydney finished her conversation with Braden. It wasn't that she wanted to spy, but recently, that had been the only way she could figure out what was going on in her daughter's life. A lump fell into the pit of Jen's stomach as she swallowed. She hated that it was that way.

"I wish I could be there," Sydney said, her body hugging the door frame.

"Well, you're the one choosing to go lounge around the badlands," Braden said.

"It's not the badlands, Braden. My dad says West Clear Creek is amazing. Green and everything. And there's a creek with deep, crystal-clear pools."

"Whatever. All I'm saying is that you never know what'll happen when you're gone."

Sydney placed one foot over the threshold and leaned forward. "What?"

"Crystal's gonna help me set up."

Sydney swatted past the door frame. "Don't tease me like that, Braden. It's not funny."

Jen frowned, taking a step forward. "Sydney?" she called. "Oh good, you're home."

Sydney glared at her. "Mom, what are you doing?"

"I'm on my way to bed, just like you should be. Say goodnight." Jen waved at Braden and walked down the hall, stopping in front of Sydney's bedroom. Maybe the rest of the date had been better than the last thirty seconds.

A minute later, Sydney stormed around the corner. "So this is where you sleep now?"

Jen folded her arms. "I haven't made it to my room yet." She dropped her arms and bounced once on her feet. "I wanted to see how your date went."

"Fine."

Jen sighed. "Syd, I don't like"—

Sydney, who had started to walk into her bedroom, turned and faced Jen, her scowl deepening.

—"it when he treats you that way," Jen said.

Rolling her eyes, Sydney turned away. "It's fine, Mom. He was just teasing."

As Sydney slammed her bedroom door, a burst of air hit Jen's face, and she took a step back. A sting pricked the corners of her eyes. What had she done wrong this time? It probably didn't matter. She shrugged off the ache in her chest the best she could and dragged her feet down the hall. Sydney was only stretching her wings, right? Learning to fly?

Jen's time in the bathroom only took a minute, then she climbed into bed, the cool sheet falling back against her body as she curled against Blake. Somehow, doing so always helped her relax.

The next morning, a stream of harsh light touched Jen's face, and she clenched her eyes tighter, pulling the blanket over her head.

Blake didn't know the value of sleep, but she did. "Too early," she mumbled.

"Come on, beetle, it's time to go."

The middle of the blanket lifted as Blake tried to rip it from the bed, and Jen's muscles burned as she clung to the covering with her hands and pushed her feet into the end that she'd wrapped under her heels. "I want to sleep." She giggled, refusing to give in.

Blake sighed. "Fine, if that's what you want. See you Saturday."

Jen popped up from under the comforter. "Don't forget to take the kids," she called out.

The bedroom door clicked shut, and Jen sighed, forcing the tension from her shoulders. As much as she'd tried to sleep, thoughts of roaring rivers and temperamental teenagers had rippled into her dreams. Anxious nerves often kept her awake before a trip, but this time it seemed worse. Different. She shook her head and exhaled heavily.

She'd been fighting dream-Sydney for weeks, and the weight of Sydney's door slamming in her face the night before still hung across her shoulders. How could she get out of bed—lift her head off the pillow—with such a miserable load to carry? Sinking deeper into the covers, she searched for a happier memory to cling to.

"Momma, I don't want to go to bed," Sydney whined. Five years old and she already had a mind of her own.

"Oh. Well, what do you want to do?" Jen asked.

"Tell me a story." Sydney bounced on the bed.

"Do you have a book?"

"Not from a book, Momma. Tell me the story. About Little Bird."

Jen wrapped her arm around her oldest daughter and leaned in closer. "After that—"

"I go to sleep." Sydney nodded vigorously.

"Okay then, how does it begin?"

10

Sydney tucked her head into Jen's side and pulled the covers up to her chin. "Up in the tippy, tippy, tippy top of the very greenest tree . . ."

"Ah, that's right." Jen touched her nose and continued the story. "Momma Bird sat upon an egg in a nest made up of twigs."

"Tap, tap, tap . . ." Sydney giggled.

"Momma Bird heard, and she shifted left to right. Then the tapping, soft and loud—"

"Grew and grew . . ."

"Until Momma Bird had to move. One more tap and the egg cracked wide. A little yellow beak pushed through, and Momma Bird's baby chick soon chirped a howdy-do." Jen pulled Sydney closer and hugged her tight. "Day and night and night and day, Momma Bird watched her baby chick grow. She fed and cleaned her and always gave her hugs and kisses. Momma Bird protected her chick from hawks and snakes and bears. And every time her chick peeped a peep, Momma Bird flew through the air."

"And she protected her from everything," Sydney said, "like rain and wind and owls." Sydney cocked her head. "Do owls eat little birds?"

"I'm sure they do," Jen said, gently pushing Sydney back down to her pillow. "Are you ready for more?"

Sydney nodded.

"The baby bird grew yellow feathers with green upon her wing. 'I'm just like Momma,' she announced, and she flitted to be free.

"Momma Bird didn't argue. Instead, she pulled her chick close and tweeted a simple song, 'It's almost time, Little Bird, but for now, you're only mine. Mine to hold and to teach. My lullaby to reach.'"

"What's a lull-lull . . ." Sydney looked at Jen and yanked on her sleeve. "What is it again?"

"A lullaby is a goodnight song."

"Like a story?"

"For birds, it's just like a story." Jen tucked her daughter back into bed. "Let's finish the story, then it's time to sleep, okay?"

"Okay."

11

"Momma Bird looked upon her little one and blinked deep, holding back a tear. The time had finally come. Little Bird had to leave the nest.

"Oh, Momma wasn't ready yet, but Little Bird had to go. With hidden tears, Momma flapped her wings, flicking them to and fro. 'Out, out with you,' Momma Bird said, 'it's time for you to fly.'

"Little Bird, a scared look upon her face, puffed out her feathers, then froze. Momma Bird both happy and sad, wrapped her in her wings. 'It's time. Go build a nest of twigs and listen well. For when you hear the lullaby, you'll know just where to fly.'"

Sydney kicked at her blankets. "Little Bird doesn't want to go. She wants to live with her momma forever, just like me."

"Maybe so." Jen grinned. "Lie back down please."

Sydney harrumphed once, then settled back against her pillow, snuggling even closer to Jen than before.

Jen touched her daughter's nose before continuing. "Little Bird twisted, twirled, and stretched, then perched upon a limb. 'If I want to be like you, Momma, I have to fly, but how can I with such wobbly knees?'

"'My knees are often just like that,' Momma Bird said with a soothing trill. 'I promise, you won't fall. Just sing that little lullaby, and know I'll hear your call.'"

Sydney turned to Jen. "Like you hear me when I need you?"

"Just like I hear you. But don't go growing up too fast," Jen said.

"I won't. I want to live with you forever." Sydney hugged Jen's arm.

A warmth filled Jen's heart. "Well, you won't always feel that way. But I'll keep you right here with me until you're ready, and that's going to be a long, long time from now." She glanced at Sydney and tucked the blankets tighter around her. Then she slipped off the bed and moved toward the door, indicating the end of the story was near.

"The ground looked close, and the air was cold, and Momma . . . well, she was nowhere. Little Bird cocked her head and begged for help. Then listening close, she heard the song—the lullaby her momma tweeted all day and all night *long. Little Bird flapped her wings and up she soared, following Momma Bird's call. Then, together, they flew high, singing their lullaby."*

Jen sighed and lowered her heavy feet from her bed to the floor. Sydney had asked for that story for years. Then, one day, she'd pronounced herself all grown up. But she wasn't grown up, not all the way, and Jen no longer knew how to connect with her daughter. What notes did she have left to sing? Her scoffing caused her to cough. Jen had never been able to sing. Maybe that's why Sydney didn't want anything to do with her anymore.

Parenting Poison

Family outings are "non-negotiable." Sydney tapped the send button and watched the text appear in a green bubble under Braden's plea for her to stay home.

Lame.

Biting her lip, Sydney read his response. Her family wasn't that bad, and she liked backpacking. *I like hiking.*

Hot and sweaty 😜

What did he mean by that? *Eew! NO! The forests n creeks R pretty.*

Whatev's. I'll par-tay w Crystal.

What? No! Braden.

Why would he say something like that? It was bad enough that he'd let Crystal hang all over him in science class. She stared at her phone. Was he joking?

She's nice.

Sydney's heart thumped once, then caught. *She h8s me.*

It was a pencil.

Three weeks ago, during finals week, Crystal had taken Sydney's mechanical pencil in the middle of class, dumped out all the lead and *accidentally* broke it into tiny pieces. After that, Sydney had no way to finish her in-class study guide. It didn't help that Braden had refused to lend her another pencil—he claimed he couldn't risk Crystal confusing it with Sydney's. When he found Sydney crying at her locker, he'd finally apologized.

She sighed, remembering the feel of his hand along her cheek as he wiped away the tears and the hurt in his eyes when she didn't immediately fall into his arms.

I wish we were together. She texted back.

When R you back?

Sat night.

Sydney dropped her phone into her lap and leaned her head against the car window. He didn't text back. No *I love you* or *Can't wait.* No *See you soon.* He didn't even bother with *goodbye.* Her bestie, Bria, swore that all guys acted like that. She'd also said, *all guys flirt.* They all seemed to flirt with Crystal. That much was true.

Closing her eyes, Sydney tried to push the rambling thoughts away. After texting with Bria until midnight and getting up before the crack of dawn, she was tired enough. And they'd just passed Sunflower. If West Clear Creek was anywhere near Payson, it meant they were getting close.

As the pricks and prods about Braden slowed, Sydney's muscles grew heavier. Finally, her mind . . .

Something poked her in the gut, causing her heart to jump toward her throat as her body lurched against her seat belt. "Hey! What was that for?"

"You were snoring." Max giggled.

"I'm tired, Max!"

"Sydney, stop yelling," Mom's worn-out voice called from the front seat.

16

Sydney huffed. "He poked—"

"Just don't yell," Mom said.

"Fine. Whatever." Sydney rolled her eyes.

Mom never cared why she did what she did or said what she said. She only cared that the house ran smoothly and everyone let her do her own thing. And she was a snoop—spying on her and Braden.

Sydney closed her eyes and slouched down further in her seat, but it wasn't long before the car turned off the pavement. She cracked her eye open, not sure what to expect. Ponderosa pine, fir, and scattered oak trees dotted the landscape as Sydney's dad navigated the spiderweb of dirt roads. Some trails were nothing more than two-track paths worn by all-terrain vehicles. Others, though wide, lacked the smooth surface of a well-maintained road.

"Da-ad," Sydney whined as their gray SUV dropped from a large rock to the dirt below, her head bouncing against the window.

"Oh, that was nothing but a pebble." He chuckled.

Rubbing her head, Sydney picked up her phone. No service. Figured. Dad said they wouldn't *get even half a bar in the canyon.* She slipped her phone into the seat pocket in front of her, then watched as they passed tree after tree. With each one, her mind cleared a bit. As much as she wanted to spend time with her friends, she couldn't help but recognize the pull of the mountains. The trees, lichen-covered rocks, and occasional deer had that effect on her. By the time her dad had parked, curiosity about the hike had urged air into her lungs and energy into her arms and legs. She opened her door and got out before the engine had time to settle to a stop.

"How far is the water?" Tessa asked, climbing out of the car after Max.

"Oh, not too far. About half a mile," Dad said. He grabbed a fishing pole and slid it into the top flap of Sydney's pack, just below the life preserver Mom demanded everyone have. "You're in charge of catching tonight's dinner."

"Great." She gave him a crooked smile, acknowledging his joke.

"Let's go." Dad sauntered toward the trailhead. "Half a mile of trail takes us down seven hundred feet to the refreshing, crystal-clear water at the bottom."

The word *crystal* coated Sydney's mood in murky oil. Braden probably had Crystal over helping him set up for his party already. Crystal would ogle his muscles and pet him with soft compliments. Then he'd lie in her lap like a gentle little puppy dog.

Pain exploded through Sydney's foot, and she stumbled forward, catching herself before tumbling into Tessa and down the first steep switchback.

"You okay?" Mom asked from behind.

Warmth flooded Sydney's cheeks, and she muttered "I'm fine" under her breath.

Jen's pack fell against a large rock where she seated herself, removed her shoes, and curled her toes into the wild grass at her feet.

The kids had changed into their hiking sandals and now waded through the creek. She smiled as Tessa waved from a teetering rock seconds before losing her balance and finding herself midcalf in water.

The hike down hadn't taken long, but the heavy pack and summer temperatures had heated Jen some. Supporting herself with her arms, she leaned her head back and closed her eyes. The warmth of the sun increased the lure of the water. Taking a sip from her canteen, she glanced at her pack. Her sandals were right there, waiting for her.

18

"What do you think?" Blake sat next to her, grinning.

She scanned the canyon. Fir and oak trees joined them partway up the north bank. The clear water sparkled under the sun. And everything was so verdant. So alive. The only open soil was the narrow trail behind her.

A yellow songbird landed on a willow branch a few feet away and chirped a welcome, then took flight across the creek.

"This is amazing. Where are the dead trees?"

"Oases don't have dead trees." He winked. "Put your sandals on."

She nodded and reached for her pack.

Wearing different, more-beat-up shoes, Blake stood and hopped two of the dry rocks in the stream, then offered his hand to Jen. Glancing at Sydney, who had waded a ways off from Jen's other two children, Jen flicked a finger, indicating a change in direction. She eased off the low bank into the water, shuddering slightly at the shock the cold creek brought to her feet and ankles. "This is cold, Blake. You said it would be refreshing."

"You'll get used to it." He took several steps with her, watching her reaction to the canyon.

"So, I need to talk to Sydney." She scrunched her nose up as she looked at him.

Blake glanced at their daughter. "No lectures."

"Not at all. I just—I have a couple questions. That's all."

Blake shook his head. "What questions?"

"Nothing important. I'll be back, okay?" She shrugged away from her husband, choosing her next steps carefully.

Sydney sat down on a flat rock where water bubbled a half inch over the top. Jen's heartbeat picked up as she approached, but she wouldn't give up trying to talk to her daughter. She couldn't. Mothers were supposed to ask questions and be a part of their daughter's lives. Granted, her own mother had always been too

19

busy with her older brother, Charlie. But Jen had promised herself to never put one kid before another, regardless of the reason. And Charlie had been a good reason for her mom—his special needs hadn't left much room for Jen—still, it had hurt.

She raised her foot to the rock, then squatted and sat beside Sydney without a sound. At first.

"It's pretty here, isn't it?" Jen finally said.

Sydney shrugged. "I guess."

"Feel better about coming now that we're here?"

"No."

Jen nodded, wishing she could relieve some of her nervousness without showing weakness—bite her lip or twiddle her thumbs. Something. "Oh, it's not that bad, is it? Seeing new things, playing in the water? I mean, I know you have to see me, but—"

Sydney turned and narrowed her eyes at Jen. "What do you want?"

"I just thought it would be nice to talk with you."

"And?"

The slow rise and fall of Jen's chest didn't stop the pain. "What did you and Braden do last night?" Jen worked to keep her voice light.

"Nothing."

"Nothing? You stared at the ground all night?" She forced a laugh. "Come on, you did something. Who was with you?"

Sydney rolled her eyes and looked away.

"Was Bria with you?"

"No."

"Soo?"

"Soo, nothing. Will you leave me alone now?"

Jen stood up. "I didn't mean to bother you, but Sydney, will you do me a favor? When I'm trying to talk to you—to show that I care—please be nice."

"I am nice."

Jen closed her eyes, squeezing them tight before reopening them. "You shouldn't have slammed your door in my face."

Sydney bolted off the rock. "Leave me alone, then. Stop being so nosy."

Jen's throat tightened as she tried to swallow her surging emotion. "I just don't want you to get hurt. Do you really think a boy should treat you like that?"

"Sixteen, Mom. He's six—"

Jen jumped off the rock. "Max, that's—get out of there."

Water splashed across Sydney's middle and Jen winced as she ran toward the side of the creek where Max was traipsing through a grove of poison ivy. Hopefully her oldest would forgive her clumsiness.

Blake twisted toward their startled son. "Jump in the creek, buddy."

Max stood frozen. "I . . . I didn't know."

Jen gave her son a soft smile, her heart pounding in her chest. "Most poison ivy we see is smaller, isn't it? You'll be okay, but we need to get you in the water."

"Run on in," Blake said. "You've got to sit in the water for a good, long soak."

"I can't," Max cried, tears welling in his eyes.

Jen exhaled slowly. "You've got to. Come on."

Throwing his hands in the air, Max ran from the center of the poison ivy grove into the water, splashing everyone except Sydney, who sat on her rock across the creek, staring at the opposite bank.

Elephants and VW Beetles

Sydney stopped and shifted the weight of her pack, gazing at the view. The canyon widened, and trees met the sandstone as little as eight feet above the water. Wide ledges lined the creek with tall, natural steps leading to the northern cliff from both the water and the trail.

And it was peaceful. Sydney closed her eyes and breathed that part in.

It was way better than Max's crying.

After finally jumping into the creek from the poison ivy grove, he'd changed into his only other set of clothing—and cried. Howled. He didn't even itch yet. With how long he'd sat in the water, he might never itch. Sydney pushed her lips to the side. He'd itch. He'd been in the grove for several minutes before Mom had seen him. Why hadn't Sydney caught it? She'd been staring at him, but none of it had registered. Once the itching set in, it was all over. Max would cry nonstop.

The excitement had wound down fast enough, and it hadn't taken long for them to start hiking again. It also hadn't taken long for Max and Tessa to trod every step a little slower. When that happened, Dad grabbed Sydney to hike ahead with him. Something about needing to clear the way and find a place to sleep before Mom took his head off. He was joking, but Sydney didn't argue. She'd do anything to get away from the dragging feet of her whining siblings. Not to mention Mom's constant reminders for her to *be nice*. Like Mom had been nice to Sydney, covering her in ice-cold water when Max needed attention. Was it that hard to run *after* passing by her? Besides, Sydney was nice. She just didn't want to walk at a snail's pace, and she didn't want Mom asking any more questions. Which, of course, had started up again. *What did you and Braden do last night? Who was with you? You shouldn't have slammed your door in my face. Do you really think a boy should treat you like that?*

As she refocused on the task at hand, Sydney turned to her dad. "Do we have to swim again?" Floating her pack across the first deep pool had been harder than she had expected, and she shivered at the thought of doing it again.

"Don't you want to?" Her dad winked. "We'll camp here tonight. Head on up."

Stepping forward, her sandals scuffing the stone, Sydney grabbed a handhold and lifted herself to the top of the natural step in front of her. Buff dust clung to her fingertips as she reached for another hold. At the top of the cliff, she stared at the dense trees several feet from the edge and toed the hard stone beneath her shoes.

"What do you think, kiddo?" Dad asked.

"It's pretty, but"—she wrinkled her nose—"it's so hard."

"That's why we have air mattresses."

"You mean the two-dollar rafts? They always break."

"That's what duct tape is for."

Her dad dropped his pack to the ground and clapped his hands, then rubbed them together as he turned from the edge of the ledge and looked at Sydney. "Let's get the two tents up. After that, you can catch dinner while I hunt down your mother."

Sydney groaned, then pulled out the tent she and her siblings would use. "Can't we wait to set up until they get here?"

"Why would we do that? We're here now, and Mom's dealing with Max."

She scoffed. "He can walk. I walked."

Her dad grinned as he unrolled the other tent. "Sixteen. Ten. I see the similarity."

Once the tent poles had been strung through their sleeves, Sydney went from corner to corner, pushing at the poles and pulling at the tent tabs until the small dome popped into shape.

"You're quick," Dad said, holding out a fishing pole with a bit of tackle.

She eyed the pole. "I should be. You've made me set up my own tent since I was ten." A slight smile played at the corner of her mouth.

"A good skill to have." He wiggled the pole at her until she took the fishing gear.

"You won't stay with me?"

"Mom needs my help. I'll be back in time for a refreshing swim. And midday or not, now's the time to fish. Before Max scares them all away."

"Mom knows what she's doing," she grumbled.

Her dad cleared his throat, a clear sign he'd heard what she'd said. "Sydney, relationships and families are about taking care of one another even when you're worn out or busy."

She rolled her eyes. "Don't be selfish. Think of others. Got it, Dad."

"It's more than that, Syd. It's also recognizing how you're treated. There's a fine line between selflessness and being mistreated."

Her dad climbed down the sandstone steps and strolled quickly down the trail they had just traveled.

Wobbling her head and imitating a blabby mouth with her hand, Sydney dragged her feet to the edge of the ledge where she sat down on the hard rock and set up her fishing pole. Now Dad was getting after her too? He'd only met Braden twice. And she cared plenty about her family. She had even started to look forward to the stupid family *adventure*, then everyone turned against her. Well, her parents had. She shifted side to side on the hard rock and gripped the pole a little tighter.

The damp prick from her swim across the creek had dried, and her shoulders warmed as the southwestern sun kissed her freckled skin. Breathing in the pine-scented air, she allowed some of her tension to melt away. She liked fishing well enough, but nothing would bite before dusk. Dad had taught her that. Waiting until later made more sense, but whatever. She pulled back on the pole and watched the thin, clear line bounce at the surface of the water.

She didn't want to be alone, but Dad had been right; this place was incredible. The lush foliage might grow elsewhere in the state, but not in such variety. And the water below? It cascaded over a three-foot-high rock wall into a deep, slow-moving pool—the gleaming color more clear than blue, except at the deepest point. While a large cottonwood hung over some of their campsite, shading the brush behind it, Sydney focused on the smattering of ponderosa pine and fir trees on the opposite bank. She'd never seen such a thing. It was like looking at two different climate zones. Dad had said West Clear Creek was different than anywhere they'd ever been. He was right about that too.

Bored, she reeled in the fishing line. The bait had disappeared. Unsurprised, she placed two more salmon eggs on the hook and cast it into the water near the opposite ledge. Her mind wandered for a moment, then she sighed at the thought of Braden.

It was almost time for his party. Crystal was definitely at his place by now. She imagined her sidling up to him, her boobs against his arm. Mom swore what girls didn't notice, boys noticed ten times over. Sometimes Mom said smart things. Sydney had to admit that. Crystal flaunted her rounded breasts more than any other girl at the school. But she only flirted with Braden. Worse than that, he flirted back.

The last day of school, when Crystal gave the lunch crowd a show, Braden had wrapped his arm around Sydney, pulled her closer, and whispered, *lighten up* as he kissed the side of her head. Talk about mixed messages.

There's a fine line between selflessness and being mistreated. Dad's words from thirty minutes before tapped at her brain. Was Braden mistreating her? The only person Dad ever flirted with was Mom, but they were married. Social graces said he couldn't flirt with other women. She and Braden were sixteen. The comparison died. How could she compare a man married for eighteen years to a sixteen-year-old guy?

The pole wriggled, and Sydney yanked back on it as she spun the handle on the reel. Bouncing, the line dragged from left to right as a fish rose from the water. The trout flung itself against the stone wall until she grasped the line in her hand.

She grinned. Dad always knew the best time.

"I'm tired." Max sat down in the middle of the narrow trail with his legs crisscrossed.

The warm sun, two hours past its zenith, touched Jen's brow as she looked up at the tall canyon walls surrounding them. It wouldn't be long before shade covered the path that now basked in the midday light. Then how cold would it be?

They'd marked the trail back to the car with a cairn—certain to use large rocks to keep wildlife from knocking the pile over—then started downstream.

Three hours later, Jen stood above her son, wondering if Blake and Sydney would find a camping spot close enough to reach before dark.

The relatively flat trail wasn't difficult to travel—when it was there. But much of their time had been spent finding their way through foot-wide patches of lush grasses and willows. In the shadier areas, box elder and poison ivy mingled, often covering the easiest route and leaving them to pick their way through the creek or over craggy sandstone outcroppings.

When Max had started whining and Sydney had, once again, snapped at Jen over her questions, Blake suggested that he and Sydney scout ahead for a campsite while Jen and the other two took their time. In other words, Jen and the younger two were slow . . . and she needed to leave Sydney alone. Jen didn't mean to annoy Sydney, but apparently, she came by it naturally.

Looking up the trail, Jen forced out a long breath. She didn't mind that Blake had gone ahead. He'd take time to talk to their oldest daughter, and that was good.

"I know you're tired," Jen said, returning her attention to her son. "Why don't we rest for a few minutes."

Max slumped forward and stared at the ground, rubbing his hands down his legs.

Jen eyed him. "Try not to touch your legs too much. We don't know how much of the poison ivy got on you."

Max grumbled. "But I itch."

The rash and itch from the poison ivy wouldn't start for a few more hours. Maybe days. Hopefully not at all. Still, Jen bent down next to Max. "Let me pull out the cream to help with that, but don't touch your legs so much."

Once Max had soaked in the water, Blake had wiped him down with a few alcohol wipes to remove whatever oil remained from his exposure. They'd been pretty thorough, but that didn't stop the psychosomatic aspect. Suggest an itch . . . She pulled out the pink calamine lotion and placed a dollop in each of Max's hands. "Rub it where it itches."

Tessa dropped her pack to a small outcropping a foot up from the creek. She toed herself to the edge of the water, picked up a smooth stone, and skipped it across the shallow pool.

Max whipped his head up. "Wow! Can you show me how to do that?" He rubbed what little lotion remained on his hands down his pants, and jumped to his feet.

Jen smiled, grateful for the motherly instincts already appearing in her second daughter.

"Sure. Find a smooth, round, flat rock."

Jen had just climbed to a rocky resting spot when she heard scuffling footsteps and whistling from around the next bend. Not long after, Blake kneaded her shoulders with cool hands.

"I'm glad you're back," she said. "Find anything?"

"Yup. A beautiful cliff site above a deep pool about half a mile away."

"How's the trail?"

"Clear now. Ready to swim?"

Jen turned and peered at her husband's wet clothing. "I wondered about that. How is it?"

"Not bad. Syd and I got across fine. It's not wide."

"How deep is it?"

"Probably eight to ten feet."

29

Jen's heart rate picked up. "So deep." *Deep enough to lose sight of the bottom.* "Where's Sydney?"

"Fishing before our noisy herd arrives."

Jen scanned the creek, her eyes narrowing with anxious resolve. "Did you talk to her?"

"It's been a couple hours, Jen. We didn't walk in silence."

"That's not what I mean." Jen sighed. "Did you *talk* to her."

"I said a little."

"How much is that?"

Blake sat next to Jen and stared at the ground. "You need to lighten up with the questions. She shuts down."

"Lighten up? I just asked how her night went." Heat rushed into Jen's cheeks.

"I heard. And I heard you end with telling her not to slam the door in your face."

Jen fidgeted with the hem of her shorts as she blinked back the burning in her eyes. "It hurt when she did that."

"Of course it did. It hurt your mom when you did that too."

"I never got the chance. Mom was too busy with Charlie."

"Well, then you probably hurt his feelings when you slammed the door in his face."

Jen rounded her body over her legs. "I just don't see what's wrong with asking about her night."

"Nothing, Jen, but you need to accept her answers. Stop lecturing her."

"I didn't lecture her."

Blake raised an eyebrow. "All right, just keep the lectures to a sentence or less."

Jen turned away and shook her head, refusing to wipe at escaped tears. A sentence or less? How could she connect with her little bird in a sentence or less? "Fine." The word came out stiff, but Jen didn't care. Facing the kids, she called out their names.

Tessa touched Max's shoulder and pointed at Blake. A giant grin broke across the boy's face, and he dashed downstream.

"Dad, guess what, Tessa taught me how to skip rocks." He grabbed Blake's hand and tugged. "Come on."

Blake eyed Jen. He wanted to make sure she was okay; she knew that, but she needed longer than thirty seconds. As he dropped his gaze to Max, Blake said, "Just one, then it's time to leave."

Max lowered his head and studied his feet. "Can't we stay here?"

"'Fraid not, buddy. There's no place to sleep." Blake glanced at Jen again. "But we get to go swimming right around that corner, there."

Max pointed at the nearby bend, eyes wide. "That one?"

"Yup." Blake picked Max up at the waist and rushed over to Tessa where he lowered him back down to the ground. "What kind of rock do you need?"

Jen watched as Max picked up a small rock, shook water from it, and showed it to Blake. She never tired of watching her husband with their children—with any child. How did he always manage what she couldn't? Like talking to Sydney. He could talk to her. She didn't slam doors in his face. But Sydney had no problem telling Jen off and shutting her out. Jen sighed. Blake was probably right. Her approach was off. She just didn't know what other approach to take.

Leaning against the cliff, she allowed her mind to wander. Blake had always had the right touch with kids and people—with her—from the very day they'd met.

Jen shut the Saxon book, ready for algebra to end forever. Clutching the educational monstrosity to her chest, she followed the throngs through the double doors, a breeze catching the hem of her oversized T-shirt as she stepped into the courtyard and to her locker; she had another book to pick up before heading home.

"Hey." Barb, her best friend, leaned against the wall of triple-stacked lockers.

Jen offered half a smile but said nothing.

"Are you going to the game tonight?"

"Nope. Never do."

"Come on, it'll be fun."

"Sit on hard bleachers and watch guys pile on top of each other? No thanks."

"It's not about the game, Jen." Barb slouched and rolled her eyes, a piece of her bobbed hair flying into her face. "It's about hanging out."

"Sorry, Barb. I promised my mom I'd hang out at home with Charlie."

"Bring him along."

"Yeah . . . no."

"Why not?"

"Have you ever—"

A group of freshmen ran past, and Jen scanned the area until her gaze fell on her older brother, Charlie, who was surrounded by bullies, his hands on his bare head. Not his hat. *She slammed her locker shut.*

The hard concrete hammered through her Doc Martins at the soles of her feet, her heart pounding faster as she pushed through the gathering crowd. "Get away—"

Throbbing pain lit up her shoulder as she collided with a band geek, then shoved past him before he could apologize. Everyone around her quieted and dispersed as some guy crouched down and checked on Charlie before gathering the papers her brother's bullies had thrown to the ground.

Charlie stared at Jen as she went to help him stand, his fingers curling into his hair and a tear streak staining his cheek.

"We'll find it, Charlie." Jen looked up when two feet appeared in her line of sight and a hand held out a few of Charlie's papers. "Thanks," she said.

The guy she'd seen checking on Charlie and gathering his things held one page back. "Hey, Charlie, did you draw this cool elephant?"

Charlie ignored the question, then ran to the hedge lining the building.

"What's he—"

"His hat," Jen answered before the guy got the rest of the question out.

Joining her brother, she pushed at the branches, then squeezed between the hedge and the brick wall. She held the branches back six inches at a time while scanning the ground beneath.

"What's it look like?"

The guy had followed her?

Jen looked up and winced as a branch drew itself across her forearm. "It's a red bucket hat."

"Are you sure it's in the bushes?"

"No." She glanced at the next patch of ground she'd exposed. "But I don't see many other places they could have hidden it this time. Do you?"

Wincing again, Jen twisted around, using her body instead of her hands— which were fairly useless—to move the branches.

Charlie's cries echoed in her ears, causing her heart to thump maddeningly within her chest. Then the cries stopped.

She took another step.

"Jen, I want to go home." Charlie sniffed.

Slowly raising her head, Jen glanced at her brother, who now wore his hat. Her gaze swept to the guy standing next to him, then back to her brother. "We can go home. Did you say thank you?"

"Thank you," Charlie said to the stranger.

"Yeah." The guy slid a glance over to Jen. "I'm Blake, by the way."

"Jen. Are you new here?"

"Nah." He looked up, following Charlie as he started walking forward. "I'm a freshman at Arizona State, but I heard one of my old high school teachers started working here, so I came to say hi."

"Really? Must be some teacher."

"Mr. Robb is the best. Do you have him?"

33

"No. What does he teach?"

The guy's brow knit momentarily as confusion draped across his face. "English."

"Oh, I think he teaches Senior English. I'm a junior."

"So you'll have him next year, then?"

Jen stifled a laugh. "Maybe. There are three different Senior English teachers."

"Really?"

"Yeah. Where are you from?"

"Greer." He grinned. "I graduated from Round Valley High School. It's pretty small."

Jen stepped into the parking lot and looked at her Volkswagen Bug. "That's us. Thanks for your help."

"I love Beetles," Blake said.

Jen glanced at him, "What?"

"Your car. It's a Beetle."

"Right. My car." She shook her head lightly and mumbled under her breath, "a Beetle."

"What do you call it? A bug?"

Looking up, Jen wrinkled her nose. "I don't really call it anything but my car."

He chuckled, placing his hand on the roof of the car. "All right then, beetle. It's your car, but you should name it. Maybe Martha?"

"Did you just call me Beetle?"

Blake leaned over and whispered, "It's a nickname. Kinda like people call Beetles bugs."

She scoffed. "Oka-ay. Anyway, we'd better . . ." She pointed at her car.

"Yeah, sure. . . . Oh, hey Charlie, I still have your picture. It's a great elephant." Blake handed the slightly wrinkled page to Jen's brother.

"It's an Asian elephant. They are smaller than African elephants," Charlie said.

"Are they? That's pretty cool. Do you like elephants a lot?"

"They're my favorite. They take care of each other."

"Like you take care of your sister."

"Yes. And my mom takes care of me."

Blake handed the picture to Charlie, who refused to take it.

"That's for you," Charlie said.

Blake looked down at it, his eyes widening. "Wow! I can't wait to hang it up on my wall. Thanks, Charlie."

Jen bit her lip, grinning, as she opened the driver's side door. "Thank you."

"Are you going to the game tonight? There is one, right?"

"There is. But I promised my mom I'd watch Charlie."

"Watch him at the game. I thought I might come, if you're there." A pink tinge crossed Blake's nose.

Jen peered into the car. "What do you think, Charlie? Should we go to the game?"

"Can I have nachos?"

Blake leaned over next to Jen. "You bet! Do you like jalapenos?"

"No way."

"All right then. Nachos without jalapenos. My treat." He turned to Jen with questioning brows.

"Okay. We'll come. But I'll have to leave if he gets upset." Jen twisted the toe of her shoe into the asphalt.

"Seven o'clock, beetle. I'll meet you at the gate."

After more than one skipped rock, Blake finally broke the news to Max that it was time to go, recapturing Jen's attention and her frustration over his lecture on lecturing. She smiled tightly as she climbed down from her perch to the edge of the stream with no doubt of what would come next.

"I'm too tired," Max whined.

"Oh, it's not far. Come on, you get to swim." Blake ruffled the boy's hair.

Max grumbled and sat down on the rocks at her husband's feet. "I'm tired."

"So, you're gonna sleep here on your own?" Blake said. "Come on, I'll help you with your pack."

Max huffed and turned to Jen. "Mo-om."

Jen shrugged a shoulder. Maybe ten wasn't old enough. But what did she know about kids? "Gotta go. That's where your bed and food are."

Blake motioned for Jen to hand him the small backpack.

At first, Jen held the school-sized pack out to her husband, but even in her frustration, she hugged it to her chest. "Let me take the pack." Her words were flat.

Blake clenched his jaw, releasing it slowly. "You have your own pack. Let me have it."

"I can carry it in front of me." Jen narrowed her eyes at her husband.

"I'm fine." He wiggled his fingers at her. "It's light."

"Yeah, but I'm not pulling him." Jen dropped her gaze to Max, then glanced up at Blake.

"I got him too," Blake said.

Jen shook her head as she looked at Tessa—who stood ready to go—then handed Blake the pack. He slid it onto his shoulders before bending down and lifting Max to his feet. "Time to go. We've got some swimming to do."

As Jen walked down the trail, she listened to her son sniff and huff away his tears. Her feet throbbed with a bit of an ache too. Traveling over ankle-twisting rock wasn't easy, and though Jen understood the need to continue, Max didn't. What boy wanted to walk on tired feet when they could sit down and skip rocks or play in the water instead? He didn't care how pretty the canyon was or why two different types of vegetation grew along its walls. He didn't even realize that cottonwoods and fir trees grew in different climate zones. Why would he?

As Max's tears eventually waned, Jen allowed her emotions to toy with her just a little. Tessa and Max were still young. Sydney was alone, trying to catch everyone's dinner. And, apparently, Jen was a lecturer. She paused. Jen was a mother. A mother of two teenage daughters and a ten-year-old boy. Sometimes her children needed correction; sometimes they needed gentle prodding. Sometimes they needed protecting. Wasn't that her job? Wasn't that all she'd done when she'd tried to talk to Sydney? Not lecture. Talk. How was that any different than giving Max some lotion for an imaginary itch?

A short ways downstream, as they walked along a wider section of the trail, Jen saw where Blake had thinned the foliage with his machete. At home, she'd teased him about packing it.

Attempting to lighten her own mood, Jen forced a laugh. "Had a little fun along the way, did you?"

"Maybe a little." He turned around enough for her to see him wink.

The next step Jen took was a little lighter, and her feet seemed to ache a little less. As hard as things were with Sydney, Blake didn't hold anything against Jen. He'd talked to Sydney in his own way. More than that, he was acting as peacemaker. She couldn't fault him for that.

Tessa fell back toward Jen and leaned in quietly. "Do we have to swim?"

"I think so. But we'll be okay," she whispered.

Up ahead, the canyon narrowed, and Blake started pointing out the various striations in the sandstone. Each line paralleled the others, some almost swirling after being cut by the water for billions of years. The farther they walked, the higher the canyon walls rose, nearly shading the creek completely. They would have if the creek had taken a different path, but the majority of the time, it flowed west.

Twenty minutes later, Blake stopped and ruffled their son's hair again. The recently cut path ended on the bank of the sparkling water. To the west, nothing but two tall stone walls lined its edges.

Jen stared at the creek. As clear as it was, just as she'd expected, she still couldn't see the bottom. "Where does the trail pick up?" She dropped her pack to the ground, fighting off the thoughts of all that could go wrong.

Tessa leaned into her shoulder, fear in her eyes.

"The other side of that outcropping." Blake pointed downstream and across the creek.

She tried to keep herself from glaring at him. "That's a short swim?"

"It's not bad. Really. The trail starts up again right there, and it opens up the rest of the way to camp. Syd's probably got dinner caught by now." He wrapped his arm around Jen, pulling her closer as he gently tugged on Tessa's hair. "It'll be fun."

Jen nodded, straight-faced.

"Get out your floats and blow." Blake chortled. "I know you have plenty of hot air."

"Hey!" Tessa said, perking up slightly. "That's Syd, not me."

"Tessa," Jen chastised, but her heart wasn't in it.

"You're right, kiddo," Blake said. "Your air is sweet as honey. But you gotta fill up that float."

Jen watched her children as she blew into her own swimming tube. Tessa's muscles had tensed, and she stared at the water. Jen's middle child had voiced her concern about swimming in the deep pools several times while they'd planned the trip. How cold would it be? How deep? What if the current was too swift? What if her pack fell? Tessa asked every question Jen had, plus more. None of the answers alleviated the stress. For either of them. Only a successful swim could do that.

Jen puffed another long breath into her float and closed the valve. "Life jackets, you two."

The other two floats lay at the kids' feet. Tessa had already strapped on her preserver and leaned over to help Max tighten his.

"Tess, you first," Blake said. "I'll even take your pack. You can float Max's across."

She shook her head. "I don't even—"

"It's okay, Tessa. I'll go with you." Jen stepped onto an underwater ledge, holding her float.

Blake lowered Jen's pack onto the swimming ring. "There's not much current, but it'll tug you a bit. Just hold onto your tube and aim for that outcropping. You'll touch bottom just about the time you get there, and the trail's right behind it." Blake patted Tessa on the shoulder and motioned for her to get in the water.

Together, Jen and Tessa eased off the thigh-deep ledge into the icy pool. Their feet no longer touched, and as Jen straightened her legs toward the bottom, icy tendrils raced up her spine. As she leaned forward, her legs trailing closer to the surface, she kicked.

Her tube towered in front of her as she worked to control its movement. Next to her, Tessa gasped as her float rocked violently. "I . . . I . . ."

Jen could only guess what had happened. "Don't use the handles until you can touch," Jen said sharply, trying to help her daughter stabilize Max's pack. "It'll topple over."

Tessa eyes filled with tears. "I can't see."

A shiver raced through Jen. "I know. I'm sorry I snapped. You're doing great. Are you warm enough?"

The bulk of Jen's life jacket insulated her chest from some of the icy prickles. But the goosebumps lining Tessa's arm said her daughter's preserver did little more than keep her afloat. It didn't help that half the pool lay in the shade.

"N-no."

"You're doing great, Tess. We're almost there." Jen kicked her feet again, urging Tessa to do the same.

"I'm c-cold."

"We'll get to camp, and you can warm up before swimming again. Dad says there's a great swimming hole right under our cliff."

Showering droplets hit the back of Jen's head, and Tessa groaned as she kicked at the water again. "I'm not swimming anymore."

Jen laughed as she fought her way to the right side of the creek, pretty sure she didn't want to swim anymore either. "There's the trail."

Her feet scratched the rocky bottom as she got closer, and she climbed out of the creek. As she lifted the packs and floats onto solid ground, Jen heard Blake's voice.

"No Max. Don't climb on the flo—"

Something splashed.

Max wailed.

Jen hurried back into the water where she could see past the outcropping. Blake pushed an empty float toward her with one hand while holding Max with the other.

"The pack," Jen blurted out, then covered her mouth with her hands.

Tessa's pack—her clothes, food, even one of the stoves—all of it was gone. Her daughter had no pad to sleep on, no warm clothes. Nothing.

"My pack!" Tessa's face crumpled as sobs wracked her body. "Why are we here? E-everything is going wrong."

Jen stood, staring wide-eyed at the creek that had so barbarously stolen their supplies—not reacting as she should toward her daughter's worry, her own fears flooded her mind.

"Should have taken two trips," Blake muttered.

Jen took Max and the float from Blake, who immediately headed back to the middle of the pool without any flotation.

"What're you doing?" Jen's heart pummeled her chest as she furiously blinked away tears.

He eyed her incredulously. "Getting the pack."

"Can you see it? I don't want you doing that unless you can see it."

"What's Tessa going to do? Go without clothes for the next several days? I'll be fine."

"Blake."

Her husband ignored her anxious call.

"Don't drown!" she yelled.

She could hear his eyes rolling as he said, "I won't."

But people drowned doing ridiculous things like that every year. Clothing snagged on underwater brush. Hypothermia disoriented them. Some gasped for air, unprepared for the icy pricks. Jen didn't know how or why, but she knew it happened.

Entering the water for hopefully the last time, she watched as her husband took several deep breaths, then disappeared below the surface. *Why is he doing this?* Tessa carried needed supplies, but they could survive without them. They could end the trip early. Sydney and Jen could share their oversized clothing with Tessa. No one would have to die. Blake knew that. Trying to retrieve the pack . . .

Jen swatted her hand against her forehead. She was being ridiculous. Blake wouldn't risk his life for a pack filled with clothing, bedding, and what she now realized were mostly redundant supplies. He would dive eight feet down to keep his daughter happy, though.

Jen bit her lip. But would he ever resurface? She wrapped her arms around her chest while water churned with white bubbles at her thighs before rushing downstream. Where was he? How long could he hold his breath? She took a step forward.

His head popped up. "I found it. Be right back."

Jen shivered, waiting for her husband. Pricks of cold prodded her legs and feet while icy bands wrapped around her insulated chest that remained out of the water. She stepped off the raised rock and into the pool. Blake had nothing to keep him warm.

The framed pack shoved through the water, Blake struggling to keep his head up. Rapid, shallow breaths pushed past his lips, as his wild eyes met Jen's gaze.

With large strokes, Jen swam out to him and took the waterlogged pack, the weight of it dragging her vested shoulders below the water. Staying next to Blake as he paddled toward shore, she glanced at her husband. Even through the water, the pale tinge of his skin peeked through.

"We need to get you warm," she breathed.

"I'm fine. Walking to camp will do that."

"I'm carrying Max's pack, and once we get the water out of this one. Tessa can carry it."

He nodded, climbed up onto the stone beach where Tessa and Max stood crying, and patted their heads. "What's everyone crying about, huh?" He glanced at Tessa. "Help your mom out of the creek. Your stuff's fine."

Tessa shook her head, sobbing harder.

"Tessa," Blake snapped, "help your mother."

Sniffing, Tessa darted to the edge of the water.

"It's okay, Tessa," Jen said softly. "Can you just help me lift it out?"

As her daughter lifted the front of the pack from the creek, Jen used one hand to steady herself on the surrounding rocks. Grunting, they dropped the pack as soon as it was out of the water.

Jen ran to Blake and wrapped her arms around him, feeling the cool of his skin against hers. "You could have died."

"Nah."

Jen raised an eyebrow. "Yes."

"I'm fine."

"You're freezing."

"I'll warm up once we start moving. Right now, we need to get the water out of that pack." He looked at Tessa. "Open it up." When she didn't move, he cut his hand through the air toward the pack and snapped his fingers. "Come on!"

"Blake, relax. I'll do it," Jen said, opening the pack.

As she peeked inside, her warm breath cascaded past her lips. She'd forgotten about the waterproof bags. Most of them had worked, though they had lost a few bags of trail mix and a box of seasoned rice. Some of Tessa's clothes were damp, and her small towel was drenched. But those items would dry quick enough. Jen sat back on her feet. "It's fine. We still have everything we need." She glanced at Tessa. "When we get to camp, we'll want to unroll your sleeping bag in case it got a little damp and hang up your towel and clothes—that's all."

As Jen squeezed the water out of the towel and refastened the backpack, her churning stomach worked to settle itself.

Shivers with Stutters

"Up there?" Jen glanced at the low cliffs lining the creek, then glanced at the boulders in front of her.

"Yup. The tents are up and ready to go, and"—Blake glanced at the edge of the creek—"it looks like Sydney caught plenty for dinner."

Max crouched down and stuck his hand into the water. Jen motioned to Blake.

"Leave them there, buddy," Blake said.

The dead fish floated unnaturally at the top of the water, the current guiding their tails downstream, while the spike hammered into the edge of the dirt trail kept them anchored.

"I want to see how slimy they are." Max lobbed a hopeful look at his father.

"Tell you what, I'll let you help gut 'em. How's that sound?"

"With a knife?"

Blake nodded curtly.

"Yes!" Max jumped up. "Where's Sydney?"

Jen smiled and pointed up the tall sandstone steps towering before them. "Get climbing."

Following her children, Jen crested the last step and lowered her pack to the ground, then entwined her fingers with Blake's as he joined her. "Nice," she said as she took in their surroundings.

Two tents were set up five feet from the narrow cliff's edge, and a fire ring off to the side said they weren't the first to call the spot home. She eyed the small pile of wood next to the ring, obviously gathered from the thick forest abutting camp, and scanned the nearby foliage, then called for Sydney. Turning, she said, "Tessa, hang your clothes and towel in a tree and drape your sleeping bag over your tent."

"I'm tired," Tessa whined.

"Me too. But it's got to get done. Go on."

Tessa shuffled her feet toward her pack with her head hung low.

A minute later, rustling from the nearby brush announced her oldest daughter's arrival. "I thought we might need wood," Sydney said.

"Can we have a fire, Dad? Can we?" Max lunged toward the pit and grabbed some of the smaller tinder.

"Don't you want to go swimming first? Maybe go cliff jumping?" Blake asked.

Max's eyes widened as he stared at Jen. "Can I?"

Jen glanced at the creek as sweat rolled down her back. "I'm swimming."

Max froze mid-jump. "But what about cliff jumping?"

"You won't see me jumping from up here," Jen said, then she bit her lip as she scanned the area. "Maybe from the one by the waterfall."

"That's a baby cliff," Max grumbled.

"It's perfect." Jen grabbed her deflated float and plopped down to the ground, huffing long bursts of air into the plastic as she watched Tessa toss her towel on top of a bush.

Sydney, not bothering with a float, glanced at Blake, then launched herself off the cliff. Jen's heart flipped twice before hearing her daughter whoop and splash her way toward the edge of the trail.

"I'm coming up," Sydney called. "Tess, you're next."

"No, I'm not," Tessa shouted from near the tent. Fear wafting off her skin, she turned to Jen.

Another huff of air poured into Jen's float, then she closed the valve. "No pushing."

Sydney scoffed. "I don't have to push. Dad can throw her in."

With a raised brow, Blake eyed Tessa.

"Mo-om." Tessa backed farther away from the edge.

"Do you really think Dad would force you off a cliff?" Jen worked to keep a straight face.

Blake stood to the side, motionless.

"Dad, throw me in," Max pleaded.

"I know exactly who I'm throwing in." Blake narrowed his eyes at Jen, then jumped into the water.

Max rushed to the edge. "What about me?"

Rising to her feet, Jen glanced over the ledge at her husband, her brows furrowed. As his head broke the surface of the water, her shoulders relaxed and she handed Max his life preserver. "I might be convinced to toss you in."

The rosy color dropped from his rounded cheeks. "R-really?"

"Sure."

"That's okay, Mom. I . . . I'm gonna swim first."

Max grabbed his preserver and rushed to the trail, Jen only steps behind him.

"I think I'm going to jump in by the waterfall," Jen said, taking his hand in her free one. "Will you come with me and toss my tube in?"

Tension roiled through the boy's shoulders. "You won't throw me?"

"Nope."

"Okay."

Jen tightened her grip on his hand as she stepped heel to toe across the warm stone outcropping below the natural steps to their camp. To her left, shallow water lapped at the rock. Three feet lower on her right, the deep pool called to her. But she wanted to get in nearer the center—by the waterfall. She took another step. Seconds later, Jen eased her hand out of Max's and handed him her tube. "Wait for me to tell you when."

He nodded with a serious demeanor.

Crouching slightly, Jen jumped.

Cold water rushed at her pores, and goosebumps erupted across her body. Though she'd expected it, the icy water still managed to rip a gasp from her as she surfaced. The reminder of how long Blake had been under while finding Tessa's pack made Jen shiver even more. It only took seconds for hypothermia to set in.

"Okay, Max," she called breathlessly, "toss it in."

The light breeze surrounding the falls caught the tube as Max flung it, and it glided forward in a rush, landing a few feet away from Jen. With a couple of quick strokes, she grabbed one handle, then the other. Chuckles from Blake caused her to grin as she tried to shimmy onto the float.

"Don't laugh. Help me," she squealed as she tried and failed again.

"You gonna push me under the water?"

As she pulled the tube toward her husband, her brows lifted. "I wouldn't do that."

"Never." He shook his head, agreeing with her. "Unless you're still angry."

Jen gulped. "I was worried you'd get hurt."

Blake smiled tightly. "Before that."

Jen ducked her head. "Oh. Yeah. You were probably right. I should give Sydney some room." Admitting that wasn't so easy, and she scrunched her nose. "I should probably apologize, huh?"

"To me? Never. To Sydney? Can you do it in three words or less?"

Jen guffawed. "Never need to apologize to you? I probably need to apologize to you on a daily basis."

"Hey! What about me?" Max waved his arms in the air.

His yelling scratched at Jen's ears, and she twisted to face him in time for a giant splash to strike her in the face. Sputtering, she narrowed her eyes, yelled Sydney's name, and shook her finger at her daughter, but she forgot to wipe the smile from her own face in the process.

"Sorry, Mom," Sydney said as she smiled and climbed out of the water, then crossed the sandstone outcropping to Max.

Warmth tickled Jen's chest. Maybe an apology wasn't necessary.

Holding one handle of her tube while Blake held the other, Jen watched as Sydney whispered to Max, then took his hand and counted to three before they both jumped. A second later, Max's head and shoulders popped above the surface of the water like a dart.

"Again," he screamed as Sydney emerged next to him.

With the kids having fun, Jen slid around the tube and grinned at Blake. "I should find another time to apologize, huh?"

Blake nodded, one brow raised. "Timing matters."

"Fine." Jen sighed and stared at her husband. "Gonna help me get on my tube now?"

"And how do I do that?"

Jen shrugged.

Blake smirked. "Hold the handles and pull yourself up. I'll help lift your love sacks out of the way."

"Love sacks?"

He wriggled his brow.

"How about my waist." She chuckled. "Goofball."

"All right. Your waist."

Jen clutched the handles of the tube and started kicking her feet, lunging forward. Blake disappeared under the water and gave her a boost. As her body bounced onto the tube, she rolled to her back, and Blake surfaced next to her. "How's that?"

"Colder." Jen shivered. "Thanks, muscles."

"Anytime, but I think I'd b-better get ou—"

"Daddy, will you catch me?"

Jen shaded her eyes as she looked up. Tessa stood at the edge of the cliff, wearing her life jacket, her hands flapping down by her thighs.

Blake cleared his throat. "You're fine, Tess. You'll pop up like a cork with that thing on."

"I'm scared."

"You can come in from the trail." Jen put her hand down as the sun eased lower on the horizon.

Tessa flapped her hands harder. "I want to jump."

That was something Jen hadn't expected, not after the earlier excitement. She'd half expected Tessa to curl up in a tent and refuse to come out. No blame there, not from Jen. Truth was, had Jen not gotten so hot before arriving at camp, she probably would have done exactly that. Almost losing a pack, and fearing for her husband's life had been enough. Tessa's desire to jump, let alone get back in the water, impressed her.

Blake squinted up at Tessa. "I can't catch you, but I promise to save you before you die."

"Da-ad."

"What? What's gonna keep me afloat?" Blake shuddered, and Jen raised an eyebrow at him. With a wave of his hand, he shook off her concern.

"Just jump," Sydney shouted from the rock she and Max were playing on.

Tessa shook her head.

"I'll do it with you." With a huff, Sydney dove into the water and started paddling to the edge.

"No," Tessa yelled.

Jen dangled her feet toward Blake, nudging his shoulder. "She needs you, Dad," she whispered.

"What if I jump with you?" Blake asked.

Tessa nodded, shaking, though perfectly dry.

Jen trailed her toes down her husband's legs, as he left the side of her tube for the bank, his goosebumps growing under her touch. She glanced at his feet as he kicked under the water. "When was the last time your feet got sun, Blake? They're whiter than mine."

Climbing out, Blake shivered as he joined Tessa on the edge of the cliff. "On the count of three. Okay?"

Tessa nodded. "Three. Got it."

"One . . . two . . . three."

Tessa and Blake bounded off the cliff, an enormous splash drenching Jen's torso where her suit had dried. Bursting from the surface nearly as fast as she had darted through it, Tessa whooped. "I did it. Yes!" She wrapped her arms around Blake as he surfaced. "Let's do it again."

"Can't, k-kiddo. I-it's time for me to get out."

Now floating in the shadow of the cliff, Jen scanned the pool. The sun glistened at the far north edge, but nowhere else. She was cold too. "Only a few more minutes, guys, then we all need to get out and get dry."

51

"I just got in." Tessa frowned.

Jen looked at her daughter, considering what she'd said. "Jump a couple more times, but we have to dry off and warm up before bed."

"I get to light the fire," Max yelled as he hurried to get out.

Jen pushed at her hair as a gust of wind caught it, and she watched Blake climb out of the water. Close to the top of the ledge, he stumbled, but before she could react, another splash of crystal water sloshed atop her, rewetting her nearly dry hair.

Giving up, she rolled off the float, and playfully splashed Tessa, proud of her for jumping alone. "Are you jumping again?" she asked.

"Yeah."

"One more time, then it's time to get out." She turned to her other two children. "Max, Syd, after Tessa's next jump, climb out."

It didn't take long before two fully-dressed girls, bounced on their feet in front of a nonexistent fire. Jen struck a match and lit the single-burner propane stove, then handed the box of matches to Blake.

"Okay, Max, touch the match to the little sticks and pine needles at the bottom," Blake said as he handed a match to their son.

Max dragged the match across his whistle where Blake had attached a striker strip, then dropped it to the ground. "Oops."

Blake harrumphed and handed him another match. "Now, don't drop this one. They have to last us the week."

"Okay." Max struck the next match and carefully moved it toward the pile of tinder, but as the flames reached the first of the pine needles, he dropped it again. "It almost burned me."

"No, it didn't!" Blake snapped.

Jen flipped the fish in the frying pan and listened as her husband's patience waned. He'd barely held it together when showing Max how to gut the fish. Now he—

"No more Max. We'll die before you manage to start a fire." Blake struck a match and, holding it to the tinder with a shaky hand, dropped it.

Smothered by the sand and wind, the flame winked out.

Muttering under his breath, Blake struck another match and carefully touched the flickering flame to several pine needles. Motioning to Sydney to watch the fish, Jen stood. Blake's chest rose and fell sharply, and as she approached Max, Blake shuddered.

"It's okay, Max, you can try again tomorrow." She gave the boy a quick hug, then stepped to her husband.

His fingers twisted with hers, and she traced the back of his hand with her thumb and watched as he shuddered again. "How cold are you?"

"I'm fine."

"You've got to let your body shiver, Blake."

"I can't exactly stop. The fire will warm me up."

"Enough?"

"I'll let you finish the job later." He slowly winked, then dropped to the ground as fatigue took over.

With a rush, Jen sent him into the tent and out of the wind, then she hurried to get him food. Three trips through the creek, ferrying the family to the campsite with one deep dive, and a family swim. He'd hardly had time to warm up before the sun set and the evening breeze started whipping past his skin. He never would have told her how cold he really was, and if his symptoms progressed, they'd all be lost.

After Jen and Tessa finished cleaning up the dinner mess, Jen called goodnight to the kids and crawled into her tent with Blake. The air in her dollar-store-raft-turned-air-mattress shifted between chambers as she scooted deeper into her sleeping bag. Even moving around, the cold had seeped into her bones. The difference between night and day temperatures in the canyon was palpable.

Once settled, she rolled toward her husband and placed her hand on his cheek. In the dim light, she could make out his rosying complexion. Skimming his shoulder with her fingers, she relaxed with the softness of his skin, cool but not icy.

"I'm fine," he muttered as he shifted toward her.

"Are you warm?"

"Am I shivering?"

"No. But that can mean you're getting worse."

He smirked. "At that point, I wouldn't know I was cold, either."

Jen snuggled closer to him, his breath now warming her forehead. "I missed so many signs. Shivering, paled skin, moody. Stumbling." She lifted her head. "You never mumbled."

He combed his fingers through her tangled hair. "And I didn't stumble. I stubbed my toe on a rock. If I'd been stumbling it would have been a lot worse. And I definitely would have been mumbling."

Blake's chest rumbled as he groaned. "I lost it with Max."

She squeezed him tighter. "He's already over it."

As Jen's memories of the day weaved through her mind, one more question surfaced. "Did you tell Sydney to gather wood?"

"Nuh." The syllable barely made it past Blake's lips as his hand drifted away from her hair and back into his sleeping bag.

Dating's Stream

Jen lurched to a sitting position for the third or fourth time. She'd already lost count. With each jerking motion, Blake gently brought her back to him. How could he be so calm? Max climbing out of the tent had been enough for her to grab her shoes. Had he developed a rash from the poison ivy? He wasn't complaining. Then Tessa started setting up the stove to make hot chocolate. That had worried her until Sydney jumped in. Her middle child had so many strengths, but comprehending the mechanical workings of a fire-breathing appliance wasn't one of them. Now Max was holding a knife to gut a fish he'd just caught with Sydney?

"Blake, he can't—"

"He can. I showed him last night. Besides, Sydney's with him." Pressing his lips to her head, he whispered, "They're not fighting."

When the aroma of fresh-cooked trout wafted toward the tent and the buzz of the propane burner disappeared, Blake pushed out of his sleeping bag and handed Jen her confiscated shoes. "Hurry up, I need some of that," he whispered. "Save me some," he called to the kids as he unzipped the tent door.

Jen couldn't help but giggle when a plastic plate with small bits of trout topped with granulated butter met him at the flap. He sat near her feet with a grin. "Thanks, Syd. Good to know we can count on you to catch us food. This is great."

"Granola?" Sydney asked.

"Sure, I'll take some of that. Mom probably wants some too."

Jen pushed herself toward the door, her tender muscles revolting. "I would, thank you."

The first mouthful of honey-roasted oats, raisins, and pecans brought a rumble to her belly. She was hungrier than she thought.

"It's good, huh?" Blake grinned as he watched her chew.

"Yeah, but I don't know about eating it for three days in a row. I'm looking forward to my apple." Jen relished the thought of eating the juicy apples she'd packed in. Fruit was heavy but worth the extra weight. At least to her. Loving her family, she'd packed two extra— a half apple each. Three apples she could handle, five seemed excessive. She smiled at Blake. "I think I'll have mine tomorrow."

Once everyone had finished eating, Jen cleaned up the cooking mess, giving the kids a break. As they went off exploring the area around them, Blake peered through the small set of binoculars he'd brought, scanning the sky and gazing up the canyon.

"No clouds. What do you think about going up a side canyon today? We can find a spot to set up camp outside of it and hike or swim our way up. Might even find some petroglyphs."

After placing the frying pan back in her pack, Jen sat down by the empty fire ring. "I love looking at stick figures on rocks. Is there another canyon nearby?"

"From what I can tell, there's one about a mile from here."

Jen twisted her mouth to the side as she studied the landscape. "What if we left camp here?"

Blake furrowed his brow. "We could, but then all of our exploring has to be done from here. If we move up a mile or two, we don't have to move camp tomorrow and we can spend it exploring new sites."

She pulled a face.

"Come on, beetle, it'll be fun." He sidled up to her, his grin wider than the creek, and pulled her into a hug.

"Maybe we can find some softer ground?"

"There's bound to be a nice, soft place where the canyon widens."

"There'd better be." Jen poked him in the side, laughing when he yowled. "Sydney, Tessa, Max, come pack up," she yelled, her voice bouncing off the canyon walls. "Time to go."

"Can't we stay here?" Sydney asked.

The whole idea of breaking camp to set it up again an hour later sounded stupid to her. But, no matter how much she whined, her parents wouldn't budge. Realizing nothing she said mattered, she stomped into the tent and started stuffing her sleeping bag. Maybe they'd find somewhere softer to sleep. *Right*. Who was she kidding? She'd be the one who ended up sleeping with a half-inch root under her shoulder blade regardless of where they were. It was the same whether they were doing chores, watching a family movie, or camping. Sydney got nagged, lectured, and a growing root under her shoulder blade.

As Sydney pushed the mummy bag deeper into its sack, Tessa, who hadn't made a peep of complaint but had gone straight to the tent and hid, started shoving a limp hand at hers. A minute later, her sister sat back with a pout. "It won't stay down."

The prodding root grows. Sydney rolled her eyes and tied her sack off with a knot, then slid it into a waterproof bag, otherwise known as a knotted trash bag. "Hold it with your knees," she griped.

Tessa pushed the bottom of her sleeping bag into the sack, and when it expanded back out less than an inch, she threw herself down to her backside. "It never works."

Pursing her lips, Sydney ignored her. It was the same every single time. "Hurry up. We have to do the tent." When would Tessa grow up?

"Syd, look at mine," Max said.

Sydney glanced at her brother and bit back a retort. Half the bag billowed from its case. Though, he had tied a decent knot. "You'll need to punch the top in, Max."

"Can you help them, Sydney?" her mom groaned from outside.

There it was. The call to do everything her sister and brother hadn't learned to do themselves.

"I am. I told them how," Sydney said.

"Show them how."

Show them how. How many times had Sydney shown them how? If she didn't *show them how,* Dad did. But Mom never said *keep trying* to them like she had to her. Mom never rescued her. Why should she rescue Tessa and Max?

Undoing Max's knot, she gripped the billowing bag and punched it into one side of the sack, then repeated the action, forcing the sleeping bag to the other side. "Max, tie another knot for me, okay."

"Why'd you undo the one I did?"

Sydney blew her annoyance out through rounded lips. "Had to get the rest of the bag in."

"Oh."

Max took the string and carefully made a loop, then pushed another loop halfway through it.

Sydney, holding Max's stuffed sleeping bag, looked over at Tessa. Her sister still pushed at the mound of bedding, but the softness of her touch remained unproductive.

Once her brother finished, Sydney snatched Tessa's sleeping bag, which fell completely out of the sack. Tessa stared at her with wide eyes, then burst into tears.

"Stop crying, and get any air left in the air mattresses out," Sydney snapped harsher than intended as annoyance whirled in her chest. She shoved at the bag until her knees could support the slipcase, then she slammed fist after fist into it. With each punch, her anger subsided a little more until she slowed and finished by sliding the puffy fabric to each side as she turned the stiff case counter-clockwise. Maybe stuffing sleeping bags wasn't so bad.

While she knotted the sack, her dad stuck his head into the tent. "Finished in here yet?"

"No." She swallowed, quietly allowing her frustrations to boil again.

He looked at her once before glancing at Max. "Good job, buddy. Hand me your air mattress, and I'll get that rolled up and put away. Where's your pack?"

With her pack on, Sydney followed the trail as she glanced at the canyon walls, her mind filled with one question. Why had she gotten so mad at Tessa and Max? She hadn't been able to successfully stuff her own sleeping bag until three years ago. No matter how hard she'd tried, she hadn't had the strength to get the billowing fabric into a sack the size of a throw pillow.

Smaller? Younger? Were those really excuses? Did it matter?

She exhaled sharply, only somewhat from exertion, and smiled wanly as the sun touched the deep-green grapevines on the south bank. They looked so soft, and Braden's eyes were that same shade of green. The vines were a different kind of luscious beauty than Braden was though. Still memories of his soft touch on her hand fluttered into her mind.

The fact that he'd shown any interest in her still stunned her. His perfect smile caught the attention of all the girls at school, not just hers. Not just Crystal's either.

When they'd first started dating, everyone gathered around her desk and asked for details. What was he like? What did they do on Friday nights? Freshman to senior girls mentioned his eyes with a dreamy haze in their own.

But all of that died after a few months.

And so had Braden's attention.

Sydney took an extra step to catch up with her dad, not wanting to fall behind.

"So?" her dad asked.

"Huh?" She looked at him, bewildered. Apparently, he'd asked her a question.

"This is better than any silly party, isn't it?"

"Um." How was she supposed to answer that? "We could have left today instead of yesterday. Then I could have gone to the party and come here."

Dad chuckled. "There'll be other parties. Even other boys."

"Da-ad."

What other boys? No other guy had glanced her direction, let alone given her the time of day.

"What?" He raised a hand in question, his eyes gleaming. "There's lots of fish in dating's stream. Don't settle for the minnow."

"Braden isn't a fish."

"Sure, sure. He's a good guy. Maybe he can join us on a hike sometime. Go fishing on the Rim."

"Maybe." Sydney grimaced. Any time she mentioned so much as going to the park, Braden scoffed at the idea of leaving technology behind.

Dumpsters Make Dollars

Evan shut the door, then leaned over his desk. What he would give to be hiking West Clear Creek with his brother. Instead, he was in charge of keeping their company running. And the Butler job was exactly what B&E Construction Management needed. Unfortunately, dealing with Ada Butler's indecisiveness might kill him before he ever had the chance to finish and get paid. First, she'd wanted white cabinets, then gray, now it was natural ash, *but not that knotty kind.* He shook his head. The knotty kind. He scoffed as he sat down in his chair and pinched the bridge of his nose.

The Butler contract pushed his foot through the door, out of the middle-class, low-budget jobs and into the upper-class, high-budget work with custom backsplashes, claw-foot tubs, and wool rugs over polished marble floors. It meant the difference between an occasional chuck steak and an occasional upscale restaurant.

If this job ran smoothly, Ada was certain to mention his and Blake's company to her neighbors, especially with all the entertaining she did.

Resting his head on the back of his chair, with the phone to his ear, he listened to the line ring for the third time.

"R&J Cabinetry."

"Joanne, I need to change that order for Ina Street again."

"Again?"

"She read some article. Natural ash is the new platinum in kitchen standards. Something like that anyway." He tapped a pencil on his desk. "Oh, and make sure it's not that knotty ash, either."

Joanne snorted. "No knots. Got it."

Evan chuckled. "Any way I can get those by next week?"

"Friday next week good?"

A groan rumbled in his chest. "Monday?"

"No way, no how."

"Come on, Joanne, help a guy out, will ya?"

"I'm trying."

The sound of clicking on a keyboard reached him, and he puffed out his cheeks, then blew out slowly.

"I can do Wednesday, but that's the soonest I got," Joanne said.

"Tuesday? And I'll send you a fruit basket."

"Oh, I do love a good fruit basket, but no can do."

"Guy's got to try." Evan glanced at his watch. Eleven o'clock. "Go have lunch, and tell that husband of yours he owes you a big kiss from me."

"Say hi to Michelle."

"Sure will." He pulled the phone away from his ear, then pushed it back up. "You guys still coming over on Saturday?"

"Already bought my suit."

Evan punched the button on the phone. At least one project promised to end on time. The Marksam family pool would be finished within the week. His kids were biting at the proverbial bit to jump in, but shotcrete needed time to cure.

Truth be told, he couldn't wait to jump in himself. He arched his back. Though a hot tub might be better for his sore muscles.

Flipping the light switch, he stepped into the heat of midday, ready to chow down on whatever Michelle had kindly packed him for lunch. Breakfast had been replaced with fixing a safety issue at the Knox job. If the guys didn't take safety glasses more seriously, he'd have to look for different drywallers. All of it was just part of the job, and half of the work would go to his brother, Blake, when he returned from his family adventure.

Evan started his truck and relaxed his shoulders, working to ease the tension. He wondered when Michelle would agree to hike the canyon with him. Not for a while, he supposed. Her fifth pregnancy had been harder than expected, and the infection following her cesarean hadn't helped.

The drive to Nina Street was too short, and Evan stuffed half his sandwich into his mouth, intent on eating something. Pulling up, he stared at the house. Where was the dumpster? Renovations, especially after house fires, did not go well without dumpsters.

Slamming the truck door, he swallowed the last of the brown bread Michelle said was good for him, then grabbed his hard hat out of the back. "Jim!"

"Yeah, boss?" Jim yelled back, tossing a cabinet onto a growing pile of refuse.

"We can't just throw stuff in the yard."

Jim stepped over to him, lowering his voice to below a shout. "Dumpster never showed. Figured you'd want us to work anyway."

The right side of Evan's jaw popped as he ground his teeth. "Yeah, but this garbage has to stay out of the neighbors' sight. We can't afford any more complaints from this place. Move it back inside. Store it in the backyard or a bedroom or something."

Continuing to grumble, Evan punched the last digit on his phone's keypad. "Yeah, this is Evan Marksam. I ordered a forty-yard to thirty-five, fifty-seven West Nina Street, and it's not here."

"Let me look that up. One moment please."

The woman's voice was smooth, but Evan rolled his eyes anyway. He'd called to confirm the dumpster two days ago, and she'd been the one to take his call.

"Okay, I have it right here. Oh, it is late."

The sound of clacking keys tapped at Evan's ear through the phone.

"Looks like we're a driver short today. I'll put a rush on it for tomorrow."

"I need it now," Evan said. "My guys are gutting a house fire and have nowhere to put the junk."

"I understand. I'm so sorry about the confusion."

"Can anyone drive it over today?"

"I don't—one moment. . . . Hey, Joe, can you drive a dumpster to Nina Street in Phoenix? . . . Thanks.

"You're in luck," the woman said, returning to the phone call, "I can get it there by four o'clock this afternoon."

With a shuddering breath, Jen jumped feet first into the frigid water, then quickly swam for her pack as it floated away from where Blake was positioning his. Max's laughter floated toward her from downstream, and she started after him. Blake would catch up.

The towering canyon walls shaded most of the crystal-clear creek, despite it being late morning, yet the gentle tips of the rippling waves glistened. Jen shivered at the thought of swimming upstream on their way back when exhaustion would leaden their muscles.

This is nothing more than a little family adventure, not a mountaineering project. Jen shook her head and lightly scoffed as Blake's words pricked her mind. She kicked some water his direction. "Coming, mountain boy?"

His hand grabbed her foot, and she screamed.

He guffawed. "Right behind you, beetle."

As he sidled up beside her—their tubes bouncing against each other, causing Jen to tighten her grip—he said, "Isn't this great? The kids'll never get to see something like this again."

This was why Jen had agreed to the family adventure. Because it brought such an alluring smile to Blake's lips—as long as he wasn't suffering hypothermia, that was. Besides, the canyon was beautiful. Even without the stunning foliage of the riparian areas, that fact was undeniable. Waves of hardened sediment adorned the currently sheer walls, which occasionally appeared craggy. Strands of vermilion mixed with the buff sandstone at the creek's edge, and the towering bright-white cliffs above reflected in the near-still water at the center of the pool.

Jen glanced below the glimmering water to the jagged rock bottom, then up to her husband as her mind slipped into past memories.

While dating, Blake had once convinced her parents to let him take her and Charlie on a day trip to the Mogollon Rim—simply called *the Rim* by locals. Dad had nearly jumped out of his skin, but Mom helped him calm down until he'd finally relented, making Blake promise to keep both his children within sight at all times.

By the time they arrived in Payson, Charlie had had enough of the car. Without so much as a flinch, Blake parked at the McDonald's and offered her older brother a Happy Meal. Jen could hardly keep up with Charlie as he rushed inside the crowded restaurant.

As they stood in line, Blake brushed Jen's hair away from her ear and slid his arms around her from behind. "They used to have a metal playground outside. I used to play on it when we'd stop on our way to Phoenix." His words tickled her neck.

She nodded. "Charlie got stuck in the Hamburglar jail one time."

"Officer Big Mac! You've been here before?"

She giggled. "Everyone has. I burned myself on the curly slide."

"Me too!"

After lunch, Blake clasped hands with Jen and Charlie, one on each side of him. "I can't wait to show you one of my favorite swimming holes."

Jen looked up at him when he turned off the main road. "Isn't the river that way?" She pointed behind them.

"That's a different crossing."

It wasn't long, and the road turned to dirt. As Blake took the right fork, he winked at Jen. "Hey Charlie, are you ready to go on a little hike?"

"A hike? Sure." Charlie grinned, always happy to do anything Blake suggested.

Charlie and Blake got along so well that Jen sometimes wondered if she and her boyfriend would ever get time to themselves. Sometimes kisses were more fun when they weren't stolen.

With little room on the bench seat of Blake's truck, it didn't take much to lay her head on his shoulder. The energy that sparked down her back warmed her chest. Then a heavy pressure landed on her arm, and she laughed, sitting up. "Charlie, you have a big head."

"Mom says it's the biggest."

"Where else are you supposed to store all your smarts, huh, Charlie?" Blake said.

"Yeah, where else?"

A little while after crossing the river, Blake turned onto another road that ended almost immediately at a closed gate.

"Oh no," Jen said.

Blake grinned and shut off the engine. "This is it."

Jen eyed him warily. "Where's the water?"

"'Bout a half mile that way." He nodded past the gate.

Blake helped Jen out of the truck, then stuck his hand under the seat. She watched him curiously as he shook out a giant trash bag. "What's that for?"

"Cans."

She raised her eyebrows. "Cans?"

"Yup. Lots of people litter their way down to the river. I like to help clean up a bit. Besides, the cans are good for a few pennies."

Minutes later, the heat wrapped around Jen as they walked down the sunny dirt road. Along the way, Charlie gleefully climbed through manzanita and scrub oak, picking up every beer-infused can he saw. The sticky substance occasionally dripped down his arm. Jen shook her head, glad they'd be swimming.

By the time they reached the river, the black plastic bag, full of aluminum beer and soda cans, thinned at the middle. Blake stuffed it next to a ponderosa and took Charlie's sticky hand.

"Are you excited to swim, Charlie?" He watched Jen while speaking to her brother.

"Is it cold?" Charlie asked.

"Not after walking in this hot sun."

Jen stepped over the rocks, following Blake past small pools of sparkling, clear water. As she took in the beauty of a football-shaped pool, Blake nudged her until she glanced up. A few yards away, a twenty-foot waterfall cascaded into a deep, clear pool with a single rock protruding from the surface. A log with a few steps carved into it leaned against the steep rise of the slick rock incline. Even from where they stood, Jen could see the bottom.

"It's beautiful."

Blake took the lead with Charlie following behind him for the few yards they had left.

Once Charlie donned the life jacket Jen had carried for him, they enjoyed the cool of the water. The sun really had prepared them for the swim.

As much as Jen had enjoyed that day, especially the stolen kisses, her favorite part was when Blake led them a few feet past the rush of water at the top of the falls. There, the creek widened into an ankle-deep pool where a school of tiny fish darted to and fro. She'd looked past the fence that warned visitors not to trespass, wishing they could explore farther. Instead, she'd enjoyed the refreshing water at her feet and the warmth of the sun on her shoulders.

That day, Charlie had chased tiny fish while she and Blake talked quietly, dreaming of their future.

Jen's memory faded when Blake poked her in the side. "Earth to beetle."

"What was that?"

"Look up."

Jen allowed her legs to drift under the tube carrying her pack and gazed above their heads. Thirty feet up, wedged between the canyon walls, were full-sized logs.

Her mouth dried. "That's how high the water gets?"

"At least once, apparently." He looked at her. "Probably during a flash flood."

"When do those start again?"

"A couple of weeks."

Jen exhaled, remembering how he'd studied the horizon that morning. If he'd seen a single cloud, he would have turned them around and headed home. Still, what if that wasn't enough? Flash floods didn't always come with clouds; sometimes they came without warning, hence the word *flash*. A shudder surged through Jen, this one unrelated to the icy water surrounding her.

"Where are you now?" Blake nudged her again. "Ready to get out?"

"Yes," she sighed, excited to feel the warmth of the sun on her shoulders.

It had finally topped the southeastern cliff and flooded the creek with sparkling light.

Ten minutes later, a dry creek bed joined West Clear Creek. Near the confluence, a soft bed of gravelly sand invited them to set up camp. Jen watched as Sydney dropped her pack and rolled the kids' tent toward Tessa, who slumped to the ground, shivering from the long swim.

"Time to set up," Sydney said.

"I need to rest." Tessa hugged her knees.

Sydney glared at her sister. "You'll warm up better if you help set up the tent."

Tessa stood, as Jen knew she would, giving in—not to stay warm, but to keep the peace.

Their tent soon formed half a dome as Sydney waited for Tessa to connect one end of the tent pole before she connected the other. Seconds later, Sydney shooed Tessa away with a scowl, taking over completely.

The difference between Jen's daughters had become more evident throughout the week. Sydney may have fought the family hike at home, but she thrived outdoors. She pushed her physical limits, naturally seeing what needed to be done. Tessa, on the other hand, often gave Jen emotional support at home by quietly starting dinner or helping Max with homework. Jen looked forward to the day when they would work together equally without hurting one another's pride. To the day when she might better connect with both of them.

With Sydney.

Blake high-fived Max, congratulating him on a job well done. They'd set up the second tent and gathered driftwood for the evening fire.

Smiling at her husband and son, Jen's gaze drifted behind them to the southern wall of the canyon. Past young willows at the water's edge, fir trees appeared to grow out of the top of a ten-foot, vertical wall, climbing the craggy terrain higher until, once again, the sandstone sheared. A yellow bird flitted from one tree to another, trilling as it did so.

Jen glanced at the bright sky, then back at Blake. "The petroglyphs are how far?"

"They're right up there," he said, nodding at the side canyon.

Blake winked, and Jen had her answer. The ancient drawings rested on some boulder, and he didn't want to—or couldn't— divulge the distance.

"Do you remember?" she asked.

"It shouldn't take longer than an hour to get there. The hike will help finish warming everyone up."

Wiping the beads of moisture from her forehead, Jen noted how right Blake had been. At least when it came to the heat. Even Tessa had started sweating. The wide, flat creek bed of the side canyon had disappeared an hour or so after beginning their walk, and soon, the family found themselves scuttling over boulders and squeezing between stone slots. Jen was glad their camp was in the wider canyon—at least in a wider section. West Clear Creek was still plenty narrow. Her mind slipped back to images of the trees lodged between the canyon walls that she'd seen that morning. An involuntary shiver ran down her sweaty back. She shook her head. They were fine. The monsoon storms were still a couple of weeks away. She trusted Blake. Pushing the thought aside, she looked at her son.

She'd thought Max might tire or that he might develop his joyfully elusive poison ivy rash, but somehow, he had all the energy in the world, even while wearing the life jacket he'd refused to leave behind. Blake had to hold the boy back as he tried to scale a rock that was ready to tumble to the canyon's floor.

Two hours after beginning the side-canyon excursion, they finally stopped, each working to catch their breath as they stared in the direction Blake pointed. Shaded by an overhang, petroglyphs scrawled across the face of a smooth section of buff sandstone.

Max ran, stumbling over rocks as he rushed toward the ancient drawings. "What do they mean, Dad?"

Blake shrugged. "Not sure. What do you think?"

"That's a buffalo, and there's a fire." Max pointed.

"That looks like the sun going down, and—over here—this looks like an arrowhead." Sydney looked over her shoulder at Blake, straining just enough to see past the top of Max's small backpack, which held the first aid kit and other basic supplies.

Jen brushed a strand of hair away from Tessa's cheek. "What do you think?"

Tessa shrugged. "It all looks like graffiti to me. Kind of scribbly."

Jen chuckled. "Kind of."

Blake turned around, took Tessa by the hand, and tugged her toward the rock. "But unlike names carved into picnic tables or neon gang signs painted on walls, these were carved by the Sinagua to communicate. People have been coming to this canyon for thousands of years."

The corners of Tessa's mouth turned upward. "Cool. I think it says 'Buffalo see fire. Sun go down. Hunt tomorrow.'"

"What if it's read right to left? 'Hunted until sundown. Cook buffalo.'" Sydney smirked.

"What about, 'the buffalo is cold because the sun went down'?" Max jumped from one rock to another.

"You forgot the arrowhead," Sydney muttered.

He hung his head and toed a rock. "Maybe . . . 'The buffalo is cold because the sun went down. Burn the arrows.'"

Jen gave Max a cursory giggle. "Maybe."

Blake lowered himself to a flat rock. "Rest up. We need to leave in ten minutes to make it back in time for you three to cook dinner."

Groans echoed as their three children slumped to the ground.

Evan rested his eyes for a minute before opening the front door to the house that he and Michelle had built three years ago. The modicum of quiet helped brace him for the noise of four children under twelve who were about to rush his ankles. That didn't account for the cries of their youngest. If Michelle's day had gone anything like his, he'd be surrounded by whining. He hoped for laughter.

As the door cracked open, Evan's shoulders relaxed.

"Daddy, Daddy, Daddy!" Emily hurried over and wrapped her arms around his knees.

Picking her up, he tossed his two-year-old over his shoulder and bounced the rest of the way into the house.

"Dad, guess what?" Dylan said, running toward him. "I raced Davey on my bike and won!"

"That's great, Dyl. You must have been going real fast."

"I was."

"Hi, Dad." Maggie, his oldest, looked up from her book as he passed the couch.

"Mags, what're you reading?"

"Harry Potter."

"Good book. I read that when I was a little older than you."

In the kitchen, Michelle kept their four-year-old, Danni, who lunged toward him for a hug, from adding sticky sugar and cinnamon to the construction dust already on his clothing.

"Cookies? Danni, are you being a big helper?"

"Yup! Me and Momma are making *snickerwoodles*."

Evan leaned over and dropped a peck on Michelle's cheek. "Where's Ellie?"

Michelle nodded toward the swing in the corner. "Sleeping, thankfully. She cried most the afternoon again."

"Colic is hitting her pretty hard, huh?"

"Yeah."

"That's no *bueno*," he said, stealing a pinch of cookie dough and shoving it into his mouth before Michelle could slap his hand. "Has the doctor said anything?"

"Not really. He doesn't think it's reflux. Mostly it's *catnap when you can*. He obviously doesn't have five children . . . even if his wife does."

"Could be worse." He grabbed another pinch of dough as she batted at his hand again. "Could have had colicky triplets," he finished.

"Ugh. Don't say things like that. It just makes me more tired."

"Go lie down. Danni and I can roll and bake cookies." He grabbed an apron and turned the faucet on to wash his hands. "Can't we, Danni?"

"Yeah!" Danni tossed her arms in the air, cinnamon and sugar peppering the floor behind her.

Michelle eyed him. "Don't burn them. They're for the Ready Reader's bake sale."

"I got this. Go." Evan shooed his wife toward the bedroom, shoved another pinch of dough in his mouth, then rolled some into a ball and handed it to Danni.

Less than five minutes and half a tray of rolled snickerdoodles passed before Ellie's piercing wail announced the end of her nap.

"Mags, you beautiful Ready Reader, why don't you come over and roll some dough while I get Cranky McCrankerson over there."

"Momma says I can't because I have a sore throat."

Evan's brow furrowed as he turned to Dylan. "You like cookies, don't you?"

The seven-year-old nodded.

"Start rolling, and you can eat two warm cookies before dinner."

Dylan rushed to the stool to stand next to his sister, and Evan picked up three-month-old Ellie, who squirmed uncomfortably in his arms.

Bouncing on his feet and holding Ellie over his shoulder while patting her back, he soon stood behind Dylan and Danni, overseeing the cookie rolling. "A little smaller, Dylan."

Dylan dropped all but a pea-sized piece of dough back into the bowl.

"A little bigger. Here"—Evan handed him a spoon—"no less than what fits on the spoon; no more than what fits in your mouth."

Dylan dug a big scoop of cookie dough out of the bowl. "Like this?"

"Let me show you," Evan said.

Dylan handed the spoon back, and Evan dug out the perfect amount. "See how you can't see the spoon?"

Dylan nodded.

"Open your mouth."

Dylan opened his mouth, and Evan shoved the spoon into it.

"See how it will fit in your mouth?"

Dylan bent over in a fit of laughter as he nodded, and Evan handed him a clean spoon.

"Try again."

It wasn't long before the cookie makers had two trays of baked snickerdoodles and the third, and last, in the oven.

Evan moved toward the back door and gazed at the new pool, Ellie fussing at his shoulder. He and Michelle had wanted a pool for several years, but it had taken time for him and Blake to build their business . . . and Evan and Michelle to build their dream house. Now things were a little less tight, and he cherished his ability to spend the last couple of daylight hours with his family. That was something Blake had taught him. Not that his brother realized it.

Blake had always put Evan and their parents above everything else. Until he met Jen. Then he put two families above everything else. His own and hers.

Evan had just started high school when Blake and Jen met.

Blake opened Evan's bedroom door, flung himself onto the bed next to Evan, and dropped a bar of soap on him, then noisily sniffed the air. "Hurry up and wash that stink off yourself. Game starts at seven."

"I'm not going to a stupid football game." Evan scoffed and picked up the Gameboy he'd dropped.

"Look, all I'm saying is that I have a date tonight and I'm willing to give you a ride. If you shower."

What he meant was you need friends.

Blake picked up the soap from the floor, placed it on Evan's stomach, and left the room.

"You're my friend." Evan muttered on his way to the shower.

He'd meant it. Blake was his friend. Still.

The construction management business was Evan's dream, not Blake's. But when Evan had nearly killed his credit and his business, Blake had offered to help save both. Blake still ran his own yard-design business, too, claiming the two companies complemented each other. They did, to the benefit of B&E Construction Management, not Lazy Beetle Yard Designs.

Ellie bopped her head nearer to Evan's neck and attempted to suckle, then wailed again.

"Hungry, are you?" He swayed into the kitchen and made a bottle. "I know you don't like this, but it'll make the hunger go away."

Life Isn't Fair

Ten minutes passed faster than Jen wanted to admit, and her knees creaked in defiance when Blake pulled her to her feet, claiming it was time to start back. She leaned against him, the bulky fanny pack buckled to her waist getting in the way as he wrapped his dusty arms around her.

"It'll feel good to rinse off in the creek," she muttered.

"Brr." He forced his body to shiver as he pulled her closer. "As long as you promise to keep me warm tonight."

She laughed, even as an emptiness filled her chest when he dropped his arms. Hypothermia had struck him the night before, and she'd almost missed it. "You have a sleeping bag for that," she said, pushing past the unease of the memory.

"Maybe I want both." He winked as he pulled Tessa up from her rock.

"My feet hurt," Tessa whined.

Jen watched as Blake wrapped his arm around their middle child.

"Mine too," he said. "Will you rub them later?"

"Da-ad, that's gross."

A silent chuckle beat at Jen's throat over the exchange. It was gross. Luckily, he didn't mean it. Blake hated having his feet touched.

Turning to face her other two children, Jen huffed. "Max, wait for us."

Max stopped mid-boulder to acknowledge her, then scrambled to the top—Sydney only a few yards behind him.

"I'll walk with him until his energy runs out," Blake said.

"My hero. How did I ever manage to capture you?" Jen swatted at his behind, and he promptly avoided her swing.

"That was Charlie."

She crinkled her nose at him.

"You were pretty cute diving into those bushes though," he finished.

"The cutest."

After kissing her cheek, Blake hurried to catch up to Max.

"Mom, what was Uncle Charlie like as a kid?" Tessa asked.

"Hmm, what was Charlie like?" Jen stared up at the sky, then eyed Tessa and took a step forward. "Funny. Kind. Happy. Unless he was grumpy, then he was a miserable coot."

"He's older than you, right?"

"He is, but with his struggles, it felt more like I was the oldest. Grandma and Grandpa did most things for him, but I had to help occasionally. At school, Charlie was my unspoken responsibility."

"How come?"

"Because kids would tease him—pretending to be his friends— always when the teachers weren't around."

"That would suck."

Jen hid a smile. "It wasn't that bad. Sometimes it was hard for me to realize that I mattered to others, though."

"Because they always paid attention to him?"

"Because I didn't realize that his needs didn't take any love away from me." Jen sighed, and her brows pinned together. "Charlie needed a lot of attention when he was a kid. And he learned how to do things through rewards. TV time, little toy animals, stuff like that.

"He struggled to tie his shoes. When he learned how, he got to choose a new toy. When I learned to ride my bike, Grandma cheered and clapped, but then had to take care of Charlie because he fell off his scooter. Charlie would be disruptive in class, so when he had a good day, he'd get extra TV time. I'd get straight A's and a hug."

"That doesn't sound fair."

Jen shrugged and wobbled her head with a grin. "Life isn't fair."

Tessa huffed. "That's not what I mean."

Jen stepped over a rock and waited for Tessa to do the same. "I know." She smiled at her daughter. "But that stuff is more about me. You want to know how Charlie captured Dad."

"That wasn't Charlie."

"Oh, yes it was. Dad paid more attention to Charlie than me at first. Always talking to him about elephants. Giving him books about the Savanna. Taking him out for treats. We went to a football game the day we met, and Dad talked to Charlie the whole time—sometimes about me."

"You were scary, and he had a cool hat," Blake called from up ahead.

Jen and Tessa laughed.

"Besides, some of that time, I spent talking to Evan."

"That's right," Jen said. "I forgot about Evan. Dad thought Evan needed friends so he dragged him along." She nudged Tessa's shoulder. "I think he was trying to set me up with his brother."

"Oh, no, I'd—"

Blake's words cut off as Sydney started yelling. "Max, stop! Get back. Daaad!"

The sound of a whistle blowing shrieked through the air.

Blake lunged forward as Sydney screamed louder.

Jen, still unaware of what was wrong, grabbed at her neck and tried to force down the lump forming in her throat. She watched Blake bound down the dry creek bed from one rock to another. He lunged toward a stick in their son's hand. One she could barely see. As her husband curled his fist around the stick and pushed Max back, he vanished from Jen's sight. A grind and snap splintered through the canyon with the fading rattle of a snake—and Max's shrieking.

Jen ran toward her husband. Mindful of the rocks underfoot, she pushed herself faster, the surrounding landscape bouncing in and out of her vision. As she rounded a boulder, all the blood rushed from her head, leaving her weak. Queasy. Blake was on the ground, groaning, and Sydney held Max back as a diamondback slithered off the path. Tears rolled down her oldest daughter's face.

"Was anyone bitten?" Jen forced the words past the fully formed lump in her throat as she landed on her knees next to Blake.

"No." Blake clutched his leg. "It missed."

Sydney sniffed.

"Where?" Jen stared blindly forward, unable to take in what she was looking at even as she gaped at his leg, her hands frozen above his thigh.

"It's my ankle. It broke."

A blubbering gasp escaped Tessa as she joined her siblings, crying.

Jen's heart raced as she nodded at Blake. She slid her gaze down his leg to the bulging knot that had once been his ankle. How had she missed that? His foot, slightly wrenched inward, didn't even look right. She swallowed the swirling acid pushing at her throat and blinked three times in quick succession. What would they do now? A broken ankle might as well be a death sentence in the canyon, as much so as hypothermia. And they'd already weathered that. She inhaled. *One thing at a time*, she told herself as she combed Blake's hair with her fingers.

"You gotta wrap it." Blake's voice shook as he spoke, the pain written in the taut line of his mouth.

Jen closed her eyes and exhaled sharply. "Stop crying!" she yelled as she faced her children, who cowered in response. "Syd, I . . . I need the first aid kit."

Picking up two sticks that only moments before had been one, Jen bit her lip. "Tessa and Max, I need two big, long sticks that won't bend.

Opening the first aid kit, Jen gazed at the interior, her thoughts sluggish, her hands shaking. Pretending. That's all she was doing. She didn't know how to treat a broken ankle. Sure, Blake had taught her and the kids, but none of them had any real experience. Just practice on a laughing family member with a plethora of old towels. Where were the towels now?

More than that, she didn't have a clue how to get Blake out of the blasted canyon. Two canyons. Shaking her head, she tried to focus. Pain relief. He needed something for the pain, right? "Do you hurt anywhere else? Did you hit your head?" she asked.

"Just my ankle." Blake panted.

"I can do this," she muttered as she worked to control her own rapid breathing. "Stay calm."

The seal over the ibuprofen snapped as she stabbed it with a rock. "Take four of these."

"You trying to drug me, beetle?"

"Sure am. Got to do what we can to keep you comfortable. Which also means finding that ankle some padding."

Glancing at the few supplies they had with them, she bit her lip. A life preserver would probably be best, the stiff foam would help support the joint while still being comfortable under the sticks. She reached to pick up Max's, the only one they had with them. Blake took her arm. "Not that. Cut my shirt off."

"You need more padding than that."

"Fine. I'll take your shirt too." He attempted to wriggle his brows.

Jen's face crumpled. *Great. My husband broke his ankle, and I've lost my sense of humor.* She choked out a scoff. Then his joke took root in her mind. "We have suits on. The girls and I have suits on! Maybe you can keep yours."

The corner of Blake's mouth turned up as she stood and waved at the kids, two of whom carried long, thick pieces of driftwood in her direction. "Hurry. Girls, I need your shirts."

Sydney removed her shirt and knelt down next to Blake. "Tessa," she hissed.

Stumbling forward, Tessa handed Jen her shirt.

"Sunscreen up, girls," Blake winced, despite his teasing tone.

Jen eyed her husband, his attempts at humor nagging at her frazzled nerves. "We're focusing on you right now." With a deep breath, she cleared some of the fog from her mind. "I'm going to wrap Dad's ankle with your shirts first. Once that's done, you girls will need to hold the sticks tight against his leg while I wrap the ACE bandage over them and the padding." Tension rose in her shoulders. She needed those blasted towels. One flimsy ACE bandage wouldn't be enough. But she'd known that. That's what the third shirt was for. She handed her shirt to Sydney. "Rip up one side-seam, then tear it into two-inch-wide strips."

Sydney snatched the tiny scissors out of the first aid kit.

While Jen had somewhat staved the shaking in her hands, she couldn't stave it from her heart or lungs. *A family adventure. A family adventure where Max climbs through poison ivy and Blake suffers hypothermia the night before he breaks his ankle after nearly getting bitten by a rattlesnake while hiking in a side canyon four miles away from camp.*

Jen took another deep breath. She could do this. They only had to make it to camp, then she could hike out for help. The only other option was waiting for Evan to gather a search party when they didn't show up in two days. Then the rescue crews would have to find them. That was too long, especially if they stayed where they were. Without enough water, they'd . . . Maybe just a little flood.

She winced. A flood was no solution. "All right, girls, let's get those sticks in place."

Max shuffled his feet. "Momma, I was just trying to get the snake to move. That's all."

His voice pricked at her nerves. "I know, Max."

"It was where we had to walk. The bushes were everywhere else."

"I know, Max."

As Jen finished tying the shirts around Blake's ankle, she heard Max take in a jagged breath before his voice cracked into a sob. She'd thought the stress of Blake's broken ankle was enough, but apparently not. Sitting back on her feet, she dropped her shoulders. "It's not your fault, buddy. Dad'll be okay."

Max let out another anguished cry.

"Do you think you could do me a favor?" Jen forced a smile. "Could you sit by Dad's head and keep him company?"

"Hey, Max, come tell me a joke. These guys are boring," Blake said, pain still lining his voice.

Max padded over and settled himself next to Blake, who reached out and took his hand.

"Okay, girls," Jen breathed as she stared at Blake's leg, trying to form a plan, "we have to lift his leg a little to wrap it. I'll slide this rock under his foot, then I'll get the sticks tied onto him before I wrap the bandage over the bottom half. You guys need to hold the sticks in place. These ties have to be tight enough that the sticks don't slide, but loose enough that he doesn't lose circulation. So hold them still. Is that right, Blake?"

"Sounds good to me," he said tightly. "Right, Max?"

Max nodded, his crying much more contained.

An anguished groan leaped from Blake's mouth as Jen carefully lifted his leg. Tying a strip of her shirt just above the ankle first, she moved up to a spot above his knee. "Is it too tight?"

"No." Blake's voice eased.

With a few more strips of her shirt, Jen alternated which stick she tied to Blake's leg, making sure everything was well secured. Afterward, she wrapped the ACE bandage as tight as she could around his bound ankle, immobilizing the up-and-down motion of the joint. Once done, she sat back and pinched the bridge of her nose. "Can you move your foot?"

"Help me up." Blake pushed at the ground with his hands.

Jen's muscles stung as she climbed to her feet and then braced his body as he lifted himself to his feet . . . foot.

"Isn't this great, guys? It's a real family adventure now." The words sounded taut even followed by his light laugh.

Tessa's face crumpled, and Max's eyes filled with more tears.

"Oh, it's not that bad. Just a broken bone. That's no big deal." Blake motioned for Jen to help him take a step.

With his arm draped across her shoulder, he slid his injured leg over the gravel, then bunny hopped on the other, inching forward. Literally.

It wasn't possible. They couldn't do this. She couldn't do this. A tear fell from Jen's eye, and she stared at the ground while helping him with a few more steps. Four miles and boulders. How would she get him over the boulders?

"See, guys, I'm moving now," Blake said.

Tessa sank to the ground in tears.

"Tess, you've got to get up," Jen said.

"Is he gonna die?"

Blake chuckled. "Not any time soon, baby girl. It's just a little break."

Tessa flung her arms into the air. "But you can't walk."

"What are you talking about?" Blake asked. "I'm walking right now."

Sydney snorted. "I wouldn't call that walking."

With Jen's help, Blake leaned against the edge of the narrowing canyon. "I may be a little slow." He looked at his kids and Jen, his jaw clenched. "Tell you what, you kids head back to camp, catch a few fish, and start dinner."

"Fish, again?" Max whined.

"Well, only if you catch it." Blake winked. "Otherwise, we have some ramen or cheesy something-or-other pasta, which do you want?"

"Ramen," Max yelled as he rushed down the trail.

"Syd, come here." Blake tilted his head as he called their oldest over. "Keep them calm. If we're not back by tomorrow evening, leave all the stuff and hike out to the car. Find cell service and call for help."

Jen watched as tension crawled across their sixteen-year-old daughter's face. "It just means we've had to stop. That's all," Jen added.

Sydney nodded and started after Max, who was currently waiting, somewhat impatiently, for his sisters.

Rushing down the trail, Sydney caught up with her brother. Jen dropped next to Tessa, who hadn't moved. "You too."

"I wanna stay with you."

Jen stared at her blond-haired daughter. Her heart was as soft as her features. Jen gently pushed Tessa's bangs out of her eyes.

"Go with them. Sydney will need help with Max. She's more nervous than she lets on, and his energy is back. Besides, with you around, Dad will push himself too hard, trying to keep up. We need to take it slow."

Tessa dragged a finger down the crack of a rock.

"Help me out, huh?" Jen said, giving her a hug.

Rising slowly, Tessa nodded and started down the trail, dragging her feet.

"Max, slow down."

Sydney's nerves burst into flames as she watched her brother's speed ease to a moderately fast walk. She hadn't even wanted to come on this stupid hike. She'd wanted to go to Braden's party and keep his attention on her instead of on Crystal. Her throat constricted, forcing her to gasp, then cough as fresh tears flooded her eyes. Now Dad was hurt. The last thing she wanted to do was hike out and find cell service by herself.

That was what he meant, right? For her to hike out alone? She grabbed at her hair, yanking at the roots. What if he wanted her to take the other two with her? She couldn't leave them alone, then she'd lose her whole family. But they'd slow her down.

"Max, I said *slow down!*"

She slumped to the boulder behind her. He wasn't that fast, but she didn't want to walk at all. Not anymore. *It's too much.* Her heart pounded in her chest, and she coughed a few more times—as if it would clear her mind. *I've got to stop thinking about it like that. Like I could lose my family. Like I've lost my dad. Dad will be fine. He and Mom might be slow, but they'll make it.*

She nodded, an attempt to believe herself.

Max stepped in front of her. "Are you tired?"

"No, I'm fine. Give me a minute."

Tessa sat on the rock next to her, her eyes as red as Sydney's felt. Though silent, Tessa's presence comforted her, even though Sydney would never admit it. "Maybe after we catch a few fish, we can go swimming." Sydney eyed her brother.

Max wrinkled his nose. "I don't want fish."

"We might not catch any. Then you'll be in luck." She clambered to her feet and picked her way down the jagged trail to where it smoothed out again.

As Max tried to pass her, she managed to snatch his hand. "You need to stay with us. I'm too stressed out to deal with you getting hurt."

"Fine." A puff of dust billowed around his foot as he stomped on the ground. "But I don't want fish."

Sydney thrust her arms into the air. "Whatever. I don't even care. I just want to get to camp and . . . and . . ." She growled in frustration as the tears came back.

Tessa stepped past her and took Max's hand. "I don't really want fish either. I bet Mom wouldn't care if we had some ramen instead."

Max grinned, then stuck out his tongue at Sydney, who rolled her eyes with a huff. "You guys do whatever you want. Never mind what Dad said."

The pounding in Sydney's chest didn't begin to slow until she cast a line into the creek for the tenth time. This time, she'd switched to some sparkly yellow bait that caked onto her fingers as much as onto the hook. If she couldn't catch anything, they'd have no choice but to eat ramen. Somehow, she didn't mind that as much has she had before.

Staring at the sky, her mind reeled. Wait until Braden heard about Dad breaking his ankle. Not to mention her coming face to rattle with a snake. That thing was thick. Even coiled it was huge. But her worry had vanished the second scattering rocks and pounding footsteps told her Dad was coming. She'd never questioned that he would take care of everything. They'd be safe because he'd save them.

It had always been like that.

But who would save them now? Where were the people Dad said they might see?

Standing up, she padded down the bank and closer to camp. The grasses and willows grew tall nearer the confluence, where the creek widened and the water shallowed. In order to use bait, she'd had to moved upstream to a small pool. It was nothing like those they'd had to swim through. And it kept her close enough to watch her siblings.

Tessa sat on rock with a tense grin plastered on her face as Max whipped a thin willow branch through the air. She must have cut one for him. A second later, her sister lunged from the rock with her own willow branch. Her hand notched at her waist, she caught Max unaware, and parried his sword.

This was why Mom liked Tessa more. Because she knew how to entertain and care for Max. Sydney knew how to catch fish. She glanced back at the still fishing pole. Sometimes.

With a sigh, she stepped back to the pole and glanced up at the sky again. Early evening had set in. If the fish were going to bite, this would be the time to use a fly. The one thing she didn't know about fishing. How to use a fly. She reeled in the line to discover the bait missing. Of course it was. Why would it still be there? She couldn't do this anymore. Dad was hurt, and she didn't want fish anyway.

Leaving the tackle and pole there, she jumped into the water, then climbed over the natural dam and into the shallows. From there, she slapped the surface of the creek with each step she took, mindful of the rocks below.

It didn't take long for her to hear Max and Tessa running toward her. Crystal droplets caught glimmers of light as they landed in the water. Maybe, for a moment, they could forget the distance between them and their parents.

Pain Management Later

Jen winced as she pushed at Blake's good foot while he attempted to pull himself onto the next boulder. After the last one, he'd hidden his hands from her view, but she'd seen the trails of blood left from his broken fingernails.

"Put me down," he panted.

Slowly lowering him, her arms shook nearly as much as his. And she was only support.

"We're not going to make it back to camp tonight." Blake leaned against the rock and eyed Jen.

"This is the last time we have to climb up. The rest is downhill. Or down cliff." She muttered the last part as she blinked back tears, but there was no question that he knew she was crying.

He gave her a soft smile as he shook his head.

Turning away from him, her face crumpled. "They're by themselves."

"The kids? I figured you were upset about sleeping on the rocks."

The guffaw caught in her throat, and she narrowed her eyes at him. "I'm not exactly looking forward to that either."

Blake motioned Jen closer, and despite his sweat-soaked, dirt-ridden shirt, she laid her head against his chest. "Shouldn't I be comforting you?"

He squeezed her shoulders, and she felt his muscles shake with the effort. "That's why I asked for a hug."

A small giggle escaped her throat, then her gaze swept up the pile of stone they stood on. Halfway up. They had no choice but to move, and either direction would be painful for Blake.

"Which way?" she asked.

"Up." He dropped his arms and exhaled.

Jen watched his shoulders tense even as they fell. "How are you going to do this?" she asked.

"With your help. There's no other choice, unless you want Sydney hiking out tomorrow."

She swallowed a wave of nausea and nodded.

"As soon as I get my foot off the ground, start lifting me—just like before." Blake waited until Jen met his gaze. "We've got this."

"Yeah."

Shuffling to face the crevasse between two boulders, Blake gripped the first two handholds. "Aim for the hold two feet up, first."

The crevasse wasn't much to look at. Even Max had made it through without help. But Blake carried the dead weight of a leg and two dense sticks. Not to mention all the pain that went with them. Where he could normally lift his single foot into a hold, using his arms for support, he now had to use his arms to lift his entire body with no support. Two feet may as well be two miles.

"Just another pull-up," he muttered.

Jen threaded her fingers together and slipped them under his good heel as it lifted off the rock, then she attempted to straighten

94

her knees just enough to propel him into the nook. His leg shifted left, and she overcorrected, slamming his bad leg into the side of the rock as he yowled. "Don't stop," he yelled through his agonizing scream.

"I'm sorry, I'm sorry."

His good foot slipped into the nook, and Jen let go. Giving each of them a short break.

Blake glanced at his foot's placement.

"Are you—"

"Pain management later, beetle." He looked back up, moving one hand, and then the other to holds slightly above his shoulders. "This one's shorter. About six inches."

Jen eased her hand under his unsupported heel. "Ready?"

"On three. One . . . two . . ."

Jen pushed his foot upward, her heart beating rapidly as another drop of sweat rolled down her back and his body tensed.

"Good. We're close. I'm going to pull myself to the top. You guide my ankle. Then it's all downhill."

A groan escaped Jen's lips. "Like that's any easier for you."

"Hey, at least you get a little bit of a break."

"I'm not worried about me, goober."

"I'm fine."

Jen sighed. "Yeah. You ready?"

Blake nodded and tugged on some unseen handhold at the top of the pile of boulders, soon bending at the waist.

"Hang on, I need to get higher." Jen quickly maneuvered from the first to the second foothold, using one hand to balance herself while supporting Blake's leg at the knee.

She'd once broken her finger while playing water volleyball. Pain from the minor injury had surged into her forearm for days, keeping her from so much as bending her wrist. A tear dropped from her eye as Blake growled in agony. His broken ankle, deformed and wrenched slightly inward, had to feel more like being hit by a truck over and over again.

As Jen clambered to the top of the pile, she took in her husband's reddened face. It was too much for him. Too much for anyone. "Blake—"

"It's getting dark. I think I see a halfway decent spot for the night. Over by those willows." He pointed.

"You need to rest."

His jaw clenched, and his eyes darkened. "I can't do that here. Let's go."

Jen threw her hands in the air. "Take half a second."

"I did. Get down there; I need you to guide my leg and help support me."

With pursed lips, Jen crawled down the five feet to the rocky wash below. Once his ankle was over the edge of the crack, Blake rolled to his belly, groaning as he lifted his knee off the ground as much as possible. Jen winced. Why wouldn't he take five minutes? That's all she wanted him to do. Five minutes to catch his breath, to let his muscles relax. She could force the issue, but he'd probably determine to scale down the rock pile on his own, leaving her to deal with her greatest fear. Life without him.

With her hand on his good leg, she guided him to the first foothold, paying close attention to the dead weight hanging next to it. "Do you want me to turn sideways or guide you down?" Jen asked.

"I'll use the wall and your shoulder."

Jen angled sideways, shoving her foot against the side of the rock face, then reached up for Blake's hand. As he slowly lowered himself down to her shoulder, she pushed back, supporting what weight he gave her. "Just like a school bus emergency drill," she said.

Blake nodded, his breathing ragged. "Something like that."

His good foot hit the ground with a bounce, and he fell against Jen.

"That was the last one," Jen said.

"Yeah. Help me over to those willows. There's a small patch of grass."

With Blake's arm around her shoulder, Jen peered at the ground in front of them. The fine pebbles were gone. Instead, jagged stones of various sizes scattered the dry landscape. She brushed at her sweat-pocked forehead. Without flat ground, shuffling wasn't exactly an option. Jen stepped to a rock, shoring up her foot placement, then helped Blake as he prepared to hop on his good foot.

"I can't walk." For the first time, Blake's chin quivered. "And I can't hop."

"Can you put any weight on it?"

He shook his head and stared at the darkening landscape.

Hours had passed since they'd sent the kids on to camp, and Jen shuddered at the sight of the first stars beginning to light the sky above. They couldn't sleep where they were. They couldn't even rest where they were, but the jarring motion of hopping . . . Jen shivered at the thought. "Okay. Then you're going to put all of your weight on me as you take the step."

She moved under his shoulder as though they were walking down the sidewalk instead of through a rocky wash and pulled him toward herself. Willing her knees not to buckle, she inched him forward a half-step. His good foot slipped off one rock and landed on another. He groaned. Repeating the process several times, and doing their best to avoid the pointed or wobbly rocks, they finally made their way to a scraggly patch of grass that stretched along the edge of the cliff and through a wispy copse of shrub oak.

Breathing heavily, Jen eased her injured husband down. First to a rock where he could sit, then, as he supported himself with his arms, to the ground.

Before sitting next to him, Jen rummaged through the nearly empty fanny pack she'd been carrying.

"Have some water."

Blake took the water bottle, and sipped at it carefully. "This is all we have?"

Jen nodded. "Can you feel your toes?"

He eyed her from the side. "You mean aside from the throbbing?"

"Yeah. Aside from that." She handed him four more ibuprofen tablets.

"Four? You're trying to poison me again."

"That's definitely my goal." She sighed. "That's what a doctor would prescribe. I'm not giving you any more than they've given me after having a baby."

He tossed the pills in his mouth and swallowed.

"Take another sip of water, goob."

"Nope." He handed her the bottle. "You need some." Picking up a pebble from the ground, he placed it in his mouth. "This'll do me just fine," he said, talking around the rock.

"Until you can't produce any saliva."

"Oh, I can *th-hpit.*"

"Hmm." Jen curled against his good side, ignoring the rocks poking her in the ribs. "Maybe I should have hiked out for help. Taken the kids with me."

"Leave me alone in the wilderness?" Blake added to her musings.

"Ugh. Maybe left Sydney with you. Or all of them. Maybe I should have sent her out." Put even more distance between Sydney and herself. A pang twisted her heart. She would never do that. She didn't have the strength to do that. Raising her head, she stared at the space where she knew his eyes were, barely able to make out the curve of his jaw in the dark. "You can't make it out of here without help."

He rubbed his hand down her back. "Let's get to camp, and we'll figure it out. We need supplies, so that's necessary regardless. We're fine, Jen. The kids can handle a night alone."

"I can't believe we're adding to the statistics of this canyon," she groaned.

Blake chuckled. "When it's in style . . ."

Jen hid her head in his side. "That's not funny." She peeked back over his chest.

"What? You broke your finger; I broke my ankle. It's a fashion statement."

"*I* broke my finger?" Jen pinched his side lightly. "You throttled that volleyball at me."

"It was a spike, and you could have dodged."

"I should have, but I was trying to make a good impression on someone."

"Oh, you did. Charlie talked about it for weeks."

Their talking faded into the night, Blake propped against one rock, with his leg elevated four or five inches by another. His breathing deepened until Jen knew he'd fallen into a tormented sleep. She, however, stared up at the sky.

Blake wasn't the type to give into his pain. He rarely admitted he had any. But this time he had—though not like everyone else in the world would have. He always pushed too hard. Forced himself to move when he shouldn't. She could have brought supplies back to him. Or Sydney could have. What's a day of walking out of the canyon and then a few hours to get search and rescue mobilized? She blinked at the stars above.

Stupid snake.

Stupid Jen.

She should have taken better control. Told him what was going to happen instead of letting him decide to walk out. What kind of damage was he doing to himself—forcing himself to climb over boulders and *not hop* to a bed of grass and poky rocks? Jen shifted.

But she couldn't separate her family more than she already had. It had been hard enough listening to Blake send the kids back to camp. And, there, they had food and water. Ways to care for themselves. It was more than she and Blake had, and more than what was at the car.

No. The decision had been made. Right or wrong didn't matter anymore. Separating from the kids had made sense. It meant she could help Blake without worry of Max finding another rattlesnake or Tessa falling apart at the sight of her father's struggles. Besides, Blake was right—the kids could handle a night together at camp. They knew how to build a fire. There, they could relax instead of watching their dad torment himself as he maneuvered around the canyon with a broken ankle. The kids would be fine, and tomorrow, they would reunite and figure out what to do.

Jen bit her lip and attempted to stop the burning that pricked at her eyes as great heaving breaths pumped her chest. It could have been so much worse. Max or Sydney or Blake could have been bitten by the rattlesnake. Blake could have hit his head. He could have died.

But he didn't. He didn't die.

She furiously flapped her hand in front of her eyes as a tear escaped. He didn't die. He was hurt, but he was okay. Once at camp, she'd hike out to the car. That was best, wasn't it? Sydney and Tessa could keep camp running. Blake would be there to give any direction they needed. Blake wasn't dying. None of them were. Her worst fear would *not* be realized.

Nothing I Can't Handle

Evan eased down onto the green-striped cushion atop the plastic wicker sofa that Michelle had fallen in love with a few short months ago. She'd seen the patio set when they'd walked into the hardware store, and he couldn't help himself. Her yearning eyes had said everything he needed to hear. A new pool with a beautiful patio. What would they be without the perfect outdoor furniture? He would have been fine with the stackable and rather flimsy plastic chairs, but then again, the first monsoon storm would blow them right out of the yard.

He scoffed as his lips curved upward. The cushions wouldn't fare much better, but he loved his wife. She hadn't even asked. He'd simply grabbed the order tag and found an associate. And, truth be told, the furniture was comfortable enough. Way better than flimsy plastic stackables.

The sliding door slid open, and Evan scooted over, welcoming Michelle with an arm ready to dangle over her shoulder. "Did she finally give in?"

"Yes." His wife slumped next to him, then curled into his chest.

"You can always let her cry it out for a bit." Evan winked, chuckling lightly when she offered him a glare.

Five babies, and Michelle had never once allowed them to cry it out.

"Learning to find comfort in a crib is not the same as being bored with a toy. They've all managed good sleeping habits once they felt safe."

Evan nodded. "They have." Pulling her closer, he kissed the top of her head. "But they would have learned faster with me."

Laughter rumbled in his chest as she pushed him away. "You're a bigger pushover than I am. A few crocodile tears, and those kids get anything they want from you."

"I have to secure my place as the fun parent."

"Hmm." She leaned back against him and stared out at the pool. "It's almost ready. Saturday can't come soon enough for the kids."

"They can wait. But I plan on an early Saturday swim around, oh say, midnight, with my lovely bride."

"Maybe a Friday night ten p.m. swim. We can get it filled by then, can't we?"

"We can try."

Michelle stood up. "Speaking of which . . . I'm pooped."

Before she took her first step, the door slid open and bleary-eyed Danni peeked out. "Momma, Ellie won't stop crying."

Without a look back, Michelle rushed into the house as Evan stood and scooped their four-year-old into his arms. "Let's get you back to bed."

"But, Daddy, I can't sleep when Ellie cries. And she's always crying."

"That's just her way of getting help."

"She needs a lot of help," Danni grumbled.

Evan tickled her sides as he plopped her back in bed. Danni giggled.

"Shh," Evan said, "we don't want to wake up Maggie."

"Too late." Maggie rolled over and faced her sister's bed. "Ellie did that a while ago."

Evan winced. "She's a little colicky, but that'll go away pretty soon. How's your throat?"

"It still hurts a little."

"Sorry about that, kiddo." Evan ruffled her hair. "You know, Mags, you were colicky too, and now you almost never cry."

"Only when I have to look at you." Maggie giggled as Evan feigned a pout.

"And to think, you look just like me."

Maggie groaned, while Danni giggled.

"All right girls, it's time to go back to sleep. Maggie needs rest, and Momma's tired, so it's my turn with Ellie."

Leaving the door cracked an inch, Evan slipped into the family room and settled next to Michelle. The news played quietly in the background as she finished feeding the baby.

"Why don't you let me take her? You go to bed." Evan said, running a finger along his youngest daughter's tiny face, her gray eyes staring up at him.

Michelle, gently transferred Ellie to his arms. "You came home pretty bushed yourself, didn't you? Where did Blake and Jen go?"

"West Clear Creek." Evan sighed wistfully. "I had a few more fires than usual, but nothing I couldn't handle. Why don't you head to bed?"

She stood up. "Hope they don't get rained out."

"Not this time of year."

She shrugged. "The news said it's been raining on the Rim all day."

"With how dry it's been recently, that's a good thing."

Michelle yawned. "Good luck with her."

"We'll be fine. Won't we, Ellie?"

It was three in the morning before Evan placed a sleeping Ellie in her crib. Like other nights, she'd fussed and cried for several hours before passing out from pure exhaustion. As he slipped into bed, Michelle snuggled into him. Though she wouldn't say it, he knew she hadn't slept the way she needed to. She never did when one of the kids was crying.

"Thank you." She kissed him on the neck.

He pulled her closer. "Just wish you'd slept."

"I did. A little."

Evan closed his eyes and let a soft moan escape his lips. "Work comes early."

The next few hours, Evan fought to ignore Michelle's restless sleep as she twitched with every little squeak and creak in the house. Once she found a way to relax, maybe he would too.

By six o'clock, the only thing stirring in the house was Evan's cell phone as it buzzed across the nightstand and fell to the floor.

Huffing, he leaned over and picked it up. "Hello."

"Hey, Ev, it's Chuck. I've got my flooring crew over at Ina Street, and the owner won't let us in."

"Ada," Evan grumbled. *Would this woman make everything difficult?* "Did she happen to mention why?"

"Too early. Says to come back at noon."

"Noon." Evan flung his arm over his eyes. "Is that even possible? Do you have anything going on then?"

"Me? No. But I gotta keep my men happy too."

"We all stand to make a pretty penny off this job, Chuck."

Chuck swore. "Hang on."

104

As Chuck talked to his guys, Evan pushed himself out of bed and reached for his pants. "I'm coming. Just don't let them leave," he said before Chuck could tell Evan about the uproar the request had caused.

Evan didn't blame them. Ada Butler's contract stated work could begin as early as six a.m., and the contractors he worked with labored early mornings to enjoy afternoons off with their families, especially in the hotter months. Ada had assured him it wouldn't bother her in the least. Even then, he'd wondered whether she meant what she was saying. *Flounderer.*

Slamming the door to his truck twenty minutes later, Evan trod past the group of waiting men to Mrs. Butler's house and hammered at the door with the side of his fist.

"Mr. Marksam!" Ada Butler's nose poked out of the cracked-open entrance. "I've already told your men it's too early."

"Ma'am, I'm sorry to bother you, but you signed a contract that states work will start as early as six a.m. I pointed it out, and you said that wouldn't be a problem. These men won't return at noon. You'd have to schedule a different day. It'd still be a six o'clock morning."

"No. No six a.m. mornings. It disrupts Maxwell's sleep and makes him anxious."

"Maxwell?" Evan slowly brushed a hand across his forehead. "Your dog?"

"Yes, my dog. The vet says his heart is aging and that he needs more rest."

"Can he sleep outside or in the other end of the house? I can't make these men wait. These are their contracted hours."

The door slid open a little wider. "His bed is in the living room."

"By the kitchen," Evan said. "I see. What if I helped you move his bed to the other end of the house? Maybe brought him a bone or two."

105

"Not rawhide."

"Not rawhide. A natural bone, with a strip of meat or two."

The door widened, allowing Evan entrance.

"I'd have gotten him ear plugs, but he always shakes them out," Ada said.

"I don't blame him. They're uncomfortable. I don't like wearing them either."

"I thought about trying a Howler's Hoodie, but it's so hot. I didn't want him suffering heatstroke."

Evan swallowed a snort. "We couldn't have that."

Picking up the luxury pet bed, complete with a metal frame and soft sheets, Evan shuffled down the hall, following Ada into the master suite.

"Will my cabinets be in soon? I assume you've ordered them. I was starting to wonder if they come in something other than natural."

"Mrs. Butler, you wouldn't want anything less than the platinum in kitchen standards, would you?"

"Of course not."

"Then you'll want those cabinets in a natural finish. That's where it's at right now."

Always Be Prepared

The shadowed outlines of Tessa and Max came into view as Sydney cracked an eye open, hoping to find the sky pitch black or bright and sunny. One meant sleep. The other meant finally giving in to her nervous energy and starting a new day.

Even as the sun set, Sydney had found herself hoping her parents would show up. Did Mom have a flashlight in her fanny pack? Probably not. The hike to the petroglyphs was supposed to be quick and easy. Longer than expected, and wrought with a rattlesnake on top of wobbly rocks, it had been anything but.

Dad telling her she might need to hike out for help only made relaxing harder. After Max and Tessa had fallen into restless sleep, Sydney sat up, staring past the coals of the fire into the darkness. Beyond the flow of the creek, she'd heard crickets. Nothing else. She'd yearned to hear the crush of rock under footfalls but wasn't surprised when that didn't come. Dad could barely shuffle across the ground, let alone climb through that canyon and over those piles of boulders. She imagined a broken ankle made it more like scaling vertical cliffs.

Hours later, when the coals had lost their glow and the breeze cooled her skin, Sydney sank into her sleeping bag and lay there with open eyes. When her eyes didn't flutter closed on their own, she forced them closed. Something she couldn't do to her mind.

Illusory conversations between her and Braden mixed with worry for her parents.

"My dad broke his ankle, saving my brother from a rattlesnake," she *would say.*

"Cool. How many rattles did it have?"

"He broke his ankle, Braden."

"Are you ready? The guys are waiting for us."

Braden was great at some things—she shivered and clutched her sleeping bag closer—but he sucked at listening. She might have to break into tears. That always got his attention.

That was when Sydney's tears had shoved out from her clenched eyelids and run past her ears into her hair. What if her parents didn't get back? What if Mom and Dad got stuck and she had to save the family? How was she supposed to do that?

The night had been restless, to say the least.

With another glance at her siblings, Sydney huffed and climbed out of her sleeping bag. *Enough.* She couldn't rehash her thoughts from the night before any longer. It was close enough to sunrise. Unzipping the tent, she slipped out, started a fire, and pulled the backpacks closer. She had to keep her mind busy with something else. Anything else.

Pulling out any supplies left in the packs, Sydney spent time considering what she would need to take with her to the car if she had to hike out and find help. She raised her head and looked at the sky. If she hiked out by herself, what would Tessa and Max do? If they went with her, it would take longer. If they didn't, she'd be by herself and Tessa wouldn't have anyone to start the camp stove for her.

What do I do?

Her eyes burned, but she blinked the feeling away, unwilling to cry again.

They'd have to go together, but not with all the supplies. A small pack with emergency gear and snacks would have to do. She stuffed granola bars, trail mix, and the fruit Mom had brought into Max's pack. Duct tape; matches; a compass, not that she used it well; calamine lotion, just in case Max itched; Band-Aids—she scoffed as she placed them in the side pocket.

What else?

Reaching into Dad's pack, she pulled out his knife, then she placed three emergency blankets on top. They wouldn't use them, but whatever. Maybe they'd come in handy after swimming upstream. She could crinkle the ends into her ears if Tessa and Max whined too much.

As the sky brightened, she stared at the canyon wall behind her and grabbed the binoculars. Dad always looked for clouds, but the canyon walls were so high, she wouldn't see far. If she could get up a little higher, it might help. She bit her lip as she gazed at the fire. The flames were low, and the ten-foot ledge behind her was close. She'd keep her eye on the fire and yell if it somehow escaped the rock ring that sat on top of gravelly sand. The vegetation was forever away from it. No breeze either.

Next to the sandstone ledge, Sydney looked for a way up. Crags and slight handholds, nothing more. The binoculars hung between her shoulder blades as she pulled herself up, the tip of her shoed toe the only strength beneath her. As she approached the top, her foot slipped, and she landed on the ground. Stabbing pain radiated through her tail bone, well surpassing the burn of the scratches on her knees and elbows, not to mention her single ripped fingernail.

"Ow."

Once on her feet, she tried again. Her arms and legs shook as she slowly moved from one tiny handhold to another, gaining minute distances upward with each new grasp. At the top, she reached for anything that might help her pull herself over the edge, but met nothing more than dust. Ten feet. That's all. Ten measly little feet. Slightly higher than their block wall at home. It shouldn't be that hard. The nine-year-old neighbor boy scaled the back wall daily. She needed a way to push herself up.

She moved her left leg, skimming the wall with her toes to where she'd had her hand only moments before. Her shoe caught. Repeating the motion with her right foot, she hung from the wall in a crouch. Two deep breaths and she pushed with her legs and tried to catch the wall with her body or elbows. She fell to the ground.

Standing up, she dusted off and swore. She'd almost had it. One last time. The strength in her arms and legs was gone, but she had to do it. She had to look at the sky. She had to. She . . .

She crumpled to the ground. She did have to, but ten feet in the narrow canyon wouldn't make that much of a difference, and her climbing the sheer canyon wall wouldn't fix her dad. Wouldn't keep her from having to hike out. None of it would save her family from dying in the canyon while on a trip she'd never wanted to take.

She slammed her fists into the ground. Why was she there?

It didn't matter. She wasn't thinking of those things. She was climbing a ten-foot vertical ledge to look at the sky and check for signs of a storm.

As she approached the top for the third time, her arms and legs like jelly, she turned her palms inward, hoping to use what remaining strength she had in her legs to lunge above the ledge, then catch it with her hands and push herself up with her shoulder strength. Pulling herself up obviously didn't work.

"One . . . two . . ." Sydney exhaled and leaped.

Her arms wobbled as she caught herself. She could see the top of the wall. The trees were only a few feet back. Pushing upward with her feet and shoulders, working to straighten her elbows, Sydney's waist slipped over the top, and she collapsed to her belly, heaving for air, her feet dangling over the side. She'd made it.

Heartbeats pounded in her chest as she crawled to her feet and gazed at the trees in front of her. For at least a hundred yards, a mixture of pine and oak clung to the steep-but-scalable canyon, reaching toward the sky. Under some of their branches were wild grapevines, likely untouched by man. A large, flat rock atop an outcropping beckoned her forward, and once she reached it, she sat down.

The strap of the binoculars dug at her neck, and she grabbed at it, yanking the field glasses from behind her and whipping her braid out of the way. After focusing the lenses, she worked to steady her hands enough to scan what little sky she could see above the towering canyon walls. By now, the sun shone brightly in the east—too bright for her to see much—though that seemed telling enough. To the west, skiffs of lacy white clouds incapable of rain scattered lightly across the sky. A perfectly sunny summer day.

As she focused the binoculars on the camp below, the flames of the fire she'd built flickered higher, and squinting, she made out her brother's and sister's forms. Tessa stood up. "Sydney," she called through cupped hands.

Max soon followed suit.

"Up here." Sydney dropped the field glasses to her chest and waved both arms above her head, then started back down the steep wooded hill.

As Max dashed across the canyon floor toward her, Sydney worked her way down the wall, an easier burden now. She'd fallen from it enough times that the thought of it being scary barely crossed her mind.

"Sydney, Sydney." Max collided with her. "What were you doing up there? Did you see Mom and Dad?"

"I wish. I was checking for clouds."

"Did you see any? When will Mom and Dad be back?"

"Not sure," she said as she started back to camp, Max yammering at her the entire way.

Jen opened her eyes with the change in Blake's breathing. The dark sky had brightened, but it left the cool of night behind. She rubbed her hands down her exposed arms, smoothing the formed goosebumps, and tried to swallow. Her tongue was glued to the roof of her mouth. Working what little spit she could between her teeth, she looked at Blake. "How's your leg?" As if she didn't know. She pushed herself up. "Let me get you some more ibuprofen."

Blake clutched at her hand and slipped a pebble into it. "Suck on it."

She nodded. The dryness of her throat was too obvious in her voice.

Moisture formed around the pebble, helping relieve the scratchiness caused by strenuous activity and too-little water. As she dug through their meager supplies, she pushed the empty water canister aside and popped the top off the pain reliever's bottle. Four tablets rolled into her hand, and she stared at them.

He needed something stronger.

"Have you worked up enough spit yet?" She offered her husband a wan smile as she dropped the pills into his open mouth.

112

"Ugh. Enough, I guess," His words garbled as he spoke before swallowing.

"Great. We'll give it twenty minutes."

Blake wrapped his arm around her, bringing her back down to his chest without a word. The thumping in his ribcage had increased, and even with the cool air, beads of sweat had formed across his brow. Jen tucked herself in next to him, hoping to share some of her warmth. "How many times did you drag me to a football game before taking me out on a real date?"

"Three, maybe four."

"That last game was freezing."

"Should have brought a jacket."

She pulled herself closer to him. "I left it home on purpose—wanted to see if you'd finally put your arm around me."

A chuckle rumbled in Blake's chest. "Guess you got your answer."

"Sure did. You finally held my hand too. For someone who kept asking me and my brother out, you sure were a slow mover."

"Me? Nah." His heart rate evened a bit. "You, on the other hand, never called me—never sent notes home with Evan. You never did any of the things other girls did to let me know they were interested."

"You mean I didn't chase you?" She laughed. "I always dressed up for you. Who else wore a skirt to a football game?"

"Cheerleaders."

"And I always said hi to Evan."

"No wonder he always came home glossy-eyed."

"He did not."

"Well, he should have."

Jen took a deep breath to settle her nerves. "It was cold last night."

"It'll be better tonight. We'll have sleeping bags."

"You will. I hope to be at the car with Sydney. If we make it to her before she starts out." Jen had spent a good portion of the night thinking about how to handle getting help. Who she would leave with Blake and who would go with her. Part of her wanted to leave Sydney to take care of him. That had been her first inclination. That and to go alone. But the more she thought about it, the more she knew both were bad ideas. She could take Tessa, but Tessa was slow and easily stressed. Sydney was faster and more capable if something happened to Jen. Having her middle child care for Blake, who could still give instructions made more sense. It would be different if Blake were unconscious, but he wasn't. He could still parent from his sleeping bag. She hoped.

Blake brushed the hair away from Jen's cheek. "We will. It's mostly flat from here on out."

Jen forced her mind to focus on Blake's words. "Is it? I seem to remember plenty of wobbly rocks."

"Well, yeah, but those are cinches to get past."

"Right."

"Jen?"

She lifted herself up and studied Blake's pallid face. Stress and pain were anchored to the creases in his brow. "We need to go," he said. "It'll only get worse."

The shock. The hypothermia. That was what he meant. And she wouldn't leave him alone. He knew that. It's why he pushed himself so hard, so that she wouldn't have to leave him or the kids alone.

"Okay. Are you ready to stand?"

Run!

"On guard." Max held a stick out at Sydney. "I said, O*n guard*."
Sydney toed the sand at her feet.

"Sydney, I said, *On guard*!"

"Not now, Max. I don't want to play anymore."

"Wanna fish?"

"Go bug Tessa."

Max's shoulders slumped. "Tessa's crying again."

"Build a rock castle. Go pick flowers. Play in the fire for all I care, just leave me alone!" Sydney shouted.

Glistening tears filled Max's eyes, and Sydney groaned as he walked away. She didn't mean to hurt his feelings, but she couldn't handle another minute of listening to his noise or playing swords with willow branches. The only thing she wanted to do was go find her parents, but she couldn't even do that. Instead, she had to wait to see if they would show up. If they didn't, she would take her brother and sister on an emergency run to the car.

Mom and Dad had to come. She needed them to come.

The burn in her eyes returned, and she repeatedly blinked, staving off the emotion. With a groan, she stood up. "Max, wanna go swimming?"

The sun had nearly reached the top of the sky, and the heat of the day rubbed at her shoulders. If nothing else, swimming would pass the time. Or at least entertain Max.

"Yay, swimming! I'll get Tess." Max ran to the tent where Tessa muffled her sobs with her sleeping bag.

"Don't forget your life jacket. I'm not pulling your dead body out of the creek," Sydney yelled after him.

A few huffs later, Sydney watched Max lunge onto his dinosaur tube and float into the center of the creek, his bulky life vest insulating him from the splashing water.

Tessa ran into the creek from the shore until finally giving into the drag and disappearing underneath the surface long enough to wet her wind-knotted hair.

"Come on, Syd," they both called out to her.

"I'm coming, I'm coming." She held back a smile and placed her tube in the creek.

The refreshing brush of the water against her legs cooled her concerns momentarily, and she gave herself to it, allowing the water to choose her meandering trail through the pool just above their camp where they had decided to swim. Leaning back in her tube, she gazed at the sky. Deep blue—bluer than she'd ever seen at home—spread across it, except for the bright yellow of the sun that caused her to squint.

A splash of water brought a sharp intake of breath into her lungs, and she rolled off her float, charging her giggling brother.

"You, little—I'm gonna catch you."

Max's giggles echoed off the cliffs as Sydney grabbed him around the waist and yanked him backward off a rock and into the water, his body bobbing away from hers as she went under and his life jacket protested.

Floating to the top, she soon gained her footing and climbed up onto the rock that she had fished from the day before and sat down. Bits of wood and debris stuck to her arms, and she brushed them away. That was odd. She hadn't seen more than an occasional leaf in the water the entire time they'd been in the canyon. The water skimmed the bottoms of her sandaled feet, and her heart thudded hard in her chest. Her feet had been inches above the water only moments ago. She screamed, "Get out. Get out of the water, now!"

Tessa and Max turned and stared at her.

"Now. The water's rising! Get out."

Tessa started toward the edge, and Sydney lurched into the water to grab Max.

"We have to run," she panted, hoisting him out of the water. "There's something wrong."

Tessa's face blanched as she looked back at Sydney.

"The cliff." Sydney pointed to the canyon ledge she had climbed earlier that morning. "Run to the cliff, Max. As fast as you can."

Max followed after Tessa, who ran pell-mell through the sand.

Heart pounding, Sydney dashed through camp, dipped her shoulder, and hooked the backpack she had prepared in case they needed to hike out for help. As she reached the wall, she looked at Tessa. "You first."

"I . . . I can't." Tessa bit her lip as tears cascaded down her chapped cheeks.

Sydney bent down, forming a stirrup with her hands. "You have to. Put your foot in my hand. I'll help."

Tessa shook her head, turning away from Sydney.

"We don't have time for this, Tess! It's flooding. Look at the creek."

The edge of the water had reached their tents, the once-lazy flow roiling as it struck the unexpected barriers.

Tessa's foot hit Sydney's hands, and Sydney lifted. Her sister dropped back to the ground. "I can't, Syd. I can't."

"You can. I need you to do this. You have to help Max up."

Nodding, Tessa rested her foot in Sydney's makeshift stirrup. "Okay."

"One, two"—Sydney lifted her sister—"grab the edge, and hold on. Don't move your foot."

The muscles in Sydney's sides, arms, and legs screamed as she pushed past their tiredness. Tessa's foot swung outward before it rested on Sydney's shoulder, and Tessa scrambled up onto the ledge.

"Max, now. On my shoulders. I need you to climb." Sydney grabbed her brother. "Put your foot on the back of my leg."

"Why?" Max eyed her.

"*Max!* We don't have time for this. Get your butt on my shoulders." She grabbed at her face as she screamed. *Didn't he get it? Didn't he understand?*

"Max, hurry up. It's cool up here." Tessa wiped at her eyes and reached her hands down. "There are grapevines. You've got to come see them."

His foot struck Sydney's leg, and she reached behind her, grabbing his hands to steady him. "My hip, Max." Her hip burned with pain as his shoe dug into her side. "Keep going."

Feet pushed into her back, and she pulled and supported his weight with her arms until his feet rested on her shoulders.

"Stand up, Max. Grab my hands," Tessa said, her voice calmer than Sydney had expected it to be.

The weight lifted from Sydney's shoulders, and she glanced back before starting her own climb. Muddy water rushed past only a few feet away, their tents long ago ripped away.

I can't. Mom. Dad.

Clutching at the wall, she began her scramble upward. Sore muscles, tired from her attempts earlier that morning, called for her to stop. Her arms shook uncontrollably. She took a deep breath and blew it out as she reached for the final hold before having to lunge toward the top.

The cold brush of water skimmed her foot. "I can do this," she whispered to herself. "I can do this. . . . Please, let me do this."

Her legs shook. How would she push upward?

"Sydney," Tessa yelled, leaning down, trying to help.

"M-move back," Sydney said through gritted teeth.

With the little room she had, she pushed upward, her knees barely able to bend to get the height she needed. Palms facing inward, she shouldered her upper body over the edge. Tessa clutched her hands and pulled her to safety.

Ragged breath mixed with the dirt, causing Sydney to cough as she pushed off the pack and rolled to her back. "Up. Up the hill. Hurry."

A thunderous crack boomed through the canyon, and the too-little color in Blake's face drained. "Run. Get behind that outcropping."

Jen turned, following his finger. Ten feet away, a small portion of the cliff wall jutted into the dry creek bed. She shook her head—her hair striking her in the face as she dug her shoulder under his. "I'm not leaving you."

Pushing Blake to move faster than he could, she bit her lip as her heart beat higher into her throat. She refused to look toward the roiling wall of flood water rushing at them. "Faster," she breathed.

Blake screamed out in pain as his wrapped foot banged into rock after rock, the sweat already beaded on his forehead streaming down his face.

"Three more steps." The roar of the water swallowed her words even as she shouted them.

"Run," Blake yelled, "Jen, run!"

Tightening her muscles, she flung her husband toward the jutting stone and into the corner. Mist struck her bare calves, arms, and face. Jen crashed into Blake, pushing him as close to the corner of the nook as possible. An uprooted pine slammed into the exposed stone next to her, twisting as it was forced downstream. She gasped as icy water, filled with muddy flotsam surged up to her shoulders, pushing her chest into the wall while swirling around her feet and threatening to upend her completely.

"A r-rock. Behind me," stuttered Blake. "H-help me up."

Terror ripped through Jen, through both of them, she knew. How was she supposed to help him up when she could barely hold herself against the cliff? She grabbed his arm and shoved at his armpit, fighting the swirling force that tugged at his body and urged his form to disappear downstream. She felt his good foot ease onto the rock in the corner as she pushed herself back against the cliff, the water now up to her neck.

She glanced at Blake, his face white. His body racked with tremors. Mud clung to his upper chest and shoulders, no longer under water.

"Up," he said, his elbow pointing at her. "Come up."

Pushing against him for support, she lifted one foot, feeling for the edge of the rock, then she teetered as a small tree slammed into her shoulder blades. Rearing back in pain, she scrambled for a crag, any crag, to jam her feet into. She grabbed at Blake's elbow with abandon. Pain rushed from her foot into her shin as she shoved her toes under a rock.

She was going to die. People didn't survive these floods. She'd die.

"Jen"—Blake clutched her hand on his arm, and leaned into the wall—"you *cannot* give up."

Ignoring the pain surging through her legs and back, even into her head, Jen raised her free foot again. Feeling the edge of the rock where Blake stood, she pushed herself upward and tangled her body with his, forcing them both against the rock wall as she searched for any kind of handhold.

Sydney stared at the curling rapids now rushing only inches from the top of the rock wall that she had scaled twice that day. Tessa and Max stood behind her, wailing loud enough to add to the pain building in her ears—the roar of the water overwhelming her senses. Less than five minutes had passed since she'd first noticed the rise of water. Not a drop of rain had fallen, and the sky held nothing but the same wispy clouds she'd seen that morning.

Her chin quivered. How would Mom and Dad get back to them now? She refused to think of the other possibility—that the side canyon they were trapped in had also flooded.

She turned to her siblings, their reddened faces crumpling further.

Grabbing the pack she'd managed to rescue from camp, she pushed her way farther into the forest. The steep terrain loosened with every step. Still she persisted, clutching at trees, bushes, rocks, and soil as she forced her way higher. She had to know, to see. Maybe there was a way.

Tessa screamed, begging her to come back. The sound of Max's rustling footsteps fell away. But she continued. *Mom. Dad.* Atop the large outcropping, she twisted, facing the mayhem below.

The roar of the floodwaters that had washed away their tents, sleeping bags, and packs, also carried full-sized trees ripped from the earth. It roiled thick with slurry as it tumbled boulders.

How long would it take? How long until the water receded? Until rescue efforts began? Would they have to wait until they were late returning home?

Air squeezed painfully from Sydney's chest, and she forcefully rasped it back in. What about Mom and Dad? From where she stood, Sydney could see the entirety of the confluence where they'd set up camp—the terrain was completely changed.

Her worst fears realized.

Muddied water from the once-dry canyon that they had hiked the day before now mixed with the slurry flowing from upstream. If her parents were alive, they were not okay. They were dying. And there was nothing she could do.

The canyon wall steepened above her, making climbing much farther impossible. She turned in a circle, haphazardly scanning the canyon walls. She had to get out of there. She had to find help. She had to . . .

She fell to her knees as a painful wail escaped her throat. Tears fell in large droplets, forming mud on the top of her sandals. Climbing out of the canyon any way other than a known trail meant never being found. At this point, authorities would expect more bodies than survivors. Even at sixteen, she recognized that.

"Mom, Dad!" Her scream ripped from her chest, but she knew it went unheard.

Her parents had told her of past floods at Water Wheel and of some flood that took place in Antelope Canyon near Lake Powell when they had been kids. Survivors were nearly unheard of.

Her parents were dead, and she didn't know what to do. Dad had spent tons of time teaching and training them, but she couldn't think straight. Not without him there to make her feel safe. Not without Mom.

Curling into a ball similar to the one Tessa had rolled into earlier, Sydney closed her eyes and wept. Nothing else helped. Crying didn't help either, but what else did she have to do?

The chitter of a squirrel sounded in a nearby tree. Another answered from a few trees over. *They're talking to each other, making sure the other is okay,* Dad had once said. *You scare them, but even fear won't keep them from caring for their family.*

Sydney scoffed. She doubted squirrels checked on each other because people were around. It was more likely they were saying something like, *Do you see their food? It's mine.* But somewhere in Dad's little story, he'd made his point. Even when things are scary, you take care of each other.

That's what she was supposed to do—make sure her siblings survived. But what she wanted to do was run. She wanted to find her parents, to throw herself into the safety of their arms.

But she couldn't do that. Not yet. First, she had to be a squirrel.

Standing, she picked up the small backpack. One day. Less than twenty-four hours, then Uncle Evan would report them missing. Then a search would definitely begin. One day.

Where did that leave her?

Sydney shivered as a breeze blew past. They'd been in the water when she'd realized the creek was rising. And though her swimming suit was dry and the sun shone where she stood, the deep shade of the forest had kept her chilled. So they'd need a fire. It would help rescue crews locate them too.

She paced along the rock, trying to clear her mind.

What else?

Food. She opened the bag she'd grabbed in the mad dash to "find a way to her parents." Eight granola bars, three apples, and two small baggies filled with trail mix. No water.

Tossing a bag of trail mix back into the open pack, she pursed her lips and narrowed her eyes. How would they get water? Even if they could collect it, they had nothing to boil it in. There were plenty of grape leaves. Sydney's tongue parched at the thought of eating raw leaves, but if she cooked them . . .

If she cooked them, maybe they'd be more palatable. She groaned at the thought. If only the grapes were more than tiny buds just starting to form.

Tessa and Max were crying again. She could hear the shrieking as it splintered through the canyon. Slinging the pack over her shoulder, she started back down. Firewood, some sort of leaf *bowl*, and a place to sleep—or at least to wait out the night. With those things on her mind, maybe she could better ignore the aching knot in her chest.

Stay With Me

Evan glanced at his watch. Babysitting Mrs. Butler and her dog wasn't exactly how he'd wanted to spend his day. The Nina Street and Cheyenne jobs needed a bit of attention too. The final walk-through on the Cheyenne house was scheduled for Monday, and none of his crews worked Sundays.

"Would you like a drink, Mr. Marksam?" Mrs. Butler asked. "I appreciate your help with Maxwell's bed. He's sleeping nicely. I gave him another blanket, just to be sure."

"A water would be great, thanks."

As he took the water, he smiled at Mrs. Butler. "I checked on my guys a minute ago. The floors are coming along. The tiles are laid in the living room, and Dan is working on the decorative entry now." He checked his watch again. "They should finish for the day in about an hour."

"Oh, that's wonderful. Now, the grout lines won't be too big, will they? I don't like big thick grout lines," she shouted over the noise of the TV.

Currently, the weatherman was droning on about rain in the high country. Something about an unusual storm that had been expected to fizzle out before ever reaching the state. This time of year, it would *fizzle* fast enough. The ground was probably already dry. *Fizzle*, he thought, tuning out the rest, *Who uses a word like that?* It sounded like some kind of cold medication.

"No ma'am. We're using the recommended width. One-eighth lines."

"And they'll be easy to clean? I don't want my cleaning lady charging me extra."

"We're going to put a sealant over the grout, just like we are the marble. Remember, though, sealants get reapplied every six months."

"Six months, yes. You'll do that?"

"We can, but most people use a carpet cleaning company. They all do tile and grout now too. This is marble tile. You'll want to tell them that."

Maxwell ambled out of the bedroom and stared at Evan with sad eyes.

"Oh, look at him." Mrs. Butler rushed over to her dog. "He's come to say hello. And he's still so tired. It's all that hammering."

"The guys have to tap the tiles into place or they'll crack."

"Well, can't they be a little quieter?"

Evan shook his head. "Not if you want your floor to look as good as I know you do."

"Fine then. You said they'd leave in an hour."

"About that."

Mrs. Butler stepped back to Evan and placed her hand on his arm, meeting his eyes with her own. "Please tell them not to come before ten a.m. on Monday."

Evan scratched at his shoulder, his movement causing her hand to fall back to her side. "I can't do that, Mrs. Butler. They'll be here at six. But I've arranged for your cabinets to come on Wednesday. We'll get them installed on Thursday."

She huffed. "I guess that will be okay. Maybe Maxwell and I will find a hotel."

"That's always an option, but someone needs to be here to let the men in." Evan planted a smile on his face.

"Perhaps my husband, Malcolm, can stay home from work."

An hour later, Evan pulled away from Mrs. Butler's and drove to check on his other projects. The Cheyenne house needed nothing more than a little polish. His guys assured him they would have everything finished before the weekend.

Saturday.

Evan couldn't wait for Saturday. Crystal clear water had started flowing from three hoses into the pool that morning. A text from Michelle had confirmed it. They had everything ready. Food, friends, music, and soon, a pool. Hopefully, Maggie would feel better by then. She'd be so disappointed if she had to miss the party because of a sore throat.

With the hot sun beating down on him through his truck windows, the thought of jumping in the pool early was almost too much to bear, especially after his conversation with Michelle the night before. But it had been made perfectly clear that it had to be completely filled first.

At the house on Nina Street, he ran past the dumpster that had finally arrived and into the house. The guys had taken the time to move the junk from the back room to the dumpster. That meant paying them for the extra time. He made a note to talk to Dumpster Depot about a discount. They were late; they should cover the additional expense. Not that it would work that way.

He stopped in front of a piece of uneven drywall in the kitchen, then continued walking. It would be taped and mudded on Monday. Pushing the back of his hand across his forehead and sopping up what sweat he could, he stepped into the second of two bathrooms. The tubs had been installed on time too. Good. Now he could go home.

The chattering of Jen's teeth matched the trembling of her body as the canyon breeze whipped through her drenched hair and swimming suit. With the water receding slightly, the chill had changed. Unlike the icy water of West Clear Creek, the flood water, though cold, had been somewhat bearable. The breeze through her wet swimming suit wasn't. She clutched Blake's arm and stared into his clouded eyes. He still trembled. That was good.

And bad.

Hypothermia had set in, and with his injury, Blake's condition was worse than hers. But if he was trembling, the final stage of freezing to death hadn't set in. Yet.

Slowly releasing her grip on Blake, she eased to the edge of the rock where they stood. Water up to her thighs still coursed past them. *That i-isn't too deep.* She shook her head, trying to clear the fog taking root between her ears. Except in flood waters. And it'd be at least waist deep once she stepped off the rock. *At least the kids are upstream of this canyon.*

She clenched her eyes shut and relished the illusory, fog-clearing effect that it caused, then she cracked them open and searched downstream. A strip of dirt along the canyon wall. A crevasse notched into the sheer rock. She needed somewhere to shelter out of the water. Somewhere to help Blake warm up.

Who was she kidding? Blake was going to die. She probably would too. Hypothermia, a broken ankle, and stuck in a flash flood. The fact they'd survived this long was a miracle. That kind of luck—the kind where you had a chance at survival—never happened.

Even now, if they got out of the water, they had no real chance, not without the means to build a fire. And it was the cold that would kill them, not the dehydration or hunger. They may as well give into the truth—stand still in the cold and let the crazy take over. Their thoughts would slow, the shaking would end, and then they'd feel warm. That's all she wanted. To feel warm.

Blake squeezed her hand. "K-kids."

"Wh-what?"

"Kids," he said stronger. "N-need you."

He knew. He knew she was nearly ready to give up. He knew what would keep her going. They'd sent their kids away, and if she gave up . . .

"W-we c-can't stay here." Jen attempted to rise to her tiptoes and search the surrounding torrent for shelter, but she could barely raise a heel from off the ledge. And she was supposed to save them with a complete lack of motor skills as water rushed around her legs? Not to mention her fogging thoughts.

She shook her head, her ragged breathing catching in her throat, then she looked again for some way—any way—to survive. The creek was full of debris. Branches still floated in the sludge. And, occasionally, she heard the thunder of boulders as they careened into one another. Her gaze landed on a spot downstream and to their right as thick thoughts rambled within her mind. So cold. Charlie and his hat. Pieces of the day she and Blake had told Charlie she was expecting . . .

"Hey, Charlie, come here." Blake slung his arm around Charlie's shoulders once he got close enough. "Look at my shirt."

Charlie glanced down.

World's Greatest
(soon-to-be)
Dad

The black, permanent-markered words were scrawled across a white T-shirt in Jen's handwriting.

"Soon-to-be Dad?" Charlie glanced at Blake. "Cool."

"Charlie," Jen said, "I made you a shirt too."

"You did?"

"Yup." Jen held it out.

Instead of dad Charlie's shirt said uncle.

He looked at it with confusion. "I'm gonna be an uncle?"

Jen elbowed Blake as he chuckled.

"You sure are, buddy," Blake said. "Jen's going to have a baby."

Jen shook her head again. A baby. Her baby bird. The first of three. Sydney was certainly capable, but she wasn't ready to leave the nest. Not yet. She—all of her children—still needed their mother. With effort, Jen forced her eyes to focus. What was she looking at? Off to the right, downstream? A large rock poked out of the water. She watched as a log thudded against it, then twisted in the current on its way past.

"S-swim," she said. "We have to swim to the r-rock."

Blake shivered next to her, not reacting to her words.

She pulled air through her nose and tried to focus by counting to ten. The rushing slurry, with all that it held—with all of its force—would take them straight to the rock. It would drop them at its edge. They'd survive. She pursed her lips. The rock was in full sun. They could get warm. Then, tomorrow, they could find the kids.

They were dead if they stayed put. That thought refused to leave.

"S-swim, Blake"—Jen tangled her fingers with her husband's—
"d-don't let go of my hand."

Jen eased herself off the rock and into the water, pushing her
feet under a rock. Blake yanked his arm away as she did.

"It's w-warm, Blake. We'll d-die here. Come on."

Easing into the corner, Blake refused to get off the rock,
confused defiance clouding his eyes.

Jen's own eyes burned as long-ago dried tears found their way
to the surface. "I-it's the o-only way. We have to go."

"N-no."

"Blake, you're not thinking clearly. We have to swim. S-see the
giant rock. The water g-goes straight to it. W-we have to g-get dry."

He shook his head. "I w-want to stay here."

With her heart beating sluggishly, but faster than moments
before, Jen climbed back onto the rock. "Blake, we'll die here. We
have to go. It's our only chance."

"I like it h-here."

Jen met his cloudy eyes. She ran her hand down his trembling
body. He wasn't thinking clearly. She probably wasn't either, but . . .
What choice did she have?

She pushed her foot against his, forcing him off balance, then
she pulled him into the muddy water. Neither landed on their feet,
and the current grabbed them.

The sludge whipped through Jen's hair, and yanked at Blake's
body as he tried to pull his hand away. But she refused to let go.
Fighting both him and the water, she pushed toward what she
hoped was the surface, her mind clearing only slightly. What had
she done? Blake couldn't swim in his condition, and the roaring
flood would take them right to the rock and *murder* them.

Her head broke the surface, and she pawed at Blake's arm,
working to bring him up. Lengthening her body, she brought her
feet forward, but . . .

Then what? There was no ground, no beach. There was nothing but debris-filled water. And a rock.

Blake's head broke the surface, and he stopped fighting her as he labored for breath. She pulled him as close as she could, refusing to let go. She would *not* let go of him. "Swim, Blake. Stay with me."

The water rushed faster. She couldn't see the rock. She couldn't see anything but muddy sludge. Sludge that surged around her, beating against her skin, invading her mouth, eyes, and nose.

Everything was too swift. Too wild. Her free arm slammed against it first. The rock. She reached out, grabbing for any kind of hold. A crack was all she needed. *Blake help!* But her words were silent, unheard. Pain ripped through her fingers as she scratched at the rock, her leg, then side, skimming across its rough surface.

Then they were past it.

There was nothing more to cling to. Blake tugged her arm, and Jen realized the current had begun to slow as the walls of the canyon widened.

"S-swim." His voice was weak and scratchy.

The word momentarily floated on her mind as she grasped at its meaning. For the edge. *He means for the edge.*

No longer fighting the current, she swam diagonally through it. They were more than halfway across as it was. There was nothing to see, nothing to swim for, but she did it anyway. What else could she do?

Then she saw it—a touch of green in the distance. If they reached that, they could at least hang on to the tree. It had survived. Maybe they could too.

She kicked with all her might, Blake floating beside her. Her exhausted husband, too exhausted to fight for himself, allowed her to fight for him. Except she was exhausted too.

Her feet struck the bottom, and she found her footing.

"Can you stand?" she asked.

Blake struggled in the water as she pushed her shaking body under his left shoulder. Two steps later, Blake stumbled and then fell. But the narrow canyon had widened just enough that the water no longer reached both sides. As Jen helped Blake up, she stared at their strip of shelter—river rock crusted in twelve inches of cold mud at the foot of a giant sycamore.

"Tessa, you and Max go look for firewood," Sydney said as she ambled back to where they sat balled up and crying against some rocks.

"You left us!" Tessa lashed out. "You just took off and left us here."

"You're fine." Sydney rolled her eyes. "We need to start a fire and get warm. Go get wood."

"We didn't know what you were doing. Whether or not you'd come back." Tessa's eyes were wild with a fire of their own.

"Where did you think I was going? It's not like there's anywhere to go."

"Maybe you left to find a way back to the car or to wave at the birds. I don't know. I only know that you left."

"I was scared," Max added.

"I'm sorry, okay? I just went to see if I . . . I could get a better view of the creek. Maybe see M-mom and Dad."

Max's eyes doubled in size. "Could you?" He looked downstream, through thick forest. "Mom, Dad!" he yelled.

Sydney blinked as her jaw tightened. "They have to stay where they are for a while because of the flood." She looked at Tessa. "Dad probably can't swim through water like that with his broken ankle."

Tessa crumpled—again.

Why was she always doing that? Sydney needed her help. She couldn't always be the strong one. She wanted to cry and fall apart and scream at the world too. She needed to let all of that out just as much as her sister. "Stop! Just stop crying, Tessa. We need a fire. We need to figure out water. You need to stop crying and remember what Dad taught us. So calm the freak down and help."

Max's face turned red as he burst into racking tears.

"What? Do you guys want me to leave again? Should I just leave you here by yourselves? Because I might if it means being away from all your crying. Seriously. I can't do all of this on my own." Sydney folded her arms as a tear rolled down her cheek and her voice cracked. "And you're giving me a headache."

Tessa sniffed, her face taking on a deeper red, and she stifled her ragged breathing. Without a word, she stood up and offered her hand to Max.

"Where are we going?" he asked as he took Tessa's hand.

"Gather wood."

The two words pricked at Sydney's lungs. "Thanks," she whispered.

"Hey, Syd." Max had stopped and turned to face her. "What are you gonna do?"

"Figure out where to sleep and how to cook grape leaves. Otherwise, we have to eat them raw."

"I don't want to eat grape leaves at all," Max grumbled.

"Me either." Sydney ignored the pounding in her head and chest and shooed him away with a tense smile and a wave of her hand, then she searched the ground. Maybe she could find a bowl-shaped rock.

A bowl-shaped rock. Maybe they existed in the movies or in ancient Native American villages, but they most certainly did not exist in the breezy forest that Sydney stood in. She flung another rock to the ground, then sat on a boulder. At least she'd managed to locate a place to sleep. It wasn't super flat, and it wasn't exactly soft, but they could have a fire without burning the forest down, and there was enough open space for them to lie down without rocks or pine cones poking their backs—once she tossed the pine cones away. She and Tessa had found a few fallen pines and carried them into camp, then wove them between two forked oak trees to act as a wind barrier. It helped some. Not much. It didn't really matter; she didn't expect to sleep anyway.

After gathering some leafy grapevines to lay on the ground, she'd decided to continue her search for a concaved rock. She hadn't really expected to find anything, but she needed something to keep her mind off her missing parents. And to think that the day before she'd struggled to keep her mind off Crystal being at Braden's party. Standing up, she stepped farther up the canyon's edge.

Braden probably didn't miss her. She missed him, though. She missed how cute he was. How strong he was. How fun he could be. But she wondered what he would have done when Max discovered the rattlesnake. What if it had been her instead of Max? Would Braden have rushed to save her the way her dad had Max? Teenagers couldn't be expected to act that way, though. Dad was an adult. Still, Dad had always stood up for Uncle Charlie, even as a freshman in college. That's how he and Mom met. Maybe she should expect more.

Reaching slightly higher ground, Sydney turned as soft warbling caught her ear. A yellow bird with a smattering of green on its wings stared at her from a tree. Where was its nest? She wondered if its mother would show up at the sound of its lullaby. She scoffed at the memory of the story her mother used to tell her, bitterness coating her tongue. No matter how loud Sydney sang, her mother wouldn't hear her call. She'd tried to hear it plenty of times, but Sydney always pushed her away. Now Mom was lost. Probably dying—if she wasn't dead.

The bird flitted to another tree, closer to the side canyon where Sydney's parents were trapped. Sydney scanned the horizon behind her twittering guide. The canyon couldn't be that far away. Maybe she could hike to the edge and find her way down. She couldn't hike out of West Clear Creek because of the high water, but if she could find her parents, they could make the decisions instead of her.

Sydney tightened her hands into fists, her jagged fingernails digging into her palms. They weren't dead. They were alive. They had to be, because she couldn't do any of this alone. Not anymore.

After heaving out a breath, Sydney turned back to where she'd left Tessa and Max to build a fire. Seeing no smoke, she knew. She'd have to build the fire.

A few minutes later, as she approached their primitive camp, she made out her siblings' conversation.

"This is the last match, Max. We can't use so many," Tessa said.

Max held a match against the whistle still hanging around his neck. "It'll light this time. Just watch."

Sydney waited through the lull in the conversation, hoping Max was right.

"Oops. Just one more," Max said.

"For me." Sydney stepped over to the rocked-in pile of wood and grinned. "How many have you used?"

"How many what?" Max asked, obviously understanding her question.

"Six," Tessa said.

"Then we'd better make this last one count." Sydney took a few of the larger pieces of wood off the pile, and placed some dried pine needles and oak leaves under a few twigs that she arranged into a tepee shape. "Max, grab me the backpack."

"We can't burn—"

She laughed. "Open two Band-Aids and hand me the paper covers."

As Tessa opened the first Band-Aid, Sydney stopped her from taking off the tabs. "I just need the paper."

Tessa nodded.

After placing the paper under the tinder and making sure enough air could get to it, Sydney looked at Max. "Your turn. Light it."

"The Band-Aid paper?"

"Yup. It'll light easier than the leaves and needles."

Max struck the match and touched the end to the paper, which immediately burst into a glow of orange. As quickly as it burned, it managed to catch enough needles and leaves on fire that Sydney could feel the warmth against her face. Easing larger pieces of wood onto the flames as twigs and then sticks lit one another, Sydney soon had a large fire going. "Guys," she said, clearing her frog-ridden throat, "I couldn't find a way to cook the grape leaves, and we have no water. I think we're going to have to eat some. Well, probably just chew on them for now." She dug into the backpack. "I've got apples for dinner."

"Just an apple," Max whined.

"Just an apple, and you need to eat the whole thing down to the seeds and stem."

Do You Have Matches?

Blake collapsed to the mud-sodden ground as Jen helped him out of the once-dry wash. With painful shivers running through her and overpowering the throb of her bloody fingernails, bruised legs and back, and abraded skin, Jen wanted nothing more than to collapse next to him. But she couldn't.

"No, Blake. We c-can't sit down. We've got to get w-warm." She yanked at his shoulders, every action helping to clear her mind only slightly. "Blake, get up!"

Her husband sat on the ground with minute tremors washing over him. He raised his head for a moment before slumping further down.

"You have to get up," Jen screamed, striking his shoulders with her fists. "You can't die. I won't let you d-die!" After hastily tearing his sodden and ripped shirt from his body, she grabbed him under his arms, then leaned back, refusing to let go.

His body slid a few inches before running into an upturned rock.

"Just to the tree, Blake. That's as far as we need to go. Then . . . then I-I'll cut some branches to lay down on."

What they needed were matches and dry wood. Sleeping bags and a tent. Heating pads.

Why had she agreed to this trip? Backpacking into a known danger with her three children? Oh, her husband knew what he was doing. He'd take care of them. He'd make sure they stayed safe. But it didn't happen that way. Not once that little serpent had caused him to break his ankle and Mother Nature got her hooks into him. He had saved Max, so there was that. But now her husband was dying.

And she couldn't live without him.

She just couldn't. Neither could their kids. Especially not Sydney.

Blake was the one who always got through to their daughter. He'd always been that parent. What would happen to Syd without Blake? Max needed a dad too. Even Tessa responded to him better than Jen sometimes.

"Blake, get up." With tears carving tracks through her mud-creased skin, Jen yanked him back again, striking her tail bone on a rock as her clammy hands slipped. Sticky mud clung to her abraded legs and tattered shorts, and she slammed her fists into the sludge in defeat, the ache in her tail bone barely louder than the one in her heart. Jen flung her head back, her gaze landing on the green leaves of the large sycamore. Somehow, it had survived. Somehow, it stood tall, its branches waving in the light breeze.

Rolling over, ignoring the sludge that now covered her from head to toe, Jen focused on the tree. Debris twisted around the lower three feet of its trunk. A white, four-inch gash scarred its bark, biting two inches into the pulpy underlayers. Though heaps of mud now lay at its roots—evidence that the flood had worked

140

to fell it—the tree lived, even as muck-covered roots stuck out at odd angles. So many uprooted trees, but this one stood tall.

Jen didn't know why, and her mind wasn't strong enough to consider the reason why what she saw mattered or what it meant to her in that moment, but something about it made her clamber to her feet.

Pushing the thick slime from her arms and legs, she foraged the ground for a sharp rock, cursing the loss of the bag she'd once clipped to her waist. A piercing stone stabbed at her blood-crusted fingers, and she grabbed it, ignoring the throbbing sting it had caused. Then she stepped to the tree, fuzzy memories of lessons once taught by Blake puddling in her mind . . .

"Okay, everyone, pop quiz. This one's oral." Blake winked at Jen as he clapped and then rubbed his hands together with a twinkle in his eye.

He always had that twinkle in his eye, but this time it did nothing for her. She glanced at her watch. Late. Again. He'd promised her they'd make the movie. It would start in fifteen minutes at a theater twenty-five minutes away. With a wave, she caught his attention and pointed at her watch. He scowled and nodded. Now he was as annoyed at her as she was at him. Nothing was more important than hanging out with his little scout troop. Not even her. Even the parents had gathered, ready for the meeting to end.

Blake looked each scout in the eye. "You're lost in the woods with nothing. It's cold, and you're wet. What do you do?"

"Build a fire." Charlie sat in the front row of the gym, staring at her new husband, as enthralled with him as ever.

"That's a good idea, Charlie. How will you do that?"

"Matches."

"Do you have matches?"

"No." Charlie hung his head.

Blake put his hand on Charlie's shoulder. "Not this time. But if you did, that would be the very best thing to do."

141

"Get dry as best as you can, and build a shelter," another boy in the front row said.

"Right." Blake glanced at Jen, then continued. "Use anything you can find to get yourself off the ground. Branches, leaves, pine needles. The drier the better."

The meeting continued for several more minutes, until one of the mothers called her son away, apologizing for leaving early—as if the meeting hadn't already run thirty minutes over. But Blake finally caught on. "Okay, boys. Next week—broken bones. Everyone bring an elastic bandage."

Jen huffed as she sagged into the front seat of the truck. Charlie yammered on to Blake about how awesome class was. How could it not be? They'd worked on building fires out at the fire pit and then built a shelter using tree cuttings Blake had saved from the landscapers. The class had been amazing. It was always amazing. Blake was amazing. But what about the promise he'd made to her? What about giving her that little bit of time that she needed. That she'd asked for?

Blake's hand eased across her knee, and she looked down, then over at him.

"There's a late showing," he said. "I checked."

"Hmm."

"We don't have work tomorrow. I thought maybe we could hit up that ice cream place you like and then head to the theater. It starts in about an hour."

"Whatever."

"Jen . . ."

"You know, parents don't want to wait around for an extra thirty minutes either."

"Beetle, it wasn't—"

"It was." Jen's voice softened. "You get so excited."

"Hey, this stuff is important. It could save a life."

"Yeah, I'm sure every one of these desert-dwelling, thirteen-year-old city boys is going to end up lost and hypothermic in the freezing Superstitions."

"It can happen there too, you know."

"In the dead of winter. It's more likely they die from heat stroke."

142

"We cover that in a couple of weeks."

Jen couldn't help but laugh. "Of course you do." She glanced out her window. "You're buying me popcorn."

"And a drink. Promise."

Another large branch fell from the tree and onto the growing pile below. Jen had been sawing and twisting at the branches for a good sixty minutes, a blister forming in the soft groove between her forefinger and thumb. The work was slow, but she could feel the movement clearing her mind. A jolt of tremors ran up her neck and down her arms. If only her mind would stay clear. No longer able to reach the branches, she hoped she had enough as she hobbled over to Blake.

He'd since lain down, and while his body shook occasionally, it wasn't enough. His eyes had closed. Jen rolled him to his side, and he groaned.

"Sleep." The word slurred on his tongue, but at least he'd spoken. It was a good sign.

"We have to warm you up."

Jen pushed several tree branches underneath him, wishing she could move him closer to the canyon wall. It wasn't any better in terms of shelter, but she felt safer there, regardless.

Once the branches were in place, Jen studied Blake's leg. Everything was soaked and covered in mud. He didn't have a lot of padding around the injury, so there wasn't much she could remove, but his shorts were loose enough to slip off. Gingerly, she worked them from his waist over his good foot and then past the bulky wrapping on the other. Once the clothing was dry, she'd figure out how to redress him.

Her gaze landed on the tips of Blake's stark white toes, which were visible on his good foot now that she'd removed his shoe. She stared at them dumbly until, finally, she remembered why their lack of color mattered. Placing her fingers against the patch of pallid skin that their *swim* through the flood waters had revealed on his injured ankle, she waited. A faint blip told her the blood his body could spare was still running through the mangled limb. She slumped to the ground and glanced at the loose bands hanging from his leg. One of the supports had disappeared with the raging water. Both would have been lost had she not tied them on individually as well as together. Either way, there was nothing to do about the leg at the moment.

After a short reprieve, Jen eased to her feet and removed the little bit of clothing that remained on her body, then hung each piece next to Blake's shirt and shorts on the debris wrapped around the tree. Glancing at her mud-caked sandals, she slipped them off too. She'd put them back on later, once she was warmer and the mud had dried. If it dried. Easing herself on top of Blake, she pulled the remaining branches over them. As her movements slowed, the cold blew what warmth she'd recovered away. She fought for clear, unmuddied thoughts, clinging to those of saving Blake and her children, until finally, she couldn't hold them any longer.

The water pouring from the two hoses glistened as it reflected the light shining from the porch. Sliding the door closed, Evan padded barefoot to the water faucet. He'd already shut off the hose draped into the pool from the front yard. A high-pitched whine vibrated in his teeth as he turned the knob to the right. Then silence fell on the yard.

As he stepped back to the patio, Michelle stepped through the door.

"How is she?" he asked.

"Cranky."

When Evan had arrived home from work, the house had been in chaos. Michelle stood at the counter with a full gallon of milk in one hand and a screaming, wriggly Ellie in the other. Emily, with snot running down her face, cried next to the fridge. Dylan and Danni ran in circles, chasing each other until Danni caused a book to fall off the end table. And then there was Maggie. She had lain on the couch, her face red and her eyes glossy.

That was where Evan's concern rested now. "Strep?"

"I'm not sure. Maybe. She cries when she has to swallow, but her fever comes down with acetaminophen."

He nodded as he took Michelle by the hands and led her to the pool. "That's good."

"It'll be so cold." Michelle said, eyeing the water.

"Oh, don't worry about that." A chuckle rumbled in his chest. "I can help you there."

"I see."

His foot dropped to the first step. He couldn't stop a jolting shiver from running up his spine. "It'll warm up," he said, failing to hide his response.

"After a week, when the sun's done its job."

"Something like that." He pulled his wife closer as he stepped to the wide Baja shelf. "It's not bad."

"I'm worried about Mags. We might need to cancel the party."

"What? No. It's just a virus. It's always just a virus."

Michelle scoffed as she tucked herself against his chest. "I know, but no one else wants that virus."

"Put distance between her and everyone else. It'll be fine. She can sleep in her room." His words were facetious, though he did hope Maggie would be well enough by morning to keep their plans.

The water swished around them, and he kicked his feet until he and Michelle were a little deeper. "See, this is nice."

"It is. And when we're done, I'll pull out some hot chocolate."

"Oh, that sounds good."

"I might take her to the doctor."

"Maggie? How long has she had a fever?"

"A few hours."

Evan brought his brows together as he questioned his wife. "I thought fevers weren't a concern until it had been a couple days." Maybe he was confused.

"They aren't normally, but she has so little energy." Michelle shrugged. "Urgent care will be open in the morning."

"Let's wait and see how she's feeling before we decide."

Michelle sighed as she said, "Fine."

"Good. Now watch this." Evan dropped his hands from Michelle's waist and hurried out of the pool. Rubbing his hands down his arms and chest as he staved off a few shivers, he rounded the deep end, stood on the raised water feature, then jumped, wrapping his arms around his knees just before hitting the water. After being out in the air, warmth instead of cold caressed his skin.

When he surfaced, Michelle was wiping water from the top of her head and face, sputtering. "Thanks for that," she said, smiling. "I will get you back."

"Oh, I bet you will."

The frantic wailing somersaulted through Evan's mind as his body shook. "Wh-what? What is it?"

"Finally," Michelle stopped shaking him and dropped her arm, wrapping it back around their oldest. "Maggie's worse."

Shoving a hand over his face and through what little hair he had, Evan struggled to sit up. The sun wasn't even up. "What time is it?" His mind wasn't ready to function on a parenting level yet.

146

Michelle's was always ready. "Three. She can't swallow. She can barely mumble."

"Maybe it'd be easier if she calmed down a little," Evan said softly as he placed his hand on Maggie's back and rubbed it lightly. "Rough night, huh?"

She nodded as she leaned over, holding a hand towel against her mouth. The wailing eased to soft whimpers as she raised her eyes to meet his. Even though her body wasn't as hot as it had been, the increased pain scrawled across her face.

"Can you try to talk now? Tell me what's going on?" Evan asked, his mind clearing.

"I *cun't swa-ow*. It hurt too *mush*." Maggie's words were slow and ill-formed, hardly recognizable.

"Does it hurt anywhere else?" Evan asked, his pulse racing as he grabbed his phone. "Can you breathe?"

Maggie rubbed at her neck. "*Siff*."

"You're neck's stiff?" Michelle said. "Can you breathe okay?"

Maggie nodded, and Evan relaxed a little. "At least there's that." He opened his phone and started panning through medical sites.

"What are you doing?" Michelle eyed him, obviously exasperated.

"Looking up symptoms."

"She needs a doctor."

"Sure does. I'm just wondering if there's something we can do for her at home for a couple of hours. Even a few minutes. Something to make her more comfortable until we determine where to take her."

Michelle's tense shoulders dropped. "That makes sense." She brushed her hand down Maggie's soft hair. "Do you think you could swallow a little something. Maybe water?"

Maggie shook her head, but then stopped. "I try."

"Okay. Let's do that while we see what Dad can find out."

147

As Michelle walked Maggie to the kitchen, Evan continued his search. It didn't take long for him to discover that Michelle already had the right idea. Cold water. He could at least tell her to add some ice. The blankets fell to the floor, nearly tripping him as he hurried from the bed down the hall. "Cold water is best. Maybe a warm . . ."

He watched as Michelle took one of the fabric rice bags they kept in the freezer from the microwave and stepped over to Maggie, who sat on the couch with a glass of ice water.

"Can you swallow?" he asked.

"I have to count and force myself." Though still garbled, her words were easier to understand.

"Good." He collapsed into the chair next to the couch. "Take a little sip every couple of minutes."

Michelle wrapped her arm around their daughter and pulled her closer, gently holding the warm rice pack to Maggie's neck. "Once you're done with your drink, try to get some rest. Urgent care opens in a few hours."

The sun started to peek over the horizon about the time that Maggie fell into a tormented sleep. Evan glanced at Michelle. "They open at eight, right?"

It seemed like such a long time to wait, especially when their oldest looked so defeated. The look in her eyes that was usually so bright had dimmed, and she'd lost every ounce of energy. The fear she must have felt—waking up in a puddle of spit, no longer able to swallow. No wonder she'd been so frantic.

"Yeah. Three-ish hours. It's not that long—not once she wakes up and we get her in the car," Michelle said.

"I'll take her," Evan offered.

Michelle studied him for a minute and then nodded. "You just don't want to fight Ellie with a bottle."

"What can I say? I wasn't born with the right equipment."

"Right." Michelle sighed.

"Maggie will be all right with me." Evan raised one side of his mouth, hoping it would comfort his wife. "I'll take care of her."

A soft smile flashed across Michelle's face. "I know. It's just hard when they're sick."

"Well, do your best to rein in momma bear and enjoy the pool with the kids. I'll take Maggie, wait the three hours at urgent care, get the antibiotic, and be back in time for the party." He grinned playfully at his wife.

The glare struck him across cheek and then pummeled his chin, and he squirmed in his chair. "I was kidding." He held his hand out as he winced. "Just kidding, promise. I'll cancel."

An hour later, Evan cracked an eyelid and watched as Michelle eased out from under Maggie and shuffled down the hall. Ellie must have woken up. How his wife heard such faint whimpers still amazed him. He hadn't heard anything other than Michelle accidentally kicking over the glass of unfinished water.

She'd kicked over the water.

Evan groaned and pushed himself to his feet. The least he could do was clean up the spill before someone slipped. Whose idea had it been to tile the family room, anyway? His. *Then when the kids spill their Kool-Aid while watching TV, the flooring isn't ruined. Have you ever tried to get red Kool-Aid out of carpet?* he'd once said. He hadn't been wrong, but no one slipped on wet carpet.

After mopping the water up with a few paper towels, Evan held his hand against Maggie's forehead. Her fever had broken for the moment. That was good. He settled at the end of the couch by her feet, leaving the chair for Michelle. Whether or not he wanted to be awake, he was. Until someone joined him or it was time to take Maggie to urgent care, he may as well veg-out to some mindless TV show.

The screen flicked to life, and he rushed to control the volume, which had caused Maggie to squirm before she settled back to sleep.

The weather. *Sunny and hot,* he thought as he flipped past it to another station. That never changed—not until the monsoon showed up, and it was still a few weeks away, even if the official start date had passed.

As a kid, the start of the monsoon had been determined by the dew point reaching a certain kind of miserable for three days in a row as well as a change in the wind's direction. In recent years, the National Weather Service had decided that using set dates would keep everything unified. So the season was set to run from June fifteenth to September thirtieth. As if it were ever possible to tell Mother Nature how to do her job.

June was still hotter and drier than July and August, so in Evan's book, Mother Nature was winning. Despite all that, a little rain would be nice. In the back of his mind, he remembered Michelle saying something about it sprinkling up on the Rim the day before. It couldn't be more than that. If it were, Blake and his family would already be home. His brother would never risk hiking in inclement weather. Besides, if storms were passing from the north, the winds hadn't changed direction yet and the rain would be lighter.

He shook his head, ridding it of his ruminations. His brother was fine. After a quick glance at Maggie's sleeping form, he looked at his watch, then sat back and clicked the button on the remote again. They still had more than an hour before urgent care opened. He stopped clicking when he saw some fix-it garage show flash across the screen.

"Right there is the leak. At the top of that rust line. This radiator's been leaking a while—"

"Daddy." Danni rubbed her fist over her eye as she stumbled into the room. "Where's Momma."

"Momma's with Ellie right now. Come here." Evan swung his four-year-old daughter into his arms. "You hungry?"

"I want pancakes."

"I'm no good at cooking. How about I get you some cereal."

Danni crinkled her nose. "I don't want Toasted O's."

"Not even with sugar?"

She shook her head, then lay on his shoulder.

"How about some Chocolate Puffs." He leaned closer to her ear and whispered conspiratorially, "I know where Momma keeps them."

As Danni cuddled in closer, Evan felt her nod against his neck. "I'm on it."

"On what, Daddy?"

"Your cereal."

Lifting her head, she stared at him. "That's gross. I want to eat it from a bowl."

Evan chuckled as he set his daughter on the counter. "I guess that's okay too."

It didn't take long before Emily and Dylan appeared, wiping the sleep from their tired eyes. Evan pulled out two more bowls and poured in the sugared cereal. He'd hear about it from Michelle—he knew that—and he was already working on his head-ducking apology.

When he was three spoonfuls into his own bowl of Chocolate Puffs, he looked up and winced at his wife, who held their irritable baby. "I know, I know. I'm sorry," he said.

"My cereal?"

"They have good taste, just like their mother." He shrugged with raised brows.

"Daddy said we could have some, Momma. He can't make pancakes." Danni stared up at her mother, and Michelle rolled her eyes.

"He can too. He just won't." She tapped Danni's nose. "Well, pass me the box, Dylan. You"—she eyed Evan, a smile tugging at her lips—"get me a bowl, please."

Keep the Fire Burning

Sydney groaned as she rolled to her side. Everything hurt. Reaching out, she tossed another piece of wood on the fire, then stared at the pale blue sky above her. It had never fully clouded, yet her family had become victims of flash flooding. Pushing at the emergency blanket, grapevines, and pine needles over top of her, she crawled to her feet. She needed to check the depth of the creek and figure out what to do next. First, another piece of wood on the fire. Max and Tessa had finally fallen asleep sometime during the night, and she needed to keep them warm. Well, as warm as possible—without melting the Mylar blanket they shared.

Even Sydney had managed an hour or two of sleep. It had helped some. Not enough. She rubbed at her shoulder as she made her way down the sloping canyon wall to the ledge they had scaled for safety. The water, still muddied, no longer carried giant trees, though tiny vortexes held flotsam and twisted it in never-ending swirls. Through the night, the water had receded enough that it only lapped lightly at the muddy bottom of the ledge. Less than fifteen feet away, a few remaining willow tips poked above the current, proving the creek's depth and the dangers of entering it. Sydney wouldn't be finding her way to the car any time soon. Besides the flowing death trap, she would have to battle the change in terrain to do that, and their cairn had most certainly been washed away.

She eased down onto the ledge where the sun now shone. Warmth touched her sore arms and back. They needed to move the fire and camp to the ledge now that the danger had lessened, but that could wait until Max and Tessa woke up. Then they'd build a big fire, and she would leave to go find her parents.

Throughout her tossing and turning, it had been all she could think about. Getting to her parents. Maybe it was smart, maybe it wasn't, but she planned to hike over land and find them. If her parents were alive, they needed help now, not later. Not that she could do much for them. But she had to do something. She just had to. She blinked back the burn pricking her eyes. The question that remained wasn't whether she would go. It was how to do it without her sister and brother blubbering about being left alone.

Blubbering seemed like such a cruel word. But it was true. That's what they did. Since things had calmed down a bit and she could think a little clearer, she could understand why they cried inconsolably. She was scared too. And even though Dad was teaching Max and had taught Tessa all the same things he'd taught her, they were younger. Well, Tessa wasn't that much younger— but she was younger. And softer. Sydney loved her brother and sister, and her mom would be mad at her for leaving them. It was probably a mistake. She could get lost or fall or run into a mountain lion. Max and Tessa could start a wild fire. All of those things were true, but the only thing Sydney could focus on, right or wrong, was finding her parents.

Rising to her feet, she climbed back up the hill to where her sister and brother were. Their sleeping forms nestled against each other. If she left them, she'd have to give them something to do, but what?

"One granola bar each," Sydney said as she handed Tessa and Max the little bit of food she'd rationed for breakfast. She figured if Uncle Evan reported them missing that evening, they'd need enough food to get through the day—maybe two.

"Can't I have two?" Max asked scratching his leg.

"Sorry, buddy, can't do that."

"Syd, I'm thirsty," he whined.

"Here. Take a few of these leaves and chew on them. I think that will help." Sydney handed Max and Tessa a few grape leaves from their bedding.

"Ew." Tessa pulled a face.

Sydney held her breath as she placed a leaf in her own mouth and chewed. A light, tangy flavor washed over her tongue, and she relaxed. "They're not that bad. It's like one of those weird lettuces Mom sometimes buys."

"I don't like those." Max rubbed his hand across his thigh.

Sydney stared at him, then crawled over and peered at his leg. Tiny bumps had begun to rise in a small patch just above his knee. *Crap*. She'd have to deal with his rash after getting him to eat. "It will help you be less thirsty," she said. "Even give you a little water. You gotta chew them. You don't have to swallow the leaves if you don't want to, though."

"You're sure they're not poisonous. Didn't Dad say to be careful around grapevines?" Tessa eyed the leaf suspiciously.

"Because poison ivy can grow nearby." Sydney eyed Max again and winced before turning back to her sister. "The grape leaves are edible. If the grapes were ripe or more than tiny buds of nothingness, we could eat them, but they're not. Chew."

"Fine." Tessa placed half a leaf in her mouth and started chewing. Her shoulders soon relaxed, and she put the other half in her mouth.

"Max, you too," Sydney said.

"I don't wanna."

"Do it anyway."

"No." Max threw the leaves he'd been handed into the air, then kicked at them when they fluttered to the ground.

Sydney stood up ready to shove a leaf down his throat in the name of saving his life but came up short when Tessa reached for another leaf.

"I like them. They remind me of lemons." Tessa grinned.

Max narrowed his eyes as he watched Tessa swallow and then start to chew on another leaf.

Tessa met his uncertain gaze. "I'm not as hungry now that I've eaten one, either."

Sydney sat back down. Sometimes her sister had the right touch. More often than Sydney did when it came to what to say. Within a minute, Max picked up a leaf and twirled it in his hand. Another minute passed before he broke a sliver off and placed it on his tongue. At the third minute, he took a bite and chewed. "Mmm, lemon."

Sydney didn't taste a hint of lemon, but whatever it took to make Max eat it was enough for her.

Once finished with his second leaf, Sydney eased next to him, the tube of calamine lotion in her hand. "I noticed you scratching. You can't do that, okay?"

"You mean . . ."

"Yeah. It's the poison ivy. This will help though." She handed him the tube and watched him smear some across his leg.

"Will it get worse?" Max's bottom lip trembled.

"I don't know. Just keep the lotion on it and don't scratch."

Max nodded, then stood up and walked to the pile of firewood.

"No, Max," Sydney stopped him. "We need to let this fire burn out. We're moving camp to the ledge."

"Why?"

"So rescue crews can find us easier. We'll need a big fire there. Do you think you could keep one going for us?"

"How big?" he asked.

Sydney spread her arms out. "Really big, and smoky."

Max jumped up. "I better get lots of wood and pine needles then. The needles make it smoke more."

"Stay close, Max," Tessa called as he ran away. She pushed out her bottom lip and looked at Sydney. "I wanna go home."

"Me too." Sydney dragged her finger across the dirt in front of herself. "Let's move those trees we carried over here down to the ledge."

Tessa gave her a questioning look, and Sydney furrowed her brow, then relaxed it before meeting her sister's eyes. "Dad won't be able to walk out of here. I need you to make a raft."

"A raft? I don't know how to make a raft."

"We'll use the trees. Break off the branches and weave grapevines around them."

"We or me?"

Sydney huffed. "I'll get you started, okay. Then I'm going to go find Mom and Dad."

"No." Tessa's face crumpled, and her eyes glistened with tears. "You can't leave us again, Syd. You can't."

Sydney handed her a leaf. "You need to keep chewing on these."

"You're not leaving, and I don't want your stupid leaves." Tessa threw the leaf to the ground.

157

Sydney held out another one. "Take the leaf. You need water, Tessa. And I am leaving. Dad has a broken ankle, and they're stuck in a flood."

"No they weren't. That canyon was dry. They'll get here once the creek goes down." Tessa sniffed angrily.

"I saw it. Yesterday. Water was pouring from that canyon into the creek."

"But . . ."

"I'll help you guys move to the ledge. Then you guys can keep the fire going and work on the raft for Dad."

Tessa shook her head and flung her arms around in the air. "Oh my gosh! Mom and Dad are gonna die, and then you'll die hiking over to them."

"How?"

"I don't know. You'll fall or . . . or get eaten by a bear or something. You can't go. Don't leave us," she cried. "I don't know what to do."

"I'm telling you what to do, and I'll be back tonight. Just keep a fire burning, and build a raft. You can do this. I know you can." Sydney stood up. "Let's grab those trees."

Jen eased her eyes open as her body shuddered again. The sun was up, and a touch of warmth found the jagged circle of bare skin no longer covered by the tree branches. She lay still, holding her breath and waiting. Then it came, the slow pump of Blake's heart.

"Blake?" Her voice croaked within her throat. She sounded like a hoarse bull frog.

"Blake?" She pushed at his arm and carefully elbowed him in the ribs.

He didn't answer.

"Blake!" she shouted, shoving the branches off herself and rubbing his sternum with her fist like she'd seen EMTs do on TV.

Nothing.

She kept rubbing, her cold knuckles pushing deeper into the bone under his skin. Finally, his hand swept across hers, and she stopped. She fell to his chest and sobbed. "You're alive. You're alive." She shook her head. "Blake? Please. Tell me what to do."

"Hot."

Jen creased her brow. "It's not hot. You're hypothermic." She crawled on top of him again and pulled the branches back over her feet and legs, protecting them from the breeze, but allowing the direct sun, which was warmer, to touch her back and shoulders. "Do you know where we are, Blake?"

"Hot."

Jen's chest heaved as she considered her husband's condition. His body was shutting down, and she had no way to help him other than to share her limited warmth. It had been hours since they'd reached land, but he was still so cold.

Hours . . .

Maybe their clothes had dried. Even the little amount of warmth they provided would help. Wouldn't it?

After clambering to her feet, Jen pushed the branches back over Blake and ambled closer to the tree. Mud clung to the soles of her torn feet, and she stumbled as her left toe caught on a rock. She flung her right arm out, her hand promptly landing in the mud. She swore as she shook the grime from her throbbing fingers, despite being grateful she hadn't fallen completely. Next time, she'd keep her sandals closer.

Once she reached the tree, Jen touched her swimming suit and shorts. Dry. She breathed out, allowing her eyelids to flutter closed in gratitude. If ever there was a time she didn't enjoy being naked with her husband, this was it. She picked up one of her sandals and

159

grimaced. It would never dry. Once dressed, she grabbed Blake's shorts, useless tattered shirt, and her muddied footwear and ambled back to where he lay.

"Blake, let's get your shorts back on so you can be more comfortable." She scoffed. *Comfortable—as if that's possible.*

After scrunching up one leg of his shorts, she gently pushed them over the toes of his bad foot, then repeated the motion on his other side. Blake groaned. Jen smiled wanly before her face crumpled. She wanted him conscious, but she didn't want him in pain.

Soon, Jen had them both dressed as much as possible—her sandals in the sun next to the makeshift bed. She eased back on top of Blake to share what body heat she could. Then she reconsidered. Skin to skin was probably still better for Blake, so she dropped the straps of her suit and pushed down the top. Even half-dressed, she felt better. At least now, if rescuers showed up, she could replace her top and straps quickly, giving her a modicum of dignity.

"Mags, it's time to go." Evan bent over his daughter and rubbed her shoulder. She'd slept for a few hours now, but he hated to wake her, especially with how terrible she felt, but waiting any longer to leave for urgent care meant one thing: a longer wait.

She didn't budge.

"Mags. Let's go," he called again.

Slowly, Maggie sat up and stared at him. Then she shook her head. "Mumma."

Three hours had passed since she'd sipped at the cold water, and her speech had become nothing more than garbled utterances again. He placed his hand on her forehead. The fever was back.

"Mom's gonna stay with the kids. But don't worry, I know how to get the good stuff from the docs," he said.

"Mumma." Maggie's chest heaved as her breathing became ragged.

"Ev, you better take Ellie while I gather Maggie's stuff." Michelle laid the crying infant in his arms, then rushed down the hall.

"What stuff?" He shook his head.

"*Buchs,*" Maggie said.

That made sense. Maggie was always reading. Books often littered the floor of the room she shared with Danni. And it wasn't uncommon for him or Michelle to find Danni snuggled up next to Maggie as Maggie read to her.

"What are you reading now?"

"Harry Podder."

"Still? You were reading that a couple days ago. Figured you'd be done."

She held up three fingers. "Thir *buch.*"

"Oh. That makes sense. How many are there again?"

She held up three fingers on one hand and four on the other.

Evan raised his eyebrows. "And you've read them all?"

This time, she held up two fingers.

"Twice?"

She nodded and closed her eyes as she leaned back against the couch.

"Momma's getting your stuff, and then we'll go," Evan said, fingering a strand of hair off her face, upsetting Ellie further.

Maggie's chest heaved as tears fell from her eyes. "I want Mumma t'go."

"I know, baby girl, but I can't feed Ellie."

"Mumma."

Ellie wriggled in his arms, joining her sister in ear-piercing howls. Evan boosted Ellie up to his shoulder and bounced lightly on his feet, patting her back. "Mags, I promise I'll be nice. Maybe we can pick up some ice cream on the way home. It'll feel good on your throat."

"Cun't swa-ow!"

Ellie's crying subsided for a few seconds, then doubled in volume as a gooey warmth spread across Evan's shoulder. He closed his eyes and took a deep breath, the tension in his jaw building.

"I better take Mags," Michelle said as she reentered the room and took their oldest by the elbow. "It shouldn't take that long. An hour, maybe two. Ellie'll fall asleep soon."

Evan nodded, then started down the hall. "Daddy needs a clean shirt because of you, little girl. I better get a really big smile when your belly feels better."

Sunlight cascaded through the trees as Sydney checked her compass again. She'd taken a reading from the outcropping of rocks she'd stood on the day before when she'd studied the confluence. Working the compass wasn't her best skill, but if she kept the needle on *S* and walked in the direction of the 220, she was pretty sure she'd run into the edge of the side canyon, somewhere just south of the confluence.

Tessa and Max had cried, begging her to stay as she'd left. But she couldn't stay. She had made certain that the fire was large and smoky and away from any trees or brush. Max had gathered a large pile of wood, and she and Tessa had gone over the importance of keeping the fire going at all times.

Tessa had the three trees they'd gathered down by the ledge now. Plenty of grapevines grew nearby, and Sydney had shown her how to weave them back and forth between the tree trunks, bringing the trunks close together and knotting the vines. The whole raft would be less than a foot wide, but that didn't matter. Sydney had given her sister busy work, nothing more. The water level was too high and dangerous to try hiking out. They had no choice but to depend on Uncle Evan.

By midmorning, Sydney had started walking with the backpack slung over both shoulders. She carried her daily ration of food, her Mylar blanket, the unopened blanket, two matches, and the duct tape. The knife and other supplies she'd put in the small backpack before the flood had been left with Tessa and Max.

With the needle on *S*, Sydney corrected her course, picked a tree that was close to the number 220 in the distance, and walked toward it. The slant of the ground pulled at her feet, calling them downward and causing an agonizing ache in both ankles. She checked the compass again. Their camp had originally been at the confluence, but climbing the canyon wall had taken them slightly east. Slow as a tortoise. That's how she moved. Any faster meant getting off course or sliding downhill. And she remembered how some of the canyon walls seemed to climb straight toward the sky. The last thing she wanted to do was slide downhill.

The arduous walk left Sydney with plenty of time to think. Think about all the things she didn't want to think about. Braden, leaving Tessa and Max, her dying parents—or were they dead?

No, she defiantly refused to think about that.

She stopped to catch her breath and pulled out a grape leaf to replace the pulp in her mouth. The leaves didn't provide a ton of moisture, but they did help her body circulate what she had, easing the scratchiness in her throat.

She wiped at her forehead. That was the other reason she had to move slowly. She could still sweat, which was a good thing, but she remembered Dad telling her something about sweat causing more problems than not when hypothermia was a risk. She couldn't quite remember what the risk was, but she knew to avoid sweating. Still, it seemed to her that warming up and sweating would be a good thing.

She rolled her eyes.

Dad would be right, whether or not she knew why.

A few feet farther, and Sydney looked up. A vertical wall stood in her path.

Is That a Crying Baby?

"All right, little one, none of that. I'm coming," Evan said.

It hadn't taken long for Ellie to fall asleep again that morning—once Evan had managed to calm her down. A bit of rocking, a warm bath, and lots of cuddling seemed to help, but there was no hidden truth; she'd passed out from pure exhaustion, and now she'd awakened from her nap.

"Everyone on the play step." Evan climbed out of the pool.

His three middle children paddled their various toys to the wide step.

"Daddy, is Ellie going to swim?" Danni asked.

The idea had crossed his mind, and he stopped to consider it again for a minute before slowly shaking his head. "Maybe in a week or two, but the water's still too cold for her."

"Oh." The corners of Danni's mouth fell.

"Hey, none of that," Evan said, looking back at Danni as he picked up a screaming Ellie from the stationary swing he'd brought out with them.

Tears filled Danni's eyes as her face pinched together.

Hand at his waist, Evan smiled wanly at his daughter. "What are you crying for, Dan-Dan?"

"I want you and Ellie to come swimming."

"We're going to watch you swim, okay. Just remember, if I'm not in the pool, you have to be on the step, and if I'm not watching you swim, then you have to get out."

"I can watch the girls, Daddy, if you need to get something for Ellie. I already know how to swim," Dylan said.

Evan chuckled. "You're a great swimmer, Dylan, but what's the rule?"

Dylan's eyes rolled to the left before he raised his gaze back to Evan. "No one in the pool unless you or Momma are watching."

"Right. We don't want anyone getting hurt."

The ringing phone pricked Evan's ears. Perfect timing. "Everyone out. Right now, hurry."

The three kids, faces hanging low, climbed out of the pool. Evan handed each one a towel and ushered them off the gated pool decking to the lawn. With the gate soon locked and Ellie still screaming, he rushed into the house. How could he have forgotten his phone?

By the time he managed to grab the phone from the kitchen table, it had stopped ringing. Glancing at the missed-call notification, he expected to see Michelle's name pop up. Instead, he stared down at Mrs. Butler's number. *Not today.* He rolled his eyes. What could possibly be wrong now?

He dialed her number.

"Mr. Marksam," Ada Butler answered, "there is a crooked tile in my entryway."

"I'm sorry to hear that. Can—"

"Is that a crying baby? I can barely hear you."

"It's my daughter."

"Well, I can't hear you."

Evan shifted Ellie to the other arm. "Sorry about that. She misses her mother—"

"Well, where is she?"

"My wife?" Evan shook his head. "Can you send me a picture of the tile, Mrs. Butler?"

"Of course I can."

The phone line went dead as his three middle children clambered into the house. "I'm hungee, Daddy," Emily said.

"You are? I think Ellie might be too."

His phone dinged, then immediately rang.

"Just a minute, okay, Emily?" Answering the phone, he motioned Dylan to the couch and laid Ellie in his lap.

"Do you see it?" Ada Butler said.

"I just received it. Give me just a minute here."

"Daddy, I don't want to hold Ellie," Dylan announced loudly. "She stinks."

Evan put a finger to his lips as he met Dylan's gaze. "I'm not sure which tile you're looking at, Mrs. Butler."

"The one on the left—"

"Daddy," Emily cried.

He rushed to the kitchen and pulled out the bread, glancing at his phone again. There was nothing wrong with the tile.

"The tile, Mr. Marksam, is crooked. I measured it, and the top is one thirty-second of an inch different from the bottom."

"W-why did you—there are going to be some minor differences. Did it look crooked before you measured it?" He rushed to spread peanut butter on a slice of bread.

"No, Daddy," Emily fell to the floor.

"She doesn't like peanut butter," Danni said.

"Daddy, Ellie—"

"Mr. Marksam, what is all that noise?"

"It's Saturday, Mrs. Butler. My wife took my oldest to the doctor, my youngest needs a diaper change, and my other three are hungry. Could you tell the tile was crooked before you measured it?"

"No. But I can't unsee it now."

The fridge slammed shut as Evan unwrapped a piece of cheese. Emily cried harder.

"I can have my guy out there on Monday to redo the tile, but I'll have to charge you for his time."

"Why? He's the one—"

"Because one thirty-second of an inch isn't visible unless you check it with a tape measure."

"Well, I see it."

"I'm sure you do." Evan covered the phone's microphone and groaned, then returned to the call. "Tell you what. I'll fix it myself, but I can't get there until Monday."

"Fine, fine." Mrs. Butler paused and silence fell between them. "Mr. Marksam, please feed your children. They obviously need you."

"Obviously. Thank you. I'll see you Monday."

Evan dropped the cheese on the floor, then flung his hands in the air. "I give up. Do you guys want to go to McDonald's?"

"Yay!" the girls yelled.

"Daddy, Ell—"

"Stinks. I'm coming right now."

Staring at the cliff, Sydney sank to the ground. She'd gone maybe half a mile in about two hours. She was close, she knew it, but she couldn't scale the rock outcropping, and she didn't know how far she'd have to go to get around it. Or if she could.

The ragged, vertical climb made her stomach churn, yet she wondered if she should try it, handhold by handhold, nail-biting by leg-shaking step. Was there any way to make it easier? She had . . . duct tape. She scoffed. MythBusters may have put their trust in duct tape, but she sure didn't. Besides, what was she supposed to do, tape herself to the rock? As she shifted, the tired muscles in her arms reminded her of the truth. Climbing the facade was a death sentence.

Sydney eased to her feet and carefully paced to the north. Two choices: turn around and go back to Max and Tessa or try walking around the cliff on the northern end. If she did that, she could—presumably—continue with her compass heading. Maybe.

She wasn't turning back.

At the edge of the white stone, which no longer gleamed in the sun, she started her downward shuffle north, back toward West Clear Creek. Fatigue bit at her muscles while her thick tongue begged for water. She placed another grape leaf in her mouth.

From their camp on the ledge, and even from farther up in the forest, Sydney had seen no sign of the cliff she now paralleled. Everything had looked steeply inclined away from the river; she'd expected that. But a vertical wall pushing out from the mountain? That, she hadn't expected.

Originally, her family had camped at the confluence. How far apart could two canyons run from their intersection point? Sydney lifted her sandaled foot, ready to stomp it into the ground, but instead, she found herself sliding two feet down the mountainside. She beat her fists into the earth as she landed on her backside. The dust from the forest floor gritted her lungs, and she coughed as another plume surrounded her. As she shoved to her feet, she focused on the shadows of the canyon below. They haunted her, toying with her emotions as they touted the deep crevasse in front of her but continued to hide the one to her left.

A rustle shook a top branch of a tree next to the cliff, and a yellow bird trilled as it flew to a neighboring tree a few feet away. Sydney flung her head back, squinting at the bright sky and studied the top of the tree where the songbird had landed. Words from the story her mom had told her as a child floated into her mind: *Just sing that little lullaby, and know I'll hear your call.* The bird's melody grew within the branches of the tree. Sydney hadn't allowed her mother to hear her song. She'd pushed her away so many times. Too many times. But she didn't have to do that anymore. She shouldn't have done it in the first place. Now Sydney was alone and scared, and she was calling for her mom, begging to be heard. But where did that get her?

She shaded her eyes as she stared at the bird and then at the tree where it perched. The overgrown fir stood a needle or two higher than the rock. Was the tree crazy tall, or was the wall shrinking? The bird soared into the air, landing in another tree to the north. *Then listening close, she heard the song—the lullaby her momma tweeted all day and all night long.* And the cliff seemed shorter.

Please be shrinking, Sydney thought.

Quickened by her hope, she pushed herself harder down the hill. The beat of her feet matching that of her heart. The bird disappeared, but Sydney's hope only grew. The wall was shrinking. The excitement thwarted her forward, and then she stopped.

For a short distance, the craggy stone dipped lower before climbing again. Twelve, maybe fifteen or twenty feet. Sydney wasn't sure, but she eyed it closely. If she continued north, what were her chances? Eventually, the ridge had to end; the wall of the side canyon faced west. *But this stone face could still plummet into West Clear Creek.* Mapping out handholds, Sydney studied the facade. Unlike most of the wall, the hand and footholds were deep and close together. She ground her teeth, then fit her hand into the crack above her head and lifted her sandaled foot onto the three-inch cut-out two feet above the ground.

She had to try.

The minutes passed, and Sydney eased herself from the ground. With each push upward, her heart beat a little faster. If she fell, her family would be divided into three when the rescue teams arrived—if she survived, that was. Tessa would never forgive her if she didn't. Sydney pursed her lips. Tessa's whining drove her crazy, but if Tessa hadn't been there to help with Max the night before, Sydney would have lost it a lot worse than she had. Her sister did a lot of good, though it hurt to admit it. Even to herself.

Why, she didn't know.

Sibling rivalry? That's what Mom would call it.

Be nicer to Tessa, Sydney.

Don't hurt your sister, Sydney.

Help her, Sydney.

The image of Mom wrapping her arms around Tessa, pulling her close, and promising they would have special time joined her memory.

Sydney never got special time. She spent most of her time at home alone. Unless they were on a family outing—where Tessa whined even more—Sydney was left to her phone and her room. Mom said she hid, but the truth was that Sydney didn't have any reason to be anywhere or do anything else. No one even noticed when she sat in the family room. Two maybe three words were all she ever heard from anyone. Except occasionally from Dad. He would quiz her on outdoors stuff. That was kind of fun.

She moved her hand up to the next hold, then lifted her foot, but as she brought her foot down, it barely scuffed the edge of the nook. Her leg struck the rock, and stinging pain thudded into her kneecap. She hung there, breathing deeply as a stone formed in her throat, then landed in her gut. What if she was on the wrong path?

What if she should have stayed on the ground? What if she should have ignored that bird?

Thoughts of her mother entered and ravaged Sydney's mind as her fingers and triceps cried out in pain. Why didn't she get special time? Wasn't she important? Didn't she deserve her mother's love? She slid her foot into the hold and panted, relaxing what little she could before moving for what she hoped was the last handhold before the top. Even as she concentrated on not falling, her ruminations pummeled her.

Special time or not, Sydney couldn't question her mother's love. At least she shouldn't. Mom loved her. If she didn't, Mom wouldn't worry about how Braden treated her. She wouldn't wait outside Sydney's bedroom door, trying to talk to her. Guilt banded Sydney's chest, and she breathed out. Mom *had* offered her special time. And by not *singing*, Sydney had done more than push Mom away. She had refused to accept the gift that she craved most of all. But Mom had never stopped tweeting. Mom had never stopped offering.

Two minutes later, when Sydney crested the ridge, she lay in the dirt and cried. Exhaustion, physical and emotional racked her body. She let it ease through her. Taking it in just long enough that she could dismiss it. She had to keep going.

She lifted her head off the ground. A few feet in front of her, the forest climbed upward, then disappeared, replaced by sky. Once on her feet, Sydney dug the compass out of the backpack. As she twisted the dial, everything looked, or at least felt, wrong. South seemed much farther behind her, and the sun was in a completely different place than she expected it to be. Moving northward without taking a reading had messed everything up.

Still, the canyon had to be right over the next ridge. Everything definitely angled downward where the forest disappeared. Why else could she see sky?

The sun had dipped below the southwestern horizon, and Jen tried to wake Blake again before pulling the leafy branches onto her back. He groaned. It was the most she'd gotten out of him for several hours.

Earlier that afternoon, she'd taken a few minutes to haphazardly weave the layer of branches together, making them easier to move off her back. That's what she told herself. In reality, it had given her something to do while the sun warmed Blake.

Once finished, she'd crouched down at the edge of the receding stream, which was nothing more than a muddy trickle. With cupped hands, she scooped up some water and stared at it. Her stomach churned at the filth. Only a day ago she'd wished for a little flood— some way for them to get water in the dry canyon. But not anymore. If she drank this water, she risked dehydrating faster from diarrhea. Didn't she? If she got sick?

Blake once told a story of a body that was discovered next to a cow pond. The lost hiker had been right there next to the water, but he'd died of dehydration because he refused to drink from the stagnant pond. She didn't want that to happen to her, but . . . She'd glanced at the sludge again, and then she'd slumped down on a rock next to Blake, unable to bring herself to drink it.

Jen's hard shivering had returned minutes after the sun retreated to the west, but the relief she'd received from the sun's warmth had boosted her cognizance. She was no longer sure that was what she wanted, regardless of whether or not it was best.

Scattered through two canyons, her family now fought for their lives. Were her children even alive? If she had the ability to make tears, they would have poured from her eyes, but at most, she managed a little glistening blurriness. She switched the pebble in her mouth from one side to the other.

Blake was dying. He wouldn't last the night unless she discovered a way to warm him up. No matches or dry wood—the green branches she had might smoke, but they wouldn't burn. No blanket. No clothing. The clothes they'd used to pad Blake's ankle had finally dried, but his back was still exposed to the coolness rising from the ground through the branches he rested on. That couldn't be comfortable.

When she lay down, she did so on top of Blake, soft and . . . well . . . warmer than the air. She'd cut the leaves and smaller branches from the limbs beneath him, trying to make him more comfortable, but her focus remained on keeping him alive. She imagined the crook he'd have in his back. He'd be asking her to rub it out every night for the next six months.

Her face crumpled. He'd better. She might kill him herself if he didn't.

What if rescue parties didn't find them in time? What if the kids were left alone in the world? What would happen to them? Evan would take them in, but would he and Michelle love them like she and Blake did?

Sydney needed a special kind of love. One that Jen wasn't sure she always knew how to give. Sydney needed to feel special. Needed. The problem was that Sydney only wanted to help herself. She had little desire to help anyone else. Especially Tessa. When she did help, however, she tended to brighten a little bit. Jen also found it difficult to talk to her. No matter what she said, Sydney rolled her eyes and walked away. An ache settled into Jen's chest, one that didn't come from a careening tree or a giant rock.

Maybe Michelle would do better. Maybe it was all for the—

A familiar sound interrupted Jen's thoughts. The sentence that had begun to form in her mind cut off as she listened, urging herself to hear it again.

"Mom, Dad!"

"Syd. Sydney, over here. We're here!" Jen called out. She pushed the branches off her back, yanked up her swimming suit, and quickly recovered Blake. "Over here, Sydney! Over here."

She turned and stared at the thirty-foot-high canyon wall, scanning its sheer edge as she backed closer to the muddy remnants of the flood water.

"Mom! Mom!"

Her heart thumped wildly as she waved at her oldest daughter. "Sydney!"

Sydney stepped to the edge, a little to the right of the tree. "You're alive. I . . ." Her voice cracked, and her face crumpled.

"I'm so glad to see you, Syd!" Jen said as loud as she could, hope and worry colliding. "Tessa and Max? Where are they?"

"On a ledge above where our camp was," Sydney yelled back. "W-we lost most everything, but I saved some stuff." Panic crossed Sydney's face as she studied the area around Jen. "W-what about Dad? W-where is he?" Sydney's voice rose.

Jen pointed. "He's under those branches." The prick of tears burned Jen's eyes, but still refused to come.

"There's no way down!" Uncontrolled tones rose higher in the air. Sydney was crying. "I-is he . . . ?"

Jen gazed at her daughter, wanting so much to hug her, to tell her it would all be okay, but she couldn't. She slumped to the ground, the moisture from the crusted mud cooling her freezing backside further. "No. B-but he's not good. He groans if I rub his chest hard enough." She hung her head. "Syd, I d-don't know what to do. I can't help him, but I can't lose him either." Losing control of her faculties, Jen's body shook harder than it had all day, the strength she needed for her daughter, succumbing to fear and exhaustion.

"Here," Sydney called. "Take this food. Eat it. And here's a Mylar blanket."

The space blanket crinkled as Sydney put something—likely food—within its folds. She dropped it to the ground. "There're some grape leaves in there. Chew them. Dad said they'll help with hydration. I can sleep up here."

"No. No, you can't! You have to get b-back to your sister and brother. They can't do any of this without you."

Sydney dropped to the ground out of Jen's sight. "I can't go back. Not now. Not tonight. They're fine. They have a fire and a blanket, and I . . . I left them food. Don't make me go back! Please don't make me."

Sydney was frantic, and for the first time in several years, Jen listened as her oldest daughter cried for comfort. Cried because she didn't want to leave her side. Or was it that she didn't want to leave Blake?

"Can you talk me through using this blanket for your dad?" Jen softened the edge to her voice, working to think clearly.

"You'll want to put it under him and then make sure that it tucks around his feet and over his body." Sydney sniffed. "It traps body heat, so if you crawl in with him, it'll help."

The information wasn't new to Jen, but it gave her time to think. "You have to stay warm too, Sydney? How're you going to do that if you stay here?"

"Build a fire."

"With what?"

"I have two matches and Band-Aids."

"Two matches?" Curious at the mention of Band-Aids, Jen decided not to bring that up quite yet.

"Yeah, I brought matches."

Jen looked at the dusky sky. "All right. Syd, stay tonight. But figure out how to get me one of those matches and gather enough wood for two fires."

The crying had stopped the second Evan mentioned McDonald's. All except Ellie's. She had taken a little longer, but after a diaper change, and after Evan convinced her to take at least a portion of a bottle, she had calmed down too.

Now he sat at a McDonald's table with Ellie snuggled into his arm, her face scrunching up every few minutes as her legs pulled into her belly. Emily called to him from above. "Daddy, watch this."

He looked up and waved. Swinging herself out of sight, Emily appeared at the bottom of the slide a moment later. A large smile planted on his face, Evan gave her a thumbs-up.

His pocket buzzed. *Finally.* "Michelle?"

"They're sending her to the hospital."

"What? Why?" Every ounce of exhaustion Evan felt doubled, combining with a new surge of worry. "What does she have?"

"Mono," Michelle sighed.

"The kissing disease?"

"Don't use that phrase with her. She doesn't think it's funny."

"Not the kissing disease, got it. Why the hospital?"

"She needs some medication—some kind of steroid is what they said. They could give it to her orally if she could swallow better, but she falls apart the second anyone suggests it. After trying to convince her, the doctor said to take her to the hospital. Apparently, they'll admit her for a day or two until the swelling goes down and stays that way."

"For mono."

"For mono."

Evan grunted. "But she'll be okay?"

"Oh, she'll definitely be okay. She's still breathing good and all that. They'll give her something for the pain while we're there. She's scared but fine."

Evan blew out a long breath. "All right then."

"How are you guys doing?"

"We're great. We went swimming, and now we're at McDonald's. I even got Ellie to take a little bit of formula."

"Good. At least one of us has the day under control."

Evan laughed and pushed his hand over his head. "I don't know if I'd go that far, but we'll be okay. What's your plan?"

"She's not going to let me leave."

"So you'll be sleeping at the hospital?" Evan glanced outside, preparing himself for what the rest of the day would bring.

"I think so. I don't see any other way."

Sydney's stomach squeezed tighter with hunger as she watched the orange flames flicker in front of her. At the moment, she sat on the ground near the cliff's edge, where she could talk to her mom a little easier. *Talk* was a bit of an exaggeration. In reality, any conversation they had involved raising their voices. Thirty feet high and in the open, like Sydney was, left little for the sound to bounce off. With the canyon walls surrounding her, her mom didn't have to strain her dry, croaky voice quite as much.

"Can you see their flames or smoke?" her mom yelled up.

Sydney turned and studied the eastern horizon, the last of the sun falling quickly in the southwest. Only black met her gaze.

She wasn't surprised. As she'd left her sibling's camp, she'd climbed at least a half mile up before skirting to the west. Worry of meeting the side canyon too far down and missing her parents had caused her to take a somewhat southernly direction as well. The unexpected outcropping she'd rounded may have made her journey longer, but not by much. If nothing else, it had given her a better idea of the lay of the canyon. Regardless, she had traveled farther west than she'd expected, and a portion of that was a slight downward slope to the side canyon's edge. Seeing Tessa and Max's fire wasn't likely, even at night.

"No. I'd have to walk up the hill to do that," she answered.

"But you told them to keep it going?"

"Yes."

After eating half a granola bar and getting her own fire started, Mom seemed to shake a little less. Getting the wood down to her had been a bit like throwing a firecracker into a rotten tree trunk. Each log Sydney threw down risked splintering into a thousand pieces. At first, Mom stood nearby, ready to rescue each one, but it didn't take long for her to take cover under the thin emergency blanket with Dad. Sydney shrugged at the recent memory. At least she had had tinder to gather. With only one match each, they didn't exactly have second chances.

"How's Dad?" Sydney asked.

"He's still breathing, and he squirms when I rub his chest hard enough." Mom's voice cracked a little more as she spoke. "He's always taken care of me." After a short pause, her mom added, "You know, we met when I wasn't much older than you."

"Yeah, I know." Sydney didn't roll her eyes like she normally would have. "You and Uncle Charlie and the hat."

"Yeah. Dad was cute, but so were a lot of boys."

Sydney sometimes thought about what it would be like to meet her future husband in high school. She'd wondered if maybe she and Braden would get married, but that thought brought as much pain as it did pleasure. "So what was it then?"

"What was what?"

"How was Dad different?"

"Well . . ."

Her mom stopped talking for a second, and Sydney caught a gleam of light reflecting off the space blanket as her mother shifted.

"He was the first guy to help me with Charlie," she finally finished.

"I thought he helped *Charlie*?"

"Yeah. He did. And by doing that, he helped me."

Sydney looked down at the little camp where her parents were. The fire burned only a foot or two away from where they lay—Mom on top of Dad. They were always together. Both of them talked about Uncle Charlie. But Sydney didn't see how her dad helping Charlie had helped her mom.

"How?"

Mom didn't answer right away, and Sydney wondered if maybe she'd fallen asleep. But then she spoke. "It was my responsibility to make sure Charlie was okay at school. Kind of an unwritten rule. If we hadn't found his hat, I would have had to figure out how to get him home in the middle of a meltdown. Then I would have had to spend the evening with him whining and crying. I was babysitting him that night. Instead, we found his hat and had fun at the football game." She let out a dry cough. "Dad talked more to Charlie than to me that night."

"Why?"

"I like to think he was nervous, but it was probably because Charlie kept talking to him."

Sydney glanced into the canyon. The only sound was Mom's voice, the only light a small fire. Even the trickle of water had stopped before Sydney got there.

She thought again about her parents. They fought on occasion, but not often. Sydney smiled as she remembered Mom getting really mad when Dad had used her kitchen knife on some drip-line hoses. She'd handed him the knife and told him he could figure out how to trim the chicken and cut the vegetables. Dad had laughed and pulled her into a hug, promising to buy her a new knife soon.

And he'd chopped the vegetables.

"So he's always been that way?" Sydney asked.

"What way?"

"I don't know. Caring and stuff."

"He's always been that way with everyone. Not just me. Your dad's respectful." The blanket over Sydney's parents crinkled as her mom shifted again. "That's an important trait, I think."

"I guess."

"I've never understood why someone would want to be in a relationship with someone who didn't respect them."

"You mean Braden." Sydney rolled her eyes and stood up.

"I didn't say that."

"No, but you implied it."

"I didn't. But I would be sad to find out he didn't respect you."

Sydney pursed her lips. "He's young."

"So was Dad."

Exhaling, Sydney plopped another piece of wood on her fire and slumped back down to the ground. "I guess."

"Guys your age will mature. I'm sure the guys who mistreated Charlie grew up. One of them even has a son with a disability. He apologized to me when I ran into him at the grocery store a few years ago. But that doesn't mean teenage girls should put up with being treated poorly. You and every other girl out there deserve to be treated right." Mom paused, raised her head and looked in Sydney's general direction. "I dated before I met your dad."

"You did?"

"Yeah." Mom laughed. "Paul Merrick. He was the guy who taught me what I didn't want."

"What'd he do?"

"Well, a lot of stuff. I ignored the way he teased Charlie. But the day he broke into my locker and copied my homework—that was the day *we* ended. I should have ended it sooner."

"He broke into your locker?"

"And called me dorky. And made me feel bad when I didn't want to kiss him. And laughed at me when I tripped."

"That sucks."

"It did, but I was completely enamored with Paul. His disarming smile and, boy, did he have a following of girls waiting for him to dump me. Then I dumped him."

The knock on the door brought Evan's head up off the back of the couch. He flicked his eyes open and stared at the kids, who had stopped watching some cartoon character jump from one mound of pink dirt to a purple one and now stared at him.

"I'll get it," he said, his mind a little fuzzy. He glanced at Ellie in the swing and gave her a little smile, then focused. *Who on earth could be at the door?*

With his eye near the peephole, he swallowed the urge to swear. He'd forgotten to cancel.

"Joanne. Rick. How're you guys. I'm sorry, I totally forgot to call," he started, after opening the door.

The smiles once plastered to his friends' faces fell as they waited for him to finish.

"Michelle had to take Maggie to the hospital this morning. Turns out she has mono."

Rick chortled. "Isn't she a little young to be kissing boys."

"That's what I thought. Turns out, catching mono doesn't require kissing. Go figure," Evan said. "Anyway, the party's canceled."

Joanne laughed. "Of course it is. Do you need any help with anything?"

"Not unless you're lactating."

"Nope. Can't help you there."

"That's what I figured. We're good. Thanks."

Joanne and Rick turned to leave, and Evan glanced at his watch. Party had been scheduled for seven. He needed to call Blake. With all the craziness, he'd lost track of ti—

When the door had nearly clicked shut, Evan caught the end of Rick's next comment.

" . . . fished two out of the creek."

Evan yanked the door open. "What was that?" he asked.

"Just curious how Blake is. Joanne mentioned he and his family were up north. Apparently, there was a mad flood through West Clear Creek yesterday. Didn't you hear about it?"

"No." Evan swallowed the lump forming in his throat.

"Yeah, turns out they yanked two bodies out near Bull Pen this afternoon," Rick said.

"Any idea who they were?"

Rick cleared his throat. "None. But I guess it was pretty bad. Water flowing ten to fifteen feet higher than normal in some places. Plenty of those side washes flooded too."

"The Rim got that much rain?" Evan's heart thudded painfully in his chest. "When I heard there was rain, I figured a few sprinkles—but flooding this time of year . . ." Evan's words fell away as a sour taste puddled in his mouth.

Rick rocked back on his feet, concern appearing on his face. "Tons of rain. Covered a lot of the watershed for the area."

"Crap." Evan ran to his phone, his stomach souring, and dialed Blake's number. Blake would have come home early. He wouldn't keep his family in a canyon surrounded by storms. *Unless* . . . "He didn't know it was raining," Evan mumbled as he listened to the fourth ring. He hung up and tried again. "I've got to . . ." He raked his hand over his head as he scanned his children's frightened faces. "It's okay, guys. D-dad's just got to . . ."

"Come on," Rick said, "I'll drive you over there. Joanne'll watch the kids."

A few minutes later, Rick parked his truck outside Blake's house. Not only was it dark, but the family car was missing.

Evan picked up his phone again and dialed Blake's number. "He's not answering."

He dialed Jen. Then Sydney. Then Tessa.

No one answered.

Evan yanked open the truck's passenger door, then grabbed at his hair and twisted around, facing his brother's house. "I've gotta . . . gotta . . ."

Rick grabbed his arm. "Ev, calm down a bit, buddy. Let's start with nine-one-one."

It took some time for Evan to get through to someone who could give him any answers—so long that he and Rick had arrived back at his house before the 911 operator had taken any information from him. It hadn't done much to calm his nerves.

The news blared in the background as Joanne played with and occupied the kids. Thank heavens for good friends.

From his phone, a voice droned into Evan's ear. He held it just far enough away for Rick to listen in. "The flooding is extensive, especially for this time of year," the officer who had introduced himself as Officer Howard said. "The roads were barely dry enough for us to get into Bull Pen to check for those other guys who were reported missing. Where did you say your brother parked?"

"At the Calloway Trailhead." Evan glanced at Rick.

"It's pretty remote that way." The officer cleared his throat. "You described them as a family of five. White, average heights, healthy weights. Girls sixteen and thirteen and a ten-year-old boy?"

"Yeah." Evan wiped at his face with the back of his hand.

"None of that matches the two we pulled out today. Two young-adult Hispanics. Their friend wasn't near the creek and

184

managed to get to higher ground and call. Bodies were several miles from where they started."

"When will you look for my brother's family?"

"Tomorrow morning."

Officer Howard seemed like a nice guy, but Evan wanted to wring his neck, despite knowing searches often broke at dark. In wilderness areas like West Clear Creek, they could be even spottier. No one wanted to risk injuries—especially when everyone expected they'd only find bodies.

"Fine. I'll be there at daylight."

"Mr. Marksam, please stay home. We prefer that the search and rescue teams work without having to worry about someone else."

"So what am I supposed to do? Sit here and twiddle my thumbs?"

"Let us know if your brother arrives home."

"Yeah," Evan mumbled.

"Stay there and take care of your family. We'll do everything we can, but, sir . . . most people . . . they don't survive these floods."

Evan hung up. He'd failed his brother again. How would he ever look him in the eye? If he ever got another chance. He bit down on his fist, the fleshiness of his index finger taking the brunt of his agony. He hadn't paid enough attention to the news or Michelle. He'd made light of the weather report as he'd sat on the couch with Maggie just that morning. He hadn't even bothered to watch it, just brushed it off, announcing to himself that it would be hot and sunny. Now his brother's family was missing—his best friend. And all he could do was sit on his haunches and do nothing? Wait for search and rescue to call him back? None of it sat well with him.

"I've got to get up there."

Rick turned and stared at Evan. "You did just hear what that officer said, right?"

"I heard, but I can't sit here. I'll drive to Payson or Verde Valley. What hospital would they be taken to anyway? Flagstaff?"

Joanne stood up. "Ev, you need to sit for a beat. Take a breath. You can't go rushing up there. You don't even know where to go."

"It doesn't matter. Any one of those places is closer than here."

"What about Maggie and Michelle? You're just going to make Michelle come home to deal with these kids? They can't exactly stay home alone."

Evan stared at her, hoping she'd see the pleading in his eyes.

Joanne stuck her hand in her back pocket and sagged her hip. "Don't you think your babies will feel out of sorts without you around? Especially little Ellie."

Evan slumped to the couch. "You're right. They love you, but Michelle would kill me for leaving them."

Rick put his hand on Evan's shoulder. "You can't do any more up there than you can from down here. The last thing you want is to be in the way."

"It's my brother, man." Tears swelled in Evan's eyes and he wept.

"Why don't we stay and help put the kids to bed," Joanne offered.

Evan nodded, then wiped at his eyes before shutting off the TV and corralling the kids down the hall.

An hour later, after Joanne and Rick had gone, Evan finally felt like he could call Michelle without bursting into unintelligible tears. Sitting on the edge of the couch, he dialed her number.

"Evan?" Michelle's tired voice answered the phone.

"Blake's missing."

Evan heard Michelle shift on the plastic recliner she was sleeping on. "Missing?" she asked.

"It flooded up there, and they never came home."

"They're . . ."

"No one knows. They think so." Tears welled in his eyes again. "They want me to stay home, but I can't, Michelle. I can't."

The line fell quiet.

"Of course you can. I can't leave Maggie, and what can you do with four little kids? They told you to stay home for a reason."

"B-but—" Tears rolled down Evan's face. "My brother."

"Ev"—Michelle's voice was sweet, soft—"you know the likelihood of survival."

"I know."

"It could be days."

"You're right." He paused. "How's Mags?"

"Maggie's fine. She's finally able to swallow some. I think we'll be home by tomorrow evening."

"Good. That's good," he mumbled.

"Evan, you have to stay home. How would you handle Ellie and her crying? And the other three running around?"

"I don't know."

"You can't. Stay home. Be patient."

"Right."

Hanging up the phone, Evan's breath caught in his throat. He couldn't go to sleep in a comfortable bed while his brother was missing. Maybe someone could take the kids. Joanne had said no. Other than Jen, she was the only person Michelle really trusted, especially with Ellie. What about his parents? Michelle could handle that. He clenched his jaw. He didn't want to worry them the way he was worrying. They didn't need that. He couldn't even bring himself to call Jen's parents to tell them their daughter and grandchildren were missing. And it would be super weird to ask them to watch his kids. Wouldn't it? It didn't matter much; years ago, they'd moved to another state where they could get better care for Charlie. If only Michelle's parents were still alive.

He pounded his fists against his mattress, then wiped at his eyes and jumped out of bed.

Clothes, diapers, formula. The kids could find toys. Snacks. If no one could watch the kids, then the kids would go with him. He was supposed to stay. Everyone told him to stay. But he couldn't. He'd tried. He'd tried keeping the kids entertained and waiting patiently for someone to call. They hadn't even started searching for Blake.

Patience was not a virtue he had at the moment. He grabbed the duffel bag from the closet and started throwing supplies into it. Staying home marked him as useless. But he wasn't useless. Even if he was, he couldn't stand the feeling of uselessness. He needed to do something. Anything. It wasn't like he was going to drag his four kids toward the flood waters or into the canyon to find Blake. But he had to be there. Be where he could have communication with search and rescue. Be there when Blake was found and brought out. Be there to identify . . .

He clenched his jaw. They weren't dead. Blake couldn't be dead.

With everything he could think to gather in the bag, he shook Dylan awake. "Hey, buddy, we're going on a little trip. Grab a couple of toys, okay?"

Dylan nodded, then his eyes fluttered closed.

"Dylan, wake up. Come on."

Dylan rubbed at his eyes and looked at Evan. "How come?"

"We've just got to go on a little trip. Come on."

Ten minutes later, with the kids in the car, Evan sagged in his seat. Somewhere along the line, people would forgive him for leaving home. He counted on that because he couldn't sit there any longer.

To the Rescue

"Mom."

The wind ripped through Jen's hair, and she pulled the emergency blanket higher. Had she heard something else?

"Mom, wake up."

The voice snapped with the wind, but Jen couldn't focus.

"Mom! Why won't you wake up? You have to wake up!"

"S-Sydney?"

Sydney burst into tears. "I thought . . . Put some tiny pieces of wood on your fire."

"I . . . I'm okay. Just really tired." She didn't mention her increasing headache. Instead, she crawled to the fire and put a few splintered pieces of wood on top of it, then softly blew at the coals below. She couldn't have blown any harder if she'd wanted to. Not with the way her stomach rolled with hunger and her throat and mouth stung with thirst. The blustery wind, however, could. It whipped right through the hot coals, lifting sparks into the fresh tinder.

Jen popped a pebble into her mouth. It stuck to her dry tongue. The grape leaves were not enough, and Blake hadn't even had those. She thought of the sludge she'd stared at the day before and cringed.

Once the flames curled a little higher, Jen stood and faced Sydney, who stared over the cliff, shivering. "You're cold," Jen said, shading her eyes with her hand.

"I . . . I'm fine. My fire died last night, but I have a blanket."

"Syd, you have to go back to Tessa and Max."

"No."

The wind slapped at Jen's face. "You have to. You have nothing but what you brought here. No way to care for yourself. And they need you."

"They're fine."

"They aren't strong like you. You have to go back."

"I . . . I'm not strong. I don't want t-to be strong. Dad's sick. You're stuck. And they're always crying. When is it my turn? When do *I* get to fall to the ground and have someone else pick me up?"

Sydney was right. She was crying for help. Calling for Jen. And Jen couldn't do anything.

Her oldest was the reason she and Blake had survived the night. She wanted nothing more than to wrap her arms around her daughter, pull her close, and let her cry into her shoulder. Sydney had to be exhausted. She'd hiked up and downhill, scaled a rock wall, and gathered enough firewood to keep two fires going through most of the night—enough for Jen to keep a small one going for at least another day. And she'd done it all without much food and with only the fluid her body could take in from a few crushed grape leaves. The physical strain was enough to kill her—anyone—let alone the mental anguish it all caused, especially for a sixteen-year-old. But if the family had to be divided, then Jen needed her oldest with her other children. Sydney's cool head and outdoor prowess was all they had to keep them alive. And Jen needed them alive.

Sydney had made it once. She could make it again. She had to. Because if she didn't, Jen would never forgive herself for sending her back.

"Syd, I know you're tired. I know it's hard, but sometimes you just have to bite the bullet and do what's necessary to survive. You've kept us alive. Tess and Max need you. *I* need you."

"Fine." Sydney flung her arms into the air. "I'll go. I'll leave you here to die with Dad. He's dying, right? And we can't say goodbye?"

"Sydney—" Jen shifted her weight, her bruised back and leg throbbing.

"No, Mom. Don't. I know the truth. You're right. I need to leave. I need to babysit Tessa and Max. If they die and I don't, I'd feel pretty crappy. It won't be any different if you and Dad die though."

"Stop it! You can't think like that."

"Why not? How should I think?"

Jen dropped the hand that shaded her eyes and stared at the ground. "You *are* strong, Sydney. Look at all that you've done over the past three days. No one else could have done those things. No one else would have thought to have Tessa build a raft, not because we need one, but to keep her mind busy. No one else would have hiked across such steep land and up a cliff while hungry and suffering from dehydration. No one. You've done amazing things, and if anyone dies, it won't be your fault, regardless of what you do right now."

Sydney sniffed. "I know."

"Please don't think like that anymore. This was a freak act of nature. No one had control. We took all the necessary precautions. No one is at fault, especially not you. Okay?"

"Yeah, okay."

"I know this is still hard for you." Jen furrowed her brow and let the bit of peace that had snuck into the conversation hang momentarily. "I'm sorry to ask you to do more, but I have to. Go back. Take care of them. Please."

"Who will take care of you?" Sydney's voice cracked again.

"I will. I'm strong too, remember? Do you think Dad would have brought us down here if he didn't think we could hack it?"

"No."

"I'll take care of me and Dad, okay? We have the space blanket, and I'll get some water from a puddle. You do that too, as soon as you can."

"But—"

"Grape leaves are good, but they're not enough. We have to risk drinking what's available."

"All right." Sydney turned away from Jen, but turned back a few minutes later. "I'm gonna head along this canyon until the canyons connect. I think it will take less time."

Jen watched as her oldest daughter shuffled away. Sydney hung her head with her shoulders rounded. Every bit of her posture and gait a tell of her tiredness. Jen looked toward the mouth of the canyon. Two miles? Maybe three? Four? The distance wasn't hard. The conditions though? They could be.

Dropping her hand to her side, she hobbled closer to what had been a roaring river less than two days ago. She and Blake had made it to safety because the canyon had widened and the water had become shallower and somewhat calmer. Now there was nothing but thick mud in front of her.

Upstream, stood the rock she had mindlessly attempted to cling to. Her body still ached from the attempt. Maybe there was something there.

Pushing through the wind, Jen started her short journey. Each step stabbed through her sandals at her feet and legs. Her lungs heaved heavier than she expected. But the pain in her head overtook almost all of her ailments. She needed water.

A couple hundred yards away from Blake, she fell to her knees at the boulder's base. The rushing water had created a depression. Jen picked up a rock and hurled it into the hole. "Nearly drown to death only to die of dehydration." She screamed past her scratchy throat into the wind, "I just want a drink! A little water."

Bending lower, she yanked at the rock, then clawed at the earth below. The furious motion caused her heart to race and her body to heave for breath even as her stomach roiled with pain and nausea. The mud clung to her hands. She kept digging—the coolness biting at her ripped and re-bloodied nail beds.

At first, it was nothing more than a seep mixing with the mud and forming a runny clay, but as she dug deeper, water trickled from the ground, filling her tiny hole. She skimmed the top with cupped hands, and brought the earth-rich water to her lips. Teeth barred, she did her best to strain what dirt she could from the water. It didn't work, but it also didn't matter. She drank it, relishing its sweep of her tongue and mouth. She brought more to her lips, enjoying the relief it brought to her throat.

She stayed near her well for an hour, digging it out as necessary and sipping a little more from its depths every few minutes— reminding herself not to guzzle it in. She hadn't peed in at least twelve hours, and she still wouldn't for a while. But she also wouldn't die from dehydration. Not right away.

As she looked back toward Blake, her smile fell. Blake hadn't improved. And he hadn't peed either.

Evan rolled over, his head landing next to Dylan's on the pillow. He'd driven to Payson and checked into the Lazy Trees Motel.

Cracking an eye, he glanced at the clock on the nightstand. Nine-oh-two. It had still been dark when they'd checked in. The blackout curtains were all that kept the sun from his eyes now.

He'd slept.

How, he wasn't sure.

Getting the kids settled into bed, helping Ellie to accept another bottle—her third—none of it had been exceptionally easy, but he'd managed it.

But now what?

As he pushed himself up in bed, three little heads popped up from their pillows.

"I'm hungee," Emily said.

"Me too."

"Yeah," added Dylan.

Apparently, the first thing on the day's docket was breakfast. "You guys want to go find some donuts?"

His three kids yelled "yeah," their eyes opening wide.

"Okay, out of bed, you sleepyheads."

Once dressed, Evan and his crew took off to find the nearest donut shop, which took longer than he'd expected it would in such a small town. After the debilitating decision-making ended, the girls each had a simple glazed donut, and Dylan ate a pudding-filled, powdered monstrosity that landed as much on his face and hands as it did on his clothes.

As Ellie finished the last of another bottle, Evan motioned for the other three to pick up their trash and put it in the garbage can. Emily reached for the hole at the top of the box trash can and dropped most of hers to the floor, including the half-drunk bottle of milk—without a lid.

"Daddy," called Danni, "Emily spilled her milk."

Evan put the empty bottle on the table. "Can you grab some napkins and help her clean it up?"

194

"Don't worry about it." A young woman with her hair in one of those elastic things, approached the garbage can with a mop. "I've got it."

"Thanks." Evan smiled as he stood to put Ellie in her car seat. "We'll get out of"—

The familiar ooze of baby barf seeped through Evan's shirt.

—"ugh . . . your hair. Just as soon as I get cleaned up."

He looked at his kids, then picking up the baby carrier, where he'd tucked a now-crying Ellie, he corralled them into the bathroom. "Everyone choose a stall."

Dylan rushed to the biggest stall while Danni hurried into the other one. Emily stood with her hands between her legs. "Daddy, I have to pee."

Evan glanced at his two-year-old daughter as he brushed a wet paper towel down his shoulder, then he glanced at the urinal hanging from the wall. "Dylan, why are you in a stall?"

"You said to choose one."

He had. That's exactly what he'd said. After putting Ellie's carrier on the floor, he hurried to the door and locked it. "Okay, Em, here's how we're gonna do this. I'll hold you, and you'll pee into that weird looking toilet."

She wiggled, her knees pulling closer together and pointed at a stall. "I like those toilets."

"No time, big girl."

Evan helped his daughter with her shorts, then balled her legs into his chest. "Don't forget to aim."

"What?" Emily said.

Evan winced. "Nothing."

Two toilets flushed just as a knock sounded at the door. "Sir, please unlock the door."

Evan quickly helped Emily with her shorts and directed Dylan and Danni to the sink. "Be right there."

The lock clicked as Evan turned it.

"This isn't a private—"

"Sorry about that. Too many kids, not enough hands. Won't happen again." Evan cringed. It would definitely happen again, but hopefully not there. As he scooped up Emily, he stepped to the sink, ignoring the dirty stare from the pimply manager. One day, the kid might understand a little better. If he were lucky enough.

"All right, guys, to the car," Evan said.

Outside the bathroom, he took Emily's hand while Danni put her hand on Ellie's seat and Dylan walked no more than two steps in front of him. "Hands on the van."

His three kids placed their hands on the van until the doors unlocked and opened. Then Evan breathed. Michelle had trained them well. How she did it twenty-four hours a day, every day, he'd never know. She'd probably handle Ada Butler better too. He chuckled, which felt good after a stressful night.

Evan still questioned the sanity of ignoring everyone he'd talked to and driving north. He couldn't exactly help Blake, but the pull to the canyon continued to drive his actions. There, he'd be immediately available for questions. He'd be there when Blake was brought out. Then, he wouldn't have to wait for a phone call.

But he still hadn't answered the pressing question: What would he do with four young kids?

Unsure of the answer, he climbed into his minivan and headed north. Eventually, he'd hit the forest roads. Unpaved, they might not even be passable, but as long as he stayed within range of a cell tower, he could stay in contact with search and rescue, which was his next phone call.

Sydney stood on a rock, studying the convergence below. No water rushed from the side canyon. Not anymore. On her way down, she'd only seen a handful of small puddles as the canyon continued to widen before joining West Clear Creek. Clear Creek, on the other hand, was twice what it had been. Though, it wasn't nearly what it had been two days ago, and Sydney wondered if maybe, just maybe, they could find a better way from one camp to the other.

Then she wouldn't have to be in charge.

She turned to the southeast and saw the smoke from the fire she'd told Max and Tessa to keep going. It billowed into the sky and was dragged east by the wind. Good. They'd listened. It wasn't far, but she still had to drop down into camp, and that required a little back-tracking. She huffed, despite acknowledging that she'd chosen to divert to the convergence.

As she started walking, she stumbled over nothing, barely catching herself before falling. The dizziness was getting worse, as was the ache surrounding her head. She stuffed another grape leaf in her mouth, wishing not only for water, but also for food.

It took less than an hour for her to reach the rock where she'd once stood and cried at the thought that her parents were likely dead. The corner of her mouth rose slightly. They weren't dead. Not yet. At least she had that good news to pass on to her brother and sister. Shuffling down the steep hill, she called to them. Stiff and scratchy, her voice was thrown back by the wind. Not even the hint of an echo carried through the canyon.

She tried again.

And again.

The fire came into view, followed by the top of Tessa's head.

"Tess, over here," she called out.

Nothing.

Max shuffled toward Tessa, grapevines wrapped around his arms, his energy levels obviously depleted. Then he turned and froze. Sydney waved.

Max waved back. His mouth moved, but the wind whipped his voice away.

From that point, it didn't take long for Sydney to reach the camp. Tessa hugged her, her eyes glistening. "I thought—"

"I found them," Sydney interrupted. "I made it to the other canyon. They're there. Alive. Well, Dad's real sick, but I dropped lots of wood down for Mom last night." Sydney slumped to the ground in front of the fire. "I need to rest, then we need to get water. Mom says we have to risk it."

"Get up, Syd. We gotta go now," Max said.

"Go where?" Sydney shook her head. "I need to rest, then we'll get water."

"No, to Mom and Dad."

"The raft is ready," Tessa said.

The raft. Sydney hadn't given a thought to it since Mom had mentioned it earlier that morning. "That was busy work, Tess. To help keep your mind off being stuck here."

"But"—Tessa's face fell—"you said it was to help get Dad."

"I know, but there's no way we can float him out of here. The water's still too high."

"That's okay, Syd. We'll go to them," Max said.

"This is the better camp. We have more water, once we get down to it, and . . . and the rescuers will see us and our fire better."

Max's eyes clouded over as his face crumpled. Sydney looked away as she struggled to keep her own emotions in check. "Come on, let's get some water."

"How will we get back up?"

Sydney turned and looked at Tessa. She hadn't thought about that. They'd climbed a ten-foot wall to get away from the flood.

Weakened from dehydration and the elements, they wouldn't make it back up.

"I . . ." Her words wouldn't come out. She didn't know. She didn't know what to do or how to do it. She didn't know how to care for her brother and sister. She didn't know how to help her parents. She didn't know what to do to survive.

"We still have matches," Tessa said. "We didn't need any more. And Max has gathered lots of wood." She nodded toward the pile of wood, enough for at least another day.

"So we drop everything down there and start another fire." Sydney considered it. "It'd be easier to spot."

"No," Max said. "What if it floods again?"

Sydney patted his shoulder with a limp hand. "That won't happen, buddy."

"How do you know?"

"I just do," she snapped.

She glanced at the pile of wood and the blazing fire. If they moved, they'd have to put the fire out. It wouldn't take long to build another one though. "All right, start dropping the wood over the side. I'll put the fire out."

Sydney hadn't given much thought to the difficulty of putting out the fire until she began to try. Without water, her only option was to smother it with dirt, and she didn't exactly have a shovel. Even worse, this wasn't a fire meant to simply keep them warm. She'd told Max to keep it big, and he had.

Taking a long stick, she untangled the pieces of wood, laying them next to each other on the rock wall. The heat caused her body to flush. Maybe she should have gotten a drink first. But that would have meant scaling the wall again, and she didn't have that in her at all.

Cool, dry dirt filled her palms as she scooped it into her hands and carried it to the closest smoking log. Other than a little sputter and a burst of sparks from the minute pieces of flammable particles in the dirt, nothing happened. After three times of the same result, she stood up straight and stared at her surroundings. Something had to change.

Her gaze fell to the backpack. The large cavity and all the time in the world offered her something a little better than nothing. While the individual logs burned down, Sydney painstakingly dug at the forest floor, scooping handfuls of dirt into the backpack. Her already tender fingers screamed at her to stop. Instead, she paused long enough to look up at her brother and sister, who worked to drop the large pile of unburned wood to the muddy ground below. There, she'd find plenty of damp soil to put out the fire. Unfortunately, the fire wasn't down there.

The bag of dirt that had dug at her fingers as much as she had at it, fell atop the first log, causing the flames to sputter out. Dropping to the ground, she began digging again. It would take another bag full to keep it from smoking.

Sydney had dumped another two bags full on the fire before Tessa and Max bent down to help her—at her insistence.

"Ow!" Tessa held her finger to her chest.

The sharp pine needles and shards of gravel had shocked Sydney at first too. Now she ignored her bleeding hands. "You'll get used to it. Just go slow at first."

Tessa nodded with glistening eyes.

Sydney suspected that her sister wanted to whine and cry and find a way out of helping, but that wouldn't happen. Not this time. She needed help. She'd decided to try something different, and so far, it was working. Sydney acknowledged her sister's difficulty and then allowed for slower progression. It was still painful for Sydney, who had no desire to shoulder most of the work, but at least Tessa was helping.

After they'd dumped enough bags of dirt to lose count, the fire no longer smoked. Tessa and Max slumped to the ground, their bodies as red as Sydney suspected hers was.

"Five minutes," she said, "then we need to get down to the water for a drink."

With her hands on her knees, she scanned the area until her gaze fell upon the raft. She stepped closer and studied her sister's work. Each grapevine was tightly woven between five thin tree trunks. The weave was so well done that she could barely see the ground beneath the raft, and the slight bends in the tree trunks appeared to have straightened—for the most part. Sydney turned and stared at Tessa.

"I added two trees," Tessa said, sitting up. "It didn't look wide enough."

Sydney nodded. "This is good, Tess. I had no idea."

"Some of the vines were harder to work with than others. That's why a few of them broke, especially at that end." She pointed toward what Sydney thought of as the top. "Then I started only using the young vines. They were shorter, but they worked better."

"This is great."

"Yeah. I thought it would help Dad."

After toeing the raft, Sydney lifted the bottom of it. It was heavy, but not impossible to lift. She pulled at the woven vines. They refused to budge.

Tessa watched. "I worried they would unravel, so I spent some time tying different sections together."

"Do you think we could carry it?" Sydney asked.

Tessa shrugged.

"Grab some more vines. I have an idea."

Max and Tessa rushed to the grapevines and gathered several of the younger strands. They obviously knew exactly what to look for. Sydney stared wide-eyed at the raft. She'd expected her sister to fail. But Tessa hadn't failed. What she had done was amazing. Sydney never would have thought to reinforce the weave. That was hard to admit.

"Tess, help me out, okay?" Sydney eyed her sister. "Can we make these vines into some sort of rope or harness or something? So that we can pull Dad around the bend?"

"You mean bring Dad here?" Max shouted with excitement, his weakened voice scratching at Sydney's ears. He needed water.

"That's what I'm thinking." Sydney took a couple of vines from him. "But I need Tessa's help." She looked at her sister. "You're the one who knows how to work with these things."

"I . . . I think we can." Tessa dropped next to the raft. "We'll need to braid the vines to make them stronger and then thread them onto the raft."

"Show me."

The back of the van fishtailed in the mud as Evan rounded a corner.

"Daddy, that's a bad word," Danni reminded him as he swore.

"You're right, Dan-Dan, I'm sorry."

Dylan laughed from the back seat. "That was fun."

Ellie started to scream, waking up as the van rolled to a stop.

"Hang on, kids. I gotta look at some stuff." Evan crawled out of the van and stared at it.

Mud caked the tires, large gooey pads of it slipping from the sides of each one. Any traction he'd once had was gone. The blue doors were splattered with a solid oatmeal-brown nearly up to the handles. His jaw tightened as he stared down the road, the strong wind stinging his eyes as he walked a few yards away to see around the bend.

Mud.

That's all he saw. Mud lined with more mud. All the sandstone rocks that would help keep him from sinking into the goop were hiding just over the top of the muddy berms running alongside the road. Maybe with four-wheel drive, but not in a minivan. He'd reached the end. A few miles lay between him and the canyon, and there was nothing he could do to get closer. He flung his arms into the air, then let his fists pound into his legs. He swore.

"Daddy, Ellie's hungee," Emily called out the open window. "I will feed her."

"That's okay, Emmy. I'll be right there."

He took a step toward the van, and his shoe squelched in the mud beneath him. Facing the sky that was filled with a blustery wind, he squeezed his eyes shut and exhaled, hoping to slow his heartbeat. As he opened his eyes, his gaze landed on a puff of strung-out, wind-blown gray. Dirty, dark gray. Smoke? He turned in a circle, his eyes wide as he took in all that that could mean. *Smoke!*

He grabbed his phone from his pocket and dialed the number Officer Howard had given him. The silence of no connection deafened him. Yanking the phone away from his ear, he stared at the screen. No service. He'd had it at the last bend, hadn't he?

He dashed behind the van, keeping his eye on the wispy plumes of gray caught in the wind. Finally, he had a bar, then two. He dialed again.

"Do you see it?" Evan didn't wait for the officer to say hello.

"See what? Who is this?"

"Evan Marksam. There's smoke coming from West Clear Creek."

"You're here?" the officer barked. "I told you to stay home."

"I'm not there. I'm on Forest Route One Forty-Nine unable to get there. That's not the point. The smoke."

"Of course you are. No, I don't see smoke. No way to see something like that through the trees."

"What about the chopper? You have one up, right? Can they see it? I'm staring right at it, blowing from the west."

Evan listened impatiently as a crackling sounded in his ear.

"The copter will be up in about thirty minutes. Wind has been slowing everything down."

"Well, I see smoke. Hold on." Evan fiddled with his phone. "My coordinates are thirty-four point fifty degrees north; one eleven point forty-three degrees west. There's smoke"—he glanced up to where the smoke had been. It was gone—"It's gone. Fire's out."

"If you really saw smoke," Officer Howard grumbled, "then anything you have can help."

"Just a sec." Evan switched to a compass app he'd downloaded. "From my location, the fire is—was—visible at three hundred, eleven degrees." He glared at the compass, then back between the trees where he'd seen the sooty plume. "I don't understand. Why would they put the fire out?"

"Not sure, but we'll keep a look out." Officer Howard cleared his throat. "Now that you're here, we can send a truck—"

"I have four kids with me."

"Daddy!" Danni screamed. "Come on. Ellie—"

"The youngest is three months old."

"You're serious?"

"And a little crazy, I think."

"I'll say." Officer Howard chuckled. "You got a place to go?"

"Yeah. The Lazy Trees Motel in Payson." Evan cleared his throat. "If they're alive, where do you take 'em?"

"Probably Flag. Verde for minor injuries."

"Guess I chose wrong." Evan dropped his gaze to the ground.

"No. You chose right. You just couldn't make it through. Next time listen. This time, head to Flag."

I'll Come Back

Sydney dipped her cupped hands into the water again and brought another mouthful to her lips. Though filled with silt, the water was clearer than it had been. She and her siblings sat at the edge of the swollen creek where it tumbled quickly over a rock. Drinking the water from there seemed to reduce the amount of mud they swallowed.

Every sip brought relief to Sydney's prickly throat and reddened skin. By the time night came around, she expected to feel quite different. Not necessarily better though. Her exertion had doubled before they'd made it to the water. Barely producing sweat, her body had heated from dehydration. But once the temperature dropped, she'd be cold again. Really cold.

But probably not hypothermic. They had everything they needed for a fire.

She took another drink and studied her brother. His poison ivy rash had only spread a bit down his leg, which was good, but his stubbornness had no bounds. "Max, listen. You're the best fire-tenderer"—Sydney paused and swallowed, the tissue at the back of her throat sticking to her tongue—"and someone will have to stay with the fire once we build it. That's you."

The argument had been circling for twenty minutes, and Sydney was ready to walk away. Unfortunately, Max had a habit of following.

"I'm strong. I'll help carry Dad," he said.

Sydney scowled. "No, you can't. I need you to stay with the fire."

Tessa gazed back and forth from Sydney to Max, then stopped, scrutinizing Sydney. "How far are they?" she asked. Her voice crackled as she spoke.

"Not far, I think." Sydney counted her breaths, attempting to soften her annoyance. "Remember when we hiked in? How the canyon narrowed about forty-five minutes in?"

"Yeah."

"They're before that part. Where it's wider."

Tessa put her hand on Max's shoulder. "That's not far. We'll make it back by tonight." She stopped and bit her lip, then took a breath. "If we can't get Dad out by then, I'll come back to be with you, okay?"

Sydney, working to keep surprise from showing on her face, looked at her sister. Tessa was not one to hike anywhere by herself. And to volunteer to leave Mom and Dad—that was a lot.

"I'll do that, Tess. You don't have to," Sydney said.

"Yes, I do." Tessa breathed hoarsely. "You know how to help Dad better. I . . . I don't."

"Sure you do. He taught you too."

Tessa turned back to Max, ignoring Sydney. "I'll come back before it gets dark, even if I'm alone."

Max glared at them from under his mud-stained brow.

"Be strong, Max," Tessa added, "for Dad."

Sydney followed Tessa's lead, and stood up. "Keep using the lotion on your rash. I'm glad it hasn't spread too much." She dropped the last bag of trail mix in Max's lap, then bent to start the fire. As she did, she wondered what had changed within Tessa. She wasn't whining or crying. And the way she helped with Max—how had Sydney not recognized the way Tessa did that so often?

Soon, thick flames from the fire lapped at the afternoon sun as Sydney looked back at Max one last time. He'd be okay. She hoped. Turning away, she leaned over the creek and closed her eyes, letting the water refresh her tongue. Now that they'd moved camp closer to the creek, the walk to the side canyon had been all of a hundred yards. Maybe two. After finally drinking something to wet their dying bodies, leaving West Clear Creek's bank wasn't so easy, but she rose to her feet and hooked her thumbs under the backpack straps at her shoulders.

"Come on," she called to her sister, who slowly backed away from the creek's bank.

Sydney understood Tessa's slow movements. Her own legs ached from her hips down to the tips of her toes. Whenever she stopped moving and paid attention, she could feel her pulse throbbing atop her shins. Bending at the knee, she reached for the coiled grapevine that Tessa had attached to the raft.

Sydney rolled her eyes. It wasn't really a raft. Now it was more of a makeshift gurney. A really heavy gurney. She pulled both ends of one of the braided vines to her shoulder and winced. Despite her attempt to keep the vines on a backpack strap and avoid friction burns, a stinging tenderness had developed within minutes of their short walk. Worse, the individual ends rubbed against her like some kind of dull knife. Still, Tessa had pointed out the added strength and lack of slippery knots in the design.

Relaxing her annoyance, Sydney reminded herself that she'd instructed her sister to build a raft, not a gurney. And lightening its blasted weight would have taken hours. Hours Mom and Dad didn't have.

Tessa slipped under the other rope. Shoulder to shoulder, they began dragging the raft up the canyon. Tessa gasped every few minutes, though Sydney wasn't sure whether it was from the rub of the rope on her shoulder or the changes to the canyon, which Tessa stared at with wide eyes.

The water was gone, but the cracked mud and overturned rocks remained—as did many of the willows and trees—though they had been ripped from the ground and were layered in mounds at the center of the arroyo, caught on misplaced boulders.

Tessa stumbled, and Sydney bit the desire to tell her to watch her feet instead of their surroundings. "You okay?"

"Yeah.

"Good. Be careful."

She couldn't say *nothing*.

It was late afternoon when Sydney saw a flourish of green next to the canyon wall. It had to be the tree. Still, she pushed forward without mention of it to her sister. If she were wrong, it wouldn't go over well.

A few minutes later, she was sure. "There"—she pointed with her chin—"they're by that tree."

"Mom, Dad!" Tessa screamed, dropping the rope and throwing Sydney off balance as the unsupported corner of the gurney fell.

"Tessa, come back." Sydney rolled her eyes, then threw her sister's rope over her other shoulder. Nothing would come of her yelling. Besides, she wanted to do the same thing. She had the night before.

Pulling the raft alone took longer than Sydney wanted, and the raw spot burned into her left shoulder made everything feel uneven, but after five minutes or so, she'd shuffled far enough up the canyon to see Tessa tightly ensconced by their mother's arms, and the fire she'd supplied wood for still flickering.

Jen sat next to the fire, watching the smoke as the wind dragged it forcefully to the east. Her hair beat against her face, and when she turned to look at the top of the tree, she thought she'd seen the trunk bend. That might have been her imagination. Her mind was as thick as the smoke.

Twisting around, she faced the waterless creek bed that had attempted to kill her and Blake. The wind bit at her eyes, scratching her already blurry vision, but she refused to shut them. Something . . . someone was in the distance. Pushing to her feet, she hobbled a step forward. Was it her imagination again?

It looked like—

"Mom, Dad!" Tessa screamed.

—her girls.

Tessa darted over river rock and around crusted mud bogs, then fell into Jen's arms.

"Wh-what are you doing here?" Jen breathed as she flung her arms around her middle child. "Where are Max and Sydney?"

"Syd's coming. . . . Oh, I should go back and help her."

Jen released her daughter and stared at her. "Help her what? Where's Max?" Worry seeped into her befuddled mind.

"The raft for Dad. Max is watching the signal fire." Tessa turned around and walked toward Sydney.

Jen shook her head. "By himself."

Her words dropped before they could reach her daughters. She knew they would. Her throat stung with dryness, and her headache was nearly unbearable. At home, it would have been. In the wilderness, she had no choice but to endure it . . . and everything that came with it.

She'd made a couple more trips to her tiny well, digging it out each time and sipping from the muddy puddle that formed. What small amount of water she could take in helped, but it wasn't enough. She needed medical attention. They all did. She couldn't imagine her children were in any better shape, and that made it even harder.

Blake's condition had improved. The heat of the fire combined with the emergency blanket Sydney had left had helped him warm up enough to squirm a little stronger when she pummeled his chest. As little as that was, it gave her hope. He had yet to fall completely unconscious—well, comatose. That had to be a good thing. Right?

She imagined the dehydration only added to his condition. As the sun warmed her further, she'd taken Blake's tattered shirt and wet it, then wiped his lips. She allowed a couple of small drops to land on his tongue, but never enough that he'd have to swallow. She couldn't risk him choking.

At the moment, she stared at her daughters, who dragged a large bundle of wood behind them. A stretcher?

"Mom," Sydney called out.

Jen waved, still struggling to take it all in and terrified for her son. "Where's Max?"

"Watching the signal fire," Sydney panted as she nodded to Tessa and dropped the stretcher to the ground next to Blake.

"You left him alone. How could you—"

"He's fine," Sydney interrupted. "We gotta go before it gets any darker."

"Go?"

Her oldest stepped over to her. "Mom, we're going to the other camp."

"No. We can't do that."

"There's water there, and look at what Tessa did." Sydney pointed at the stretcher. "She made it herself. Help us get Dad on it."

"Dad's sick."

"We know." Sydney looked at her oddly.

Jen shook her head. "Am I slurring my words?"

"It's okay," Sydney dropped her gaze.

It wasn't okay. Confusion, whether from dehydration or hypothermia had set in. But she wasn't trembling . . . not since the night before.

"Mom"—Tessa patted her shoulder—"Sydney said that Uncle Evan should have called for a search party by now."

Jen nodded.

Sydney looked at Blake and then at Jen and Tessa. "I think we have to roll him on his side, then put the gurney under him. Tessa, you take his feet—"

"Can you?" Tessa's words were soft, and Sydney didn't respond right away. In that short amount of time, Tessa added, "I don't want to hurt his ankle."

Sydney rolled her eyes, her mouth working, but she only said, "Take his head then. Mom, you take his waist."

Jen nodded, and Sydney positioned herself by Blake's feet. "One, two, three."

Together, they rolled Blake onto his side. Sydney moved nearer to Jen and pushed the stretcher underneath him, then stood, breathing heavily. Without any warning, she awkwardly sat on the ground.

"Syd." Tessa hurried to her side.

"I . . . I'm okay. Just a little dizzy. Can you center him on the raft? You can tug on the blanket. It won't rip."

Tessa nodded, then pulled on the blanket. Nothing happened. Without making a peep, she shifted her body, placed her feet on the

213

edge of the stretcher, and pulled. Blake shifted to the center of the logs.

"H-how do we keep him on?" Jen asked.

"Duct tape." Sydney pulled the tape from the sagging backpack she wore and looked at Tessa. "I'll lift the gurney."

Tessa nodded and wrapped several layers of tape around Blake and the trees she'd woven together.

"What are you doing?" Jen stared at what was happening, confusion wracking her brain.

"Taping Dad." Tessa smiled.

"But he won't be able to move."

Sydney frowned. "Yeah, Mom. That's the point."

"It is?"

"Yup. Mom, have you had enough to drink?"

She hadn't, and her daughters' worry shone on their faces. It wasn't that easy to get water from a hand-dug well. "I . . . I'm fine."

Sydney grunted as she eased the grapevine rope over her right shoulder. Why not have matching raw shoulders? It wouldn't take long for her skin to slough off her right shoulder like it had her left, but it didn't matter. They had to get back to Max, and the sun was nearly down. She'd have to ignore her trembling legs and swaying body and think about something else. Once they were back at the creek, she could have more water.

"Mom, can you help pull?" Sydney asked.

Her mom wasn't in great shape, but she was still on her feet. Her help transporting Dad would be slower than having Tessa help, but Sydney couldn't trust Mom to watch Dad. Or to keep up. If only they could carry both parents.

"I . . . I think I can. Sure." Mom cupped her hand on Dad's cheek, whispered in his ear, and kissed his cracked lips, then stepped next to Sydney. "What do I do?"

"Tessa?" Sydney eyed her sister.

"Here, Mom, let me show you," Tessa said.

Sydney listened as Tessa showed their mother how to hold the braided vines. She hadn't dared to lean over and gather her mother's rope. The dizziness she felt was enough just standing, especially after putting out her parents' fire.

Her mom looked so fragile with her ripped and muddied clothes and hair matted with grime. Glancing down, Sydney studied her mother's inflamed leg, red and swollen. She touched the back of her hand to her mother's forehead. It didn't feel hot, but would it? "We'll go as slow as we can, okay?"

As Sydney lowered her hand, Mom grabbed it, squeezing it once before letting go. Sydney gave her a soft smile, a flutter stirring within her. She was finally with her momma. Swallowing back the sudden emotion, Sydney nodded for Tessa to follow behind them.

A few feet later, the gurney caught, tilting upward and to the left. Mom dropped her rope and fell to the ground. Sydney's knees began to buckle, shaking as she forced herself to stand tall despite most of Dad's weight landing on her right shoulder.

"Hold on," Tessa shouted.

The bottom of the stretcher lifted, leveling from one side to the other as Tessa worked to help steady it. Shaky, Sydney slowly lowered herself to the ground and picked up the rope her mother had dropped.

"I'm gonna move left, Syd," Tessa said.

"Okay. I got him." Sydney allowed her sister to guide the back of the gurney. When the movement stopped, she slowly lowered her father to the ground, and joined Tessa next to her mom.

"You okay, Mom?" Sydney asked.

"I . . . I'm fine."

The worried gaze Tessa tossed Sydney's direction said everything she felt too. Mom was anything but fine.

"She can't carry it," Tessa said.

"I know, but she won't be able to watch Dad either." A prickle scorched Sydney's eyes. She fell next to her mother. "Mom, I don't know what to do. I can't do this anymore."

"I . . . I'll help," Jen whispered.

"No. You can't help. That's the problem. You and Dad are sick. And Max is by himself, and the sun is going down, and . . . and all we have is bad water and grape leaves. I'm tired of grape leaves. I can't even catch a stupid fish." She dropped her chin to her chest. "What I would give for a tiny trout." The words fell from her lips, hard and clipped, an echo of the torment she'd suffered over the past several days. She didn't want to get up. She wanted her warm bed and soft pillow. She wanted Braden—or someone—to wrap their arms around her just as they handed her the biggest, coolest, clearest glass of water she'd ever seen. That's what she wanted. Instead, she was stuck in some canyon literally trying to survive.

Tessa's small, cool hands touched Sydney's shoulders, soft against what little skin she still had there. She reached up and tangled her fingers with her sister's, holding them tight.

"It's okay, Syd. I'll help carry Dad. Mom can walk next to me."

Nodding, Sydney gazed at Tessa, who offered a small smile. Gingerly, she eased to her feet. Then, together, she and Tessa helped tug their mother from the ground.

As they walked, Tessa's soft voice pattered against Sydney's ears. Somehow, it comforted her—different than all the times it had done just the opposite. She talked to Mom about what she and Max had done while Sydney hiked over to the side canyon. She mentioned making sure Max didn't use too much calamine lotion and sleeping next to Max under the space blanket, waking every few hours to add another piece of wood to the fire. "Syd said we couldn't let the fire burn out. And we don't have many matches left."

Mom shuffled across the canyon's rocky floor, slow and swaying as Tessa spoke. But she didn't complain or stop.

"We only have to go around that corner, right there, Mom." Tessa nodded at the convergence that had finally come into view. "Then we'll see Max. He's probably a bit worried since we've been gone so long, but I told him we'd be back by dark. I said that if we didn't all come back, then I would."

"That was nice of you, Tess," Mom said.

It was nice of Tessa. Everything Tessa did was nice. A tightness eased into Sydney's chest. One she recognized. Then the next emotion surged through her. Guilt. Guilt for feeling the tightness in the first place. But what was she supposed to do about it? She was jealous. She didn't want to be, but she was. And admitting it wasn't that easy.

"Tess has done a lot, Mom. More than me." That wasn't necessarily true, but it made Sydney feel a little more pious.

Tessa eyed her from the side. "Not more."

"Well, you built a raft and kept the fire going, and you helped Max whenever I yelled at him. Or at you."

Tessa shook her head. "You found Mom and Dad and told me and Max what to do."

"That's true." She smiled at her sister, wishing she could wipe away the swirl of emotions within herself. Part of her couldn't help but feel pride after the recognition. She had done a ton, but she wasn't at all sure how. "We better pick up the pace a bit. There's not much light left."

After stopping at the creek and drinking in as much water as they dared, Sydney stood and called to Max. Within seconds, the sound of his feet slapping the soggy ground reached her ears.

"Mom!" Max flung himself into their mother's body.

She stumbled, but steadied by Tessa, recovered, and wrapped her arms around the youngest member of their family. "I'm so glad to see you."

"I saved you some trail mix."

Sydney watched as her mother's face crumpled slightly.

"Thank you, Max."

Orange flames continued to dance near Jen's side as she settled down next to Blake, glad that the wind had finally stopped whipping her mud-caked hair—and the smoke—into her face. Since arriving at the kids' camp, she'd spent an hour next to the creek, taking in as much water as her body could handle. Part of her mind had cleared, but not enough. Thoughts bounced through her brain, but only a few made sense. When her children spoke, she spent as much time trying to remember what they'd said as she did forming a response. Between the brain fog and the pounding head and body aches, Jen was pretty useless. But she could manage one thing, and that was what she intended to make her focus. Holding a piece of fabric ripped from Blake's tattered shirt to his lips, she urged him to wake up. He didn't so much as twitch.

How long had it been? Two days? That sounded right. "Two days," she whispered.

"Mom?" Tessa looked at her.

"It's been two days since the floods, right?"

"Yeah."

Jen stroked the top of Blake's head. "Why haven't we heard a helicopter?"

"I heard a copter. I saw one." Max stood up and placed his hands on Jen's shoulders.

She turned and took his hands. "You did? W-when?"

Max shrugged. "I don't know, but I waved."

"Was it still light outside, Max?" Sydney was by Jen's side now.

"Kinda."

"Did they have lights? Did they say anything?" Sydney's questions rattled around in Jen's mind, begging to be understood.

"No. They just stayed in the sky for a minute, then left."

Jen dropped his hands. "They saw you?" She laid her head on Blake's chest. Neither of them had trembled since the night before. What did that mean? "Where did they go?"

"Dunno." Max shrugged.

Jen clutched Blake's arms and squeezed. His heart beat limply near her ear. He wasn't dead. None of them were dead. Those were the thoughts she clung to. The ones she understood. "Hold on, Blake. Don't you dare give up now."

Sydney snorted, and Jen looked at her. "What?"

"Nothing." Sydney smiled.

Jen put her hand to her forehead and clenched her eyes shut. "I sounded like a TV drama."

"Little bit."

Jen laughed lightly, meeting Sydney's tired eyes. "I don't care."

She turned and rubbed Blake's chest with her fist. His hand lifted as he squirmed. It was more than he'd done all day.

"Water." Jen tried to stand, her leg throbbing.

Tessa grabbed her hands and helped her sit back down.

"Get me water." Jen forced the words past her brittle tongue.

"Here." Tessa held out her hand.

Jen raised the tattered cotton cloth, and Tessa grabbed it, rushing to the creek.

Moments later, with the cloth dripping wet, Jen held it to Blake's lips and rubbed her knuckles across his sternum. The action was so ingrained in her mind that it stole all of her energy. Forcing away her exhaustion, she watched as tiny rivulets of water rolled into his mouth and he swallowed. Air coursed into her lungs. He was alive. Really alive.

"Swallow," she said.

Had she been able to produce tears, the sobbing that fell from her lips probably would have appeared normal. But she didn't care how she looked. Blake was alive, and she'd finally grasped what Max had said. He'd been spotted.

"They're coming, Blake."

Sydney pulled her corner of the space blanket closer to her chin as she watched her mom care for her dad.

Mom laid her head on Dad's chest and spoke softly to him, ignoring the world around them. Every few minutes, she touched his face or clutched his hand. At one point, she held her fingers to his bad foot. "It's okay. I still feel a pulse. I don't know how you still have one there, but you do, even after hypothermia."

Sydney had never seen her mother so distressed. And Mom wasn't thinking of herself. The only people Mom thought about were them. Her, her sister and brother—and Dad.

"Mom, he'll be okay, won't he?" Tessa asked.

"I hope so," Jen said. "But I don't want him to suffer."

"What do you mean?" Tessa eyed Mom.

"He'll be okay," Jen said, not answering the question.

But Sydney knew what she meant. Mom would rather Dad die than live the rest of his life in agonizing pain. She wouldn't use medical means to keep him alive—not in a vegetative state. Anything aside from that, though, and Mom would take every step available to keep him alive—including sacrificing herself, Sydney suspected.

"You love him." Tessa sat next to their mom.

"I do."

"They'll come in the morning, won't they?"

Jen curled an arm around Tessa. "I hope so."

The exchange . . . the words—all of it—clutched Sydney's chest, squeezing it. Dad felt the same way about Mom. He felt that way about all of them. It's how he'd broken his ankle in the first place—sacrificing himself to keep Max safe when Sydney had screamed. Mom and Dad weren't two people living separate lives who came together whenever it suited them. They lived their lives together as one. Sydney had lived her life with that in her midst, and she hadn't even recognized it.

Throughout the week, both of her parents had spent time trying to talk to her about it. About respect. About caring. But she hadn't let their words in. Not enough.

Now, though, she knew. What they had was what she wanted in her life. Not right away. She was still young. But she wanted someone who would love her and care for her more than anything else. She wanted a relationship where both she and her boyfriend or husband—she rolled her eyes—whoever—would care for each other and what they built together more than anything else.

Mom deserved that.

Dad deserved that.

She wanted that.

Sydney bit her lip, scooting over as Tessa came to lie next to her under the Mylar blanket.

But did she deserve that?

News

By the time Evan stopped back at the Lazy Trees Motel, picked up the few belongings they'd left behind, and fed the kids dinner, night had set in. Reaching Flagstaff would have been faster had he checked out of the motel before leaving that morning. But he'd figured they would return for the night when Blake and his family were brought to Payson.

Hopeful. That's what he'd been.

Instead, he'd had to backtrack. With an average travel time of fifty miles per hour, the fastest way to Flagstaff from Payson wasn't super fast, but it was better than heading through Verde Valley and up the I-17. At least that's what Evan's GPS said. He wasn't so sure.

The two-lane road, each side lined with tall ponderosas that soaked up the gleam of his old headlights with every curve, looped through the forest past lakes Mormon and Mary. Only idiots would speed.

All four kids had fallen asleep to the rumble of the engine on the mountain road, and Evan took the time to listen to something other than the *Wheels on the Bus* album Michelle had picked up for $5.95 on a day when she'd needed time to *decompress from a stressful and depressing day.*

Evan had his own stress and depression to think about. His daughter was in the hospital, and his brother's entire family was missing. His shoulders slumped further as his mind swept through the many times Blake had been there for him before it settled on one of the few times he hadn't. All Evan had needed was a ride . . .

Evan glanced at his watch. Seven thirty-five. The college entrance exam started at eight. Pulling his jacket a little closer, he huddled under the roof of the tiny porch. Blake should be there any minute. He'd promised not to be late.

Edging through the door, Evan ran to the kitchen and dialed Blake's pager: 811-47. The eight-one-one should get him moving. The forty-seven told him it was Evan paging.

Mom and Dad weren't available to take Evan to the testing site, and when Evan had asked Blake for a ride, his brother had hemmed and hawed about having to work a late shift the night before and about Jen not feeling all that great. But as Evan expected, it hadn't been super difficult to talk him into helping out.

Back outside, Evan pushed his shoulder blades against the door and sighed. If he'd had someone else to call, he would have. His friends had taken the exams the previous month. And it wasn't like he had lots of family around. That left Blake and Jen, and recently, all Blake seemed to care about was his new wife and her tag-a-long brother, Charlie, who could barely tie his own shoe.

Evan exhaled noisily.

That wasn't fair. Charlie was a good guy, and Blake had probably taught him to tie his shoe a long time ago.

Still, he missed palling around with his brother. He missed Blake throwing things at him to get him off his bed and out to some social activity that Evan always hated, but somehow . . . didn't.

Seven fifty. Where was he?

Stepping into the spring rain, Evan walked to the end of the driveway—as if he'd suddenly see Blake careening around the corner.

It took five minutes to get to the testing site. That left Evan . . . two minutes to get into his seat.

Blake could have at least called and canceled. Or said no when he'd asked. The test cost money. Money that Mom and Dad didn't offer to pay. Anything dealing with college was on his shoulders—the same way it had been on Blake's. Forty-two dollars may not have seemed like a lot to Blake, but it was a ton of money for Evan, who had no current job.

Seven fifty-five.

Evan slammed his fist into the door, forcing it open.

One thing. He'd asked for one thing, and it wasn't that hard. Just pick him up and drop him off at the testing site. That was it. Evan would have walked, but five miles wasn't that close. If Blake had said no, though, he would have considered it.

Who cares about college anyway?

Evan threw himself onto his bed, tossing his number-two pencil across the room. He wouldn't need that anymore. Not now that he'd wasted his money on a test he couldn't take. Now that he wasn't going to college. From now on, he could do everything in pen.

A horn honked.

Now he shows up.

Evan didn't bother getting off the bed, and a few seconds later, he heard Blake call his name.

He didn't answer.

The bedroom door swung open, and Blake leaned against the door frame. "Don't you have a test or something?"

"I did. But it started"—he looked at his watch—"ten minutes ago."

"You told me eight thirty," Blake said, pushing Evan's feet out of the way and sitting on the bed.

"I said eight, and you got your panties in a wad over it."

"Yeah, pick you up at eight. I'm here."

225

"The test started at eight." Evan scowled. "I told you it started at eight, but you're late. Again. Even after promising."

"I swear you said to pick you up at eight."

"I didn't. Why would I do that?" Evan jumped off the bed and started pacing the room. "I don't know if they're even offering the test again. And if they are, I don't have the forty-two dollars to pay for it. Are you going to pay for me?"

"I . . . I don't have—"

"I know, you have to pay rent, buy groceries, pay for Jen's doctor's appointments. Save for the baby—"

"Hey, man, you don't get it. I'm married now. I have to support more than just me. I swear I thought you said eight o'clock. Back off."

Evan slumped back to the bed. "Who needs college anyway? It's not like I want to go. I'm not that kind of smart."

"Don't say that."

Evan eyed his brother. "Why don't you go home. Make sure Jen has some pickled ice cream or something."

"Yeah." Blake hit Evan's feet off the bed as he stood up. "Give you a chance to cool off."

Headlight beams struck Evan in the eye as he rounded a corner, and he glanced right, hoping to protect his night vision. His heart beat wildly in his chest, but he couldn't be sure whether it had to do with the memory or the passing car.

It had taken Evan a couple of days to cool off enough to talk to Blake after that incident—another month or two before trusting him to drive him anywhere, and three years before getting up the courage to register for the college exam again. This time, the community college placement exam.

Evan hadn't handled the situation well. Now he understood the life that Blake had been balancing as he supported his young family. He sagged in his chair. Sometimes a bit of jealousy still prodded his

226

chest. How many times had he mentioned wishing Michelle were up to hiking West Clear Creek? Too many. But no more. Never again! Now he wished for nothing more than Blake's life.

The ringing phone caught Evan's attention just as the moon appeared between the trees. Pushing the button on the steering wheel, Evan said, "Hello."

"Mr. Marksam, this is Officer Howard. I have some news."

Evan gripped the steering wheel tighter.

"The winds died down slightly, and we were able to get the helicopter in the air by late afternoon. It took a while for them to get to the location where you mentioned seeing smoke, but when they did, they saw a little boy tending a fire."

"Max?" Evan whispered, his heart thudding in his chest. "They found Max. Is he okay? What about everyone else?"

"From what we can tell, he's okay. He waved at the helicopter, and the fire was quite large. I doubt he started it on his own."

"Couldn't say. Might have." Evan slid his hand through his hair. "You found Max. Where is he? Where should I go?"

"I want to make it clear that he appeared coherent and was up and walking. The fire was large and well-placed. Unfortunately, with the breeze and the time of day, we were unable to get to him. A team will be sent to his location at first light."

Evan nearly slammed on the brakes. "First light? He's ten!"

"We understand that. If hiking in were an option . . . but it isn't. There are too many variables that come with air rescues to go tonight."

"Fine. What now?"

"Now," Officer Howard said, "We wait 'til morning. We've already alerted medical staff and emergency crews. The copter should be back in the air by five a.m. Ambulances will be waiting at Bull Pen near the lower half of the canyon where it's easier for them to get in. The boy, and hopefully the others, will be lifted out as soon as we can get to them. With luck, before breakfast."

"Breakfast." Evan relaxed his shoulders. "Can I—"

"If you can make it to Bull Pen—"

"I'll figure it out. I . . . I'll be there by daybreak."

"Mr. Marksam"—Officer Howard cleared his throat—"preferably without your children."

"Yeah . . . yeah, I'll try." He hung up.

Halfway between. Halfway. Evan had two choices, turn around and head back to the Eighty-Seven, or continue to the I-17 and I-40 interchange in Flagstaff. He stepped on the gas. Heading down the I-17 and back into Verde Valley would be fastest. After a few hours of sleep, he'd drive to Bull Pen.

But the kids?

He dialed Michelle.

One ring . . . two rings . . . three . . .

"They found Max. Max is alive." Evan gave Michelle a chance to process his words.

"Where are you?"

"Did you hear me? They found Max!"

"They found Max? Oh, thank goodness." Michelle paused. "But, Evan, where are you?"

"Ah." Evan furrowed his brow. "Between Strawberry and Flag on Lake Mary Road."

"And the kids?"

"They're with me, sleeping in the back. We're headed to Verde so I can be at Bull Pen when they pull him out. How's Mags?"

"Mags is getting released in the morning."

"Great. Great." Evan sighed. "That's just great."

"It is. All of it."

"Yeah." Evan needed to figure out the kids, but obviously, Michelle could no more drive up to care for them than he could have them at Bull Pen. "Any idea of someone who can come take the kids?"

"Have you called your parents yet?"

Did he want to call his parents yet? He'd put it off, not wanting to worry them, but now that Max had been found, maybe he should. "I'm not sure they should be driving up here so late. Do you think they could stay with Maggie?"

"Don't you think they'd want to be with Blake and the kids who almost died? Jen's parents should probably be notified too."

"I think Mom and Dad would be happy to watch Maggie. It'd be less stressful, and I think I have Jen's parents' number somewhere."

What Evan really wanted was his wife. He missed her. He needed her for his own comfort as much as for his children. His parents didn't need the stress. In their seventies, they didn't need to be driving all over Arizona so late at night, and they definitely didn't need to rush up to be with Blake when Evan was already there.

"Miss me, do you?" Michelle's voice jingled in his ear.

"Maybe a little."

"Hang on."

Evan listened to his wife's and daughter's soft voices as they discussed the possibility of his parents taking Maggie home from the hospital.

"I have to check with the nurses to make sure it's possible, but I'm guessing there's a form I can sign or something."

Relaxing his grasp on the wheel, Evan sighed. "Thanks, Shell."

"I'll call you as soon as I have an answer from the nurse."

Evan hung up and pushed the gas pedal down just a little more. He wanted at least a couple of hours of sleep, and it'd be even better if those couple of hours included holding Michelle in his arms.

The brush of Michelle's arm curling over Evan's waist, woke him slightly. She'd arrived at the motel in Verde Valley an hour or so after he and the kids had. Next to Evan, Ellie had been the most excited to see her, though the other three still refused to leave her side. Feeling her hand run across his chest, Evan rolled over and hugged her closer. "Thank you."

"For what?"

"Coming."

"I couldn't not come, Evan. This is your brother's family."

He kissed her forehead. "I know."

Sleep pushed at the back of his eyes, but something roused him further. The clock. What had it said? Forcing his eyes open, he checked the time again. He could afford ten more minutes, after that, he needed to leave. Falling asleep again was dangerous.

"Mom and Dad?" he asked.

Michelle groaned. "Were nervous and angry and more than willing to pick up Maggie in the morning. She was pretty brave too. She's worried about her cousins."

"I guess I'd be angry too."

"You didn't tell them their son and grandchildren were missing. But they also understand that you were trying to protect them."

"I was. When I remembered to think about them. Shell, I've been awful. Running off, thinking about myself and what I wanted."

"You were thinking of your brother."

"Was I?" He had, right? "I mean, yeah, but by driving up here, I spent way more money than I should have; I forced four young kids to spend nearly two days in a car, upsetting their schedules— and I risked pulling attention away from the search."

"Did you though?" Michelle asked. "It sounds to me like you were the one who pointed search and rescue in the right direction."

"Happenstance."

"I don't believe in coincidences, Evan. You were right where you needed to be. Though, calling your parents to take the kids before leaving town—that would have made sense."

"Really, I didn't want to worry them."

Michelle dragged her finger down his side. "I know."

"I have to go. It'll take some time to get to Bull Pen, even in the truck, and I want to be there when everything starts."

"Call me as soon as you know anything." She leaned over and placed her soft lips against his.

It was almost enough to convince him to stay. "I will."

Copter's Down

Evan eased his truck to the right. It would be smoother than driving through the pot hole in the center of the road. *Do dirt roads have pot holes?* He shrugged. Either way, the truck Michelle had driven up handled the rock-studded road into the Bull Pen area much better than the minivan had handled the muddy mess off the Eighty-Seven, and he'd reach his destination in a matter of minutes.

Pale yellows and oranges lined the eastern horizon. It shouldn't take long for the helicopter to take off from Verde now. He assumed that was where it would come from, if the crew was meeting at the Bull Pen day-use area—the Yavapai County side of the canyon. Officer Howard was with the Coconino Sheriff's Department, though, so Evan really had no idea. He wasn't even sure how much he cared—as long as his brother was found safe.

He had no proof that anyone was safe, except for Max. And really, he didn't even have knowledge of that. The only information Evan really had was that there was a young boy about Max's age stuck in the middle of a flooded canyon. Left there because of a little wind.

It had to be Max.

What kind of hell had Blake's family gone through for Max to be left alone? Jen would never have allowed that, not in her right mind. Blake had always taught his kids basic survival skills, and he'd mentioned working with Max on fire-building. Could Max start a fire by himself?

The questions continued to bombard Evan. Where were the girls? What about Blake and Jen? Where were they? How had Max survived?

A little pressure on the right side of the steering wheel brought Evan off the forest road to a graveled area near a large day-use-only sign. He'd arrived before anyone else.

Climbing out of the truck, he gazed up at the sky. He'd left pretty early, arriving before daybreak. Though that was only minutes away now. A light breeze blew, and he rolled his eyes. They better not have put off rescuing his nephew because of such a little breeze.

He knew they hadn't. Wind in any canyon was always stronger than it was at the top, and yesterday had been downright blustery. As much as he wanted to blame someone, doing so seemed a bit ridiculous.

At the sound of an engine, Evan turned to see a Coconino Sheriff's Department truck arrive. Ambling nearer the driver's door, he waited for the officer to get out.

"Mr. Marksam?"

Evan nodded.

"Nice to put a face with a name. I'm Officer Howard. The helicopters just left the Valley and will be here in about a half an hour."

"The Valley? Phoenix?" Evan stuttered.

"Scottsdale, this time. Seems strange, but we take 'em from wherever we can get them. Flag, Verde, Kingman, Page. They come from all over. Though, the Valley is probably more common than Page."

"Makes sense." Evan scratched his head. "So—"

"A couple of ambulances are also on their way. Once everyone's here, a copter will make a pass over the location where the boy was seen, make sure he's still there and see if anyone else has joined him. Depending on what's going on, they'll either drop a man and maybe a litter down, or come back to discuss the best option."

"But they'll get him—them—out today?"

"Well, the wind's a lot calmer than yesterday, but we're farther away than we were then. I've no idea what it's like to the east."

"What're we supposed to do? Leave them there for days because of a little wind?" Evan ground his teeth, biting back his anger.

"We're not leaving anyone. One way or another, we'll get them out."

Evan nodded, his head hung low until the sound of another engine caught his attention. Within minutes, the staging area was full of sheriff deputies and emergency crews. As the sun peeked over the eastern horizon, a rescue helicopter passed overhead only minutes before another one landed.

The sound of whirring blades whooshed into Sydney's dream, the image of her dad being lifted into the air, then dropped from a hundred feet up, rousing her consciousness. Sitting up with a start, she stared at the helicopter in the sky.

"Are you the Marksam family?" The voice echoed through the canyon from some kind of bullhorn.

Max jumped to his feet, waving and yelling "yes." Sydney and Tessa joined him, waving with more energy than Sydney had. Her entire body ached, inside and out. With that thought, she licked her swollen lips and tried to swallow. Dry slivers poked at the tender tissue of her esophagus, and she winced. Still, the excitement of the helicopter above kept her from dropping to her knees next to the dirty creek for a drink.

"How many of you are there?"

Sydney held up her right hand with all five fingers extended, her eyes begging her to cry.

"How many *cannot* walk?"

Sydney held up one finger, and yelled, "My dad!"

"How many cannot speak?"

Again, she waved her finger in the air. "My dad is hurt really bad!"

Words ran through Sydney's mind, hardly any of them worth speaking, yet every one of them bringing a rush of joy to her chest. *We're okay. We're okay. Dad's going to be okay.* Though tears refused to roll, her eyes burned with sandy grit and elation. She couldn't help but smile, and she ignored the pain of her cracked lips.

Sydney watched as a man appeared at the side of the helicopter, a harness wrapped around his legs. The sun had yet to rise above the canyon walls, but the bright sky still obscured her vision as the man began his descent to the ground. A few seconds later, he held out his hand to Jen, who had finally stood up, and introduced himself as Ryan. "Looks like Dad's hurt worst. When was the last time he spoke?"

Jen's mouth worked, and Tessa stepped closer to her, clutching her shoulder. Sydney bit her lip, meeting Ryan's eyes. "I think it was Friday."

"He hasn't spoken in three days?"

"In the afternoon, maybe evening," Sydney added. "He broke his ankle Thursday."

Ryan motioned to the helicopter, and another rescuer with some kind of soft emergency bed soon appeared in the air. "He's definitely dehydrated. Seems pretty warm now, though. Did he suffer any hypothermia? Trembling? Cold skin? The trembling may have stopped as he became more confused," Ryan said as he nimbly worked to assess Dad's needs.

Mom nodded. "Y-yes. It was pretty bad on Friday after the flood. W-we . . ."

As Mom's words trailed off, Sydney searched her face, then picked up where she'd left off. "They were in the canyon over there. M-my sister built a gurney that we used to carry him over here yesterday."

"It's a raft," Max blurted out. "She used grapevines to tie it together."

Ryan studied each of their faces, and Sydney, feeling a flush come to her cheeks, dropped her gaze.

"Walking miracles. Pretty sure that's what you guys are." Ryan looked up at his partner, who was unhooking himself from a cable. "This is my buddy Paul. He's going to ride out with your dad and make sure he makes it to the hospital okay."

Sydney stood out of the way, watching the men as they continued to assess her dad and situate him in a carrier that looked as much like a bag as a basket. The movement quickly became a blur of red and orange mixed with heart-wrenching nerves and exhaustion. She couldn't take it all in.

As she watched Paul and her dad be hoisted into the air, she overheard Ryan say her mom would be next.

Mom shook her head. "I'll go last."

"Ma'am, I'll be here with your kids the whole time. You should go next."

"No. I . . . I can wait." Mom's body shook as she tried to move away.

Sydney wanted to jump in, to tell her mom to go, but she couldn't. Fear gripped her, holding her captive. Despite knowing that her mother needed more medical attention than she did, Sydney struggled to give up the comfort she found with her nearby. She dropped to the ground, her knees already numb. Guilt swirled within her. How could she hold her mother back? Keep her from medical attention? How could she be so selfish? She couldn't. But she couldn't speak up either. She hung her head as her composure crumbled. Why wasn't she strong enough to send Mom?

Tessa's feet scratched at the ground as she stepped up to the rock where their mother begrudgingly allowed Ryan to clean and bandage her leg. "You gotta go, Momma," Tessa patted her shoulder.

Sydney watched from the side, as their mom shook her head. "He'll take care of me here. After that, a few extra minutes won't matter."

Evan stood on the outskirts of the first responders who waited for their turns to play a part in the rescue. So many had come out to help with a single boy, as far as they knew. Everyone hoped for more.

The engine of the second helicopter started and took off toward the canyon, yanking Evan's thoughts away. Within seconds, Officer Howard was jogging in Evan's direction. "Mr. Marksam, they found them. All of them. I can't believe it."

Evan dropped his hands to his knees as tears welled in his eyes. Looking up, he met the officer's gaze. "All of them? They're okay?"

"They're alive. Your brother, though, he's in bad shape. He's being short lifted here in what they call a bag. It's less bulky than a basket for rescues like this. He'll be moved inside the helicopter and then taken to the hospital in Flagstaff. After assessing his injuries, we think that's the best place to take him."

Evan nodded, allowing the tears to run down his face. "And the rest of them?"

"They're beat up, especially your sister-in-law and the oldest, but everyone's up and walking."

A bout of exhaustion surged through Evan. As much as he'd hoped, he'd not allowed himself to believe that Blake's family was alive. The realization struck him harder than he would have liked. Opening his arms, he wrapped them around Officer Howard. "Thank you. They're alive! Thank you so much." After pounding Officer Howard on the back, Evan let go of him. "I need to call my wife."

Less than five minutes passed before the helicopter carrying a litter with a dangling paramedic next to it came into view. Evan watched as his brother was lowered to the ground. Once the line was unhooked, the helicopter moved several yards away to land. Evan rushed over to his brother. "How is he?"

"He responds to stimuli. That's good," the paramedic said. "He's severely dehydrated, and he suffered hypothermia while down there. We don't know what damage that may have caused. And he has a broken ankle." The paramedic glanced at Evan. "He should be dead. I've never seen anything like this. Never."

Evan nodded. "Thank you."

All he could see of Blake was his face. Every other part of him was covered by an orange bag and black straps.

"Copter's down. We gotta move him." The paramedic pointed at the helicopter.

"See you soon, buddy." Evan stepped back and watched as a group of men carried his brother, alive, over to the waiting helicopter.

Minutes later, Evan stumbled to his truck to sit down. Michelle and the kids were already on their way home, but he hadn't had the chance to call his parents yet.

"Mom, he's alive. They're all alive," Evan cried into the phone.

"Thank you, Lord." His mother's voice trembled as she called out to his father. "They're all alive, Norm."

"Blake's still pretty bad, Mom. He's not fully conscious. They're flying him to Flag right now."

After he'd explained the situation to his mother, she handed the phone to Maggie.

"Hi, Daddy."

"Hey, Mags, bet you'll stop kissing boys now, huh?" Evan grinned, brushing leftover tears from his face.

"I haven't kissed any boys."

Evan laughed. "Oh, if you say so. Hey, Mags, I've got to check on Uncle Blake. He got hurt pretty bad. But I'm super proud of you going to the hospital and all. You sound a lot better."

"Yeah. I can swallow now."

"That's good. You keep resting, okay? I can't wait to see you. Super proud of you, Mags."

"Yeah," she said, pausing. "Daddy?"

Evan waited for her to continue.

"Will you tell Tessa hi and that the hospital isn't too scary?"

"I sure will, baby girl."

As he hung up, Evan scanned the area. A few sycamore and cottonwood trees stood in the distance. Not a single leaf swayed. The warm sun beat down on the group of men and women who had come to save his brother's family. One wiped at her forehead with a bandanna. It was weird to think of his brother suffering hypothermia when the temperatures were so warm.

Blake was alive.

The thought continued through his mind, and as much as he'd hoped for it, a part of him still struggled to believe it. In the distance, he saw a small body hanging next to a larger one from the bottom of a helicopter. It had to be Max.

As Tessa disappeared from sight, hanging below a helicopter, Jen turned her gaze to Sydney. "You're next."

Sydney's face crumpled, and she glanced between Jen and Ryan. "Can my mom go with me?"

Ryan smiled softly. "Sorry. Only one at a time."

Hiding her face in her hands, Sydney shook her head. "I c-can't."

Jen eased to her feet, every inch of her body screaming in retaliation, and she cringed, silencing her groan. As she hobbled over to Sydney, her emotions fought for attention. Joy at her family's rescue. Worry for Blake. Pain over her daughter's agony. That's where her focus was now. She laid her hand on Sydney's shoulder. Sydney grabbed her arm, and hugged it to her face, holding it like a lifeline.

"It's okay." Jen stepped closer and faced her daughter, cupping her cheek with her free hand. "You've done so much. It's time to let people take care of you. I'll be right behind you, promise."

With a gentle tug from Jen, Sydney stood up, her face twisted with fear. Jen wrapped her arms around her daughter, hugging her tight, feeling her tremble. "We'll be okay. All of us. But you have to go."

Sydney nodded as Jen let go and squeezed her hands.

"I love you," Jen said.

"Me too." Sydney fell into Jen's arms again, her body racked with tearless sobs, then, wiping at her grimy face, she stepped toward Ryan.

Their rescuer held out a harness similar to those used by Max and Tessa. "Paul's on his way. Let's get you strapped up."

A few minutes later, Jen's shoulders slumped forward with exhaustion as she watched the helicopter lift Sydney into the air. No matter what anyone said, Sydney had refused to go until Max and Tessa had. The paramedics had assumed she was trying to be brave. Jen knew the truth. For the second time in two days, her little bird didn't want to leave her side.

Her oldest daughter had done more than anyone would have thought possible: got her siblings to safety and made sure they had what they needed to survive . . . hiked over to Jen and Blake. Sydney had been one of the biggest factors in their survival. But in the last hour, Jen had watched the strength get zapped out of her daughter as she'd become a little girl again. One who still needed and wanted her mother. Even in her addled state, Jen could see the change.

Sydney's gaze hadn't left Jen. She'd even stopped answering Ryan's questions unless he specifically asked her, which forced Jen to take the lead. When Ryan had asked Sydney to leave after Blake, she'd become frantic but hadn't been able to express why. She just didn't want to was all she could say.

With everything Sydney had done, Jen didn't blame her. She herself wanted nothing more than to wrap her arms around her little bird and, once again, hold her close—this time never letting go. She wanted to do that with all of her children, but somehow, she felt a closeness to Sydney that she hadn't felt in some time. A gratitude and a responsibility—after all, Sydney was still her daughter.

"All right, ma'am, you're next."

Ryan had coordinated the rescue from their position since he'd first landed. Jen wondered if that's how it always worked. She'd probably never know. Holding out his hand, Ryan helped her to her feet. The abrasions on her leg had become infected, and putting pressure on it sent zings of agony up her bruised spine. It took away the sting that surrounded her ripped nail beds and the sticky dryness of her throat. No matter how much water she'd had, it hadn't been enough.

A little shaky—dizzy—she allowed Ryan to wrap the harness straps and what he called a strop around her.

"If it's all right with you, now that the fire's out and you're ready to go, I think I'll hitch a ride. Sound good?" Ryan put his hand on her shoulder. "You've done good, Momma. You've done good."

Jen curled her head into his shoulder, and he wrapped an arm around her and then gave the signal.

As her feet left the ground, she raised her head from Ryan's chest, embarrassment rising in her cheeks. "Thank you . . . for saving my family. For letting me go last."

"Thank you for making my job easy." Ryan chuckled. "I don't know how you did it. Entire families just don't survive stuff like this. I figured I'd spend the day searching for bodies—even after they said they'd spotted a survivor."

Jen didn't know how to respond. They should be dead. Every single one of them. But they weren't.

The air whipped through her tangled hair, reminding her of the wind from the day before—the bending of the tree. The sting on her face.

As she risked a look below, memories of roiling black sludge with entire trees tossed to and fro overtook more pleasant thoughts of floating in the cold water or taking in the beauty of the canyon with Blake.

Closing her eyes, she refused to think about any of it. All she wanted was to pull her family close and hug them. To hold Blake's hand and hear him laugh about their West Clear Creek adventure. Without opening her eyes, she rolled them. He'd laugh and talk about going again. She already knew it.

"We're about to touch down. When we do, I'll unhook you, but stay right with me. I'll help you get to the ambulance."

"Ambulance? I don't want . . ."

Ryan laughed. "Your husband is already at the hospital."

A small smile crossed Jen's face. "An ambulance."

She Needs Me

Jen sat in the bed next to Blake and wrapped her hand around his. His color was returning, and with a couple of bags of saline, he'd even opened his eyes a few times. Though Jen didn't know how much he remembered about his dream adventure in West Clear Creek. He hadn't stayed awake long enough for any kind of explanation.

Several doctors had moved in and out of the room over the past two days. Occasionally, they came to check on her, but most of the time they spent a few minutes checking on Blake. The combination of hypothermia and dehydration had not been kind to his body. Low blood pressure had led to some concern with his heart, and his kidneys had nearly shut down. Treatments that Jen would need a lot more information about to understand would lead to a slow recovery, but he would recover.

Gingerly rubbing her hand down her infected leg, Jen wondered at how close she had come to requiring the same treatments. Had Sydney not shown up—

"Beetle."

Jen lifted her head, then sat up further. "You're awake." The tears she had yearned to come so many times that week finally cascaded down her cheeks, landing on Blake's chest.

"Yeah." He swallowed thickly and took in the room, confusion, then recognition flooding his face.

"So, you slept through your first helicopter ride. How's it feel?" She pushed her fingers across her cheeks as she smiled.

"I what?"

"Do you remember breaking your ankle."

Blake cocked an eyebrow. "Yeah, but not being knocked unconscious."

Jen laughed. "That's not exactly what happened." As her heart filled with the last piece of warmth it had been missing, she told Blake the details of their family adventure.

Slowly, he nodded, processing all that she'd said. "Where're the kids now?"

"Evan took them home this morning. Once Max got some fluids in him and a prescription cream for his poison ivy, he started bouncing off the walls." Jen lifted her gaze to his, a gleam of playfulness entering her voice. "The hospital might pay us for sending him home."

He smiled. "Unlikely."

"Sydney's hands are being treated for infection. She ripped most of her nail beds open by climbing cliffs and digging in the dirt. But she's okay too." Jen dropped her head, eyeing her own split nails. "She did a lot. Kept the other two safe, found us. I . . . I realized something though."

Blake squeezed her hand.

"Going against every piece of training you've given her, she didn't stay put. She risked everything to come find us." Jen shook her head and wiped at her eyes. "I don't think it was to save us though. It was because she needed us. She needed me."

"She always will." Blake's voice sounded so scratchy, so strained.

"Maybe that need will stick around." Jen laughed. "She didn't want to leave today."

"She's still a teenager." Blake coughed. "Give it a few days."

Jen wrapped her arm around Blake's shoulders, then eased into his warmth. "Tessa impressed me too." She raised her gaze to the ceiling, quickly dropping it back to his chest where she traced the pattern on his hospital gown. "So many of my memories are hazy, but I'm pretty sure I remember her picking Sydney up and telling her that she could keep going. And there was something about getting back to Max, even if it was by herself. Blake, they left Max alone with a signal fire in way windy conditions."

Blake chuckled as he nodded. "He handled it." Then, shifting in bed, he groaned. "What is all this stuff?"

Jen grinned as she scanned the monitors and wires hooked to her husband. "Beats me. Something to do with your heart and kidneys. I was half out of it when you were hooked up. Evan handled everything. How's your foot?"

"I think it's still attached. Isn't it?" He straightened his back and looked toward his feet.

Jen nudged his shoulder. "Yes. Lucky you. I think I heard something about pins."

"You mean I've had surgery?"

The door swung a little wider. "Yes," a nurse said. "And you'll walk again soon enough. Until then, why don't you look at this dinner menu and tell me what you'd like?"

The nurse handed a menu to each of them as she ushered Jen back to her own bed.

Jen marked the page, choosing the broiled chicken breast with rice and green Jell-o, happy to finally be eating solid foods again. Handing the page back to the nurse, she looked at Blake, who glared at the menu and then at the nurse. "My options are Jell-o, chicken or beef broth, and a side of ice chips?"

The nurse scowled playfully at him. "Yup. You weren't going to get that, but when the doctor walked past and noticed you were talking to your wife, he changed your options."

With a little grumbling, Blake circled beef broth and handed the form back to the nurse. Jen giggled and held her hand out to him, wiggling her fingers until his hand entwined with hers.

As Jen relished the warmth in Blake's hand, the phone on the small table between them rang. Raising an eyebrow, she picked up the receiver. "Hello."

"Jen? Is that you?"

She grinned at the sound of her brother's voice. "It sure is, Charlie. I'm so glad you called."

"You are?"

"Of course I am. I'm always happy when you call."

"Mom said you and Blake are in the hospital. Are you sick?"

Jen looked at Blake, who sat listening to her side of the conversation. *Let me talk*, he mouthed. She held up a finger, telling him to wait.

"Blake's a little sick, and he broke his ankle. Guess what, I had to brace it like he taught us."

"Did you use a stick?"

Jen rubbed her injured leg. "Two."

"Wow! Are you sick?" Charlie asked gently.

"I'm getting better."

"Good," Charlie said.

Blake held out his hand and wiggled his fingers at Jen, asking for the phone.

248

"Hey, Charlie, Blake wants to talk to you."

"Okay. I love you. Get better."

"I love you too, buddy. I will. Hang on, okay?" Jen covered the receiver with her hand, and turned to her husband. "Not too long," she whispered.

"I'm fine, Jen. Hand it over," Blake whispered back, then, taking the phone, he said, "Charlie, I got to swim in a flash flood. I don't even remember it . . ."

Evan's truck rolled to a stop in his driveway, and he let his hands fall to his lap. Everyone was safe. Officer Howard had met him at the hospital. *You saw the smoke*, he'd said. Evan shook his head. He'd seen the smoke. He'd done exactly what everyone told him not to—did exactly what he knew he shouldn't, and he'd seen the smoke that helped find Blake's location.

They were trying to make him feel better, to bolster his mood. The minute the helicopter got into the air, they would have seen it. This time of year, rangers scoured the horizon for signs of forest fires. One of them, from some tower somewhere, would have seen the smoke too. Evan appreciated the kindness, but he should have stayed home. At least until they'd been found.

He was willing to admit that he was needed at the hospital. And since he was being honest, he'd admit that it was good for Blake's kids to see a familiar face when the chopper dropped them off at Bull Pen. Poor Sydney had been a mess—crying for Jen. He didn't blame her. He'd cried with his mom that morning too. Luckily, he'd been able to console Sydney before she was loaded into the ambulance. Jen riding in the same one hadn't hurt either.

Evan pulled out his phone and shook his head. Mrs. Butler had called him three times to find out when he was going to fix her crooked tile. He dialed her number.

"Mr. Marksam—"

"Mrs. Butler, have you watched the news recently?"

A long pause stilled the line.

"My brother and his family were pulled out of West Clear Creek after a flood this weekend. They're all alive, thankfully. That's why I haven't come to relay your perfectly straight tile."

"I didn't know."

"I figured you didn't," Evan said. "I'm going to spend the next few days with my family, if that's okay with you. Well, even if it isn't. But your cabinets should be there Wednesday, and I'll be over by Friday to fix your tile."

A momentary silence invaded the conversation, then Mrs. Butler cleared her throat. "You know, I've been thinking, I'm not sure I could ever really see that the tile was crooked. I probably mismeasured. I'm sorry to bother you, Evan."

"It's not a problem." Evan's voice softened. "You call whenever you need to, and I'll do my best to get to you in a reasonable amount of time and take care of any reasonable concerns."

"Of course. You've done a fabulous job. Maxwell and I will see you when you're available."

With a deep breath, Evan pushed the front door open.

"Daddy," screamed his three middle children.

He swung Emily up onto his shoulders, patted Danni's head, and ruffled Dylan's hair. "How's everything going here?"

"Momma's feeding Ellie, and Maggie won't let us use the TV remote." The seriousness on Dylan's face as he spoke made Evan laugh.

"Let's let Mags have the TV for a while. That way she's not out kissing boys."

"Hey!" Maggie's raspy voice called out from the other room. "I don't kiss boys."

"Not anymore." Evan chuckled as he sat on the couch next to her. "You know, guys, we have a pool party to reschedule."

Sydney fell to her bed. Now that she was home, she might be able to relax, but she still worried about her mom and dad. She guessed that was normal. Curling her fingers toward her palm, she examined her fingertips. Three of them were bandaged. The nurse told her to run lukewarm water over them twice daily for the next week. She had some pills she had to take too. Luckily, she wasn't thirsty anymore. Although, there was still no such thing as gross sounding food. Not unless someone mentioned grape leaves.

The house phone rolled into her leg as she shifted some pillows. Her cell phone was still in the car—wherever that was. Uncle Evan would take care of that—probably with Grandpa.

She wasn't sure why she'd grabbed the house phone. They only used it for emergencies, and it wasn't like she remembered any of her friends' numbers. None of them would understand anyway, though it would be nice if at least someone was around to talk to.

Grandma and Grandpa had moved their stuff over from Evan's house to help take care of them. Sydney rolled her eyes. At least Grandma was a decent cook.

The doorbell rang, and Sydney ignored it until Grandma called her. "Sydney, someone's here to see you."

Slowly rolling from her bed, she shuffled down the hall. Fully hydrated, her muscles still cramped.

As she turned the corner, she came face to face with Braden.

"Hi," she said.

"What's going on with you? Why are you ignoring my texts?"

Sydney sank into a chair. "I don't have my phone."

"Well, where is it? I wanted to take you out last night, but you were AWOL."

"You mean in the hospital after surviving a flash flood, right?"

Braden stared at her, then sputtered, "What?"

"Family backpacking trip. Camping. Canyon. Any of that ring a bell?"

"Oh, that's right. You went on that trip thing."

Sydney laid her head against the chair and pursed her lips. He'd never change. But that didn't matter. She'd made her decision. "So how'd Crystal like it when you asked her to go?"

Braden's eyes widened. "Um, I . . ."

"It's okay, Braden. We're through anyway."

He stepped back. "What do you mean?"

"I'm breaking up with you."

"What? Why?"

"Did I ever tell you that my parents met when my mom was in high school?"

Braden suddenly looked bored. "What does that have to do with—"

"They almost died this week." Sydney rubbed at a rough spot on her hand. "Watching them was so . . . so real. I don't think I'd ever done that before."

"Real?"

"Yeah. They were nice to each other."

"Okay."

"You're not nice to me, Braden."

"I—"

"I," Sydney interrupted him, "may not deserve what my parents have—yet. But I know I deserve better than you." Sydney stood up and prodded Braden toward the door. "You should spend more time with Crystal. I think she'd like that."

As Braden stepped outside, Sydney shut the door and smiled. The realization may have been long in coming, but after watching her parents care for each other, she had a better understanding of why, even as a teenager, respect mattered. More than that, she understood what a real relationship looked like. Well, the type of relationship she wanted to have anyway.

After padding down the hall to her room and easing back onto her bed, she picked up the house phone and dialed the number her mom had written down that morning.

"Mom?"

"Hi, Syd, I'm glad you called. Dad's been talking more since you left. He's been worried about you. Here, let me hand him the phone—"

"Can I talk to you for a minute first? I just broke up with Braden . . ."

Mothers and Their Daughters

Evan opened the door wide, allowing Blake—and his crutches—into the house.

"Is the job finished?" Blake asked.

"Finally. And we got five referrals to boot." Evan grinned as he swung the door closed behind his brother. "Jen, kids, everyone's outside."

"Sorry I missed out on all the excitement." Blake shuffled toward the back door.

"Mrs. Butler was anything but exciting," Evan said. "I just hope these new customers aren't quite so high maintenance."

"We don't have to take them."

"Eh. You're back in the office. It'll be fine."

The smell of hamburgers and hot dogs wafted through the humid, late-July air, and Evan rushed to the grill. "Sure you can't get in the water?"

"Oh, I'm sure I can. The brace comes off. I'm also sure that I don't have much desire to go swimming. Not this year."

Jen rushed over. "Ev, don't get him started."

Evan looked between his brother and sister-in-law. "About what?"

"Jen doesn't want to go back to West Clear Creek. Something about having had enough of an adventure for a lifetime."

Evan raised his eyebrows. "You want to go back?"

"Sure. It's not like I remember much about it," Blake said, straight-faced. "I mean, if I can handle a little flood when my mind is lost in the clouds, imagine what I could do in my right mind."

Jen shot Blake a dirty look, then joined Michelle at the edge of the pool.

"Your right mind is loony." Evan laughed.

A corner of Blake's mouth raised. "Maybe."

Evan turned away from the grill long enough to take in the chatter and laughter coming from the pool. "Where's Syd?"

"She's coming." Blake cleared his throat. "She's bringing her new boyfriend."

"Ah. Do we like this boy?" Evan asked as he pulled the hot dogs off the grill.

"I think so. Jen seems to think he's a nice guy. She and Sydney have been having late-night gab sessions recently. Sometimes with popcorn." Blake pointed out a blackened hot dog. "Pretty sure I only get about half of it."

"Popcorn?"

"Gossip."

"Mothers and their daughters," Evan shook his head, grinning. "A little mono, and Maggie doesn't leave Michelle's side."

Sydney's knee bounced as she waited for Collin to open her door. It had taken a bit for her to get used to that. Braden had never

256

opened her door, even when she could have used the help. But on her first date with Collin, when she'd jumped out of the car, he'd quietly said that his father had taught him to be a gentleman and that, if she would like, he would open doors for her. He'd been so adorable as he'd mentioned it that she couldn't say no.

As her door swung open, Sydney took Collin's hand and stepped into the blazing sun. The refreshing coolness they'd enjoyed while ice blocking had long since ended. Still, she stared at her uncle's house.

"A pool party." She shook her head. "Maybe Max will get in."

Collin chuckled. "Not so easy now, huh?"

"It's hot. That helps."

"We don't have to get in. We can just put our feet in, or hang out in the shade."

Sydney squeezed his hand. "Yeah. Let's go."

After knocking lightly on the front door, Sydney opened it wide, and together, she and Collin walked through the house and out the back door. Her mom immediately waved, smiling. Sydney waved back as she thought about how Mom had stopped skulking down the hall, pretending to be *passing by* when Sydney arrived home from a date.

"Do you want to get in?" Collin asked, bringing her attention back to him.

"I—"

Sydney was about to say she wasn't quite ready to try swimming yet, but then she noticed Tessa sitting cross-legged at the edge of the pool. Their cousin Maggie held on to the concrete deck, talking to her. Tears rolled down Tessa's cheeks, and she shook her head no.

"I'm gonna . . ." Sydney pointed at Tessa and walked away from Collin, who smiled softly at her.

Sinking next to Tessa, Sydney wrapped an arm around her. "It's tough, huh?"

Tessa nodded.

"I'm not sure how much I want to get in either, but I was thinking I'd start with my feet. At least then the sun won't feel so hot." Out of the corner of her eye, Sydney watched Collin climb into the pool with Max, who obviously had no problem with the idea of swimming. Of course, he refused to eat anything grape or lemon flavored.

"Want to do it together?" Sydney asked.

Tessa untangled her legs.

"On the count of three. We can start with our toes." She eyed her sister. "One, two . . ."

The cool water enveloped Sydney's toes, and with it, came the memory of playing in West Clear Creek after they'd walked the short trail in. She and Tessa had taken a few seconds to change their shoes just before Max fell in—without having put on his water shoes. They'd laughed so hard.

It wasn't the memory she'd expected. It wasn't the feel of cold grime brushing against her feet as she'd struggled to get up the cliff to safety. That was the memory she'd expected. She flung her foot out of the water, splashing herself and Tessa.

Tessa sputtered, then laughed. "Hey!"

A moment later, they were kicking splashes at each other until Tessa lunged off the edge and into the pool. Turning around, she pushed a wall of water at Sydney.

Sydney backed up as it struck, pulling her feet from the water.

Tessa backed up, her eyes wide. "I'm sorry. I'm sorry, Syd."

"I-it's okay. You didn't hurt anything." Sydney hadn't expected the fear to hit her quite the way it had. She hadn't been stuck in a flood. She'd only witnessed one. But the moment that wall of pool water struck her, her heart took off, pounding hard in her chest.

Flashes of their tents being ripped from the ground and dragged downstream rammed her mind. She hated it. All of it. But Tessa had jumped into the pool. She had made it into the water without reliving such trauma. Sydney didn't want to ruin that. "You're in the pool, Tess. Mags is waiting for you. Go on."

A second later, Collin pulled himself out of the pool and sat on the concrete next to Sydney. "You okay?"

"Yeah." Sydney smiled softly. "She splashed me when I wasn't expecting it. That's all."

Collin ducked his head to meet her gaze. "Do you want to go find some shade?"

"No." She exhaled. "I want to get in, but slowly."

"I can help you do that."

She nodded and eased her feet back over the edge.

"I'm gonna get in so I can help you better." Collin eased into the pool without a splash, then stood with his chest against Sydney's knees. "How about I lower you from your waist? Then there won't be any splashes, and I'll have you the whole time?"

Sydney's heart beat faster. She suspected it had as much to do with Collin helping her into the pool as it did with the idea of getting in. "Yeah, let's do that."

She scooted a little closer to the edge, and Collin took her by the waist, wrapping his arms around her and lifting her away from the decking.

As she gripped his shoulders, Collin met her gaze. "You still all right? I'm going to start lowering you now."

"I'm good."

The water rose to her waist, and then her chest. Her feet flattened on the bottom of the pool. Her heart still beat wildly, but the memories of West Clear Creek were gone. She gave Collin a quick hug. "Thanks."

"Hey, Collin, wanna play basketball with me?" Max pushed the ball toward them, a hopeful smile on his face.

Collin glanced at the hoop hanging over the pool. "Well, that depends," Collin said. "What do you think, Syd?"

"I think I'm cheering Max on. He's totally gonna whip you."

Jen jumped off the lounge chair and ran to the door the second she heard Sydney return after saying goodbye to Collin. She couldn't wait to hear about their earlier date. From what she understood, they'd gone ice blocking with a group of kids from school.

Collin, much to Jen's delight, had been nothing but respectful to Sydney. It wasn't that he opened doors for her—though he did—it was more that he put her wants and needs at the same level as his own. Sometimes higher.

Even more, Sydney didn't walk into the house looking lost anymore. In fact, she and Collin spent almost as much time at home, talking with Tessa and playing with Max, as they did on dates. It was refreshing, especially after Braden.

"Mom"—Sydney slid into her arms, giving her a hug—"guess what happened today. We ran into Braden and Crystal at the ice cream place once we finished ice blocking—oh my gosh, that was so much fun. Anyway, Crystal was hanging all over Braden, and he was trying to get away, and I couldn't help it. I kind of starting laughing. Braden got so mad, he yanked his arm away from Crystal and brushed past my shoulder. Collin pulled me out of his way just in time, then Collin kissed me on the cheek."

"He did? Was that the first kiss?"

"Mo-om." Sydney rolled her eyes. "No. I told you about that."

"Oh, that's right. That was a few nights ago when he dropped you off."

Sydney nodded. "Do you think Dad likes him?"

"Collin? Certain of it. Besides, it's not like you're going to marry him—not tomorrow anyway."

"Definitely not tomorrow, but maybe in a few years. How long after high school did you and Dad wait again?"

"In your case, not long enough." Jen put her arm around her oldest daughter, and they walked over to the lounger. Eyeing Blake, she shooed him away with the flick of her finger. As much as she needed time with him, she valued every minute she spent with her little bird.

Thank You for Reading Little Bird's Lullaby

Please take a moment to leave a review of *Little Bird's Lullaby* on Amazon.

Whether your reviews are three words or three hundred, they help others find great new reads and allow indie authors to publish more content.

Other Titles by Kameo Monson

When Love Is Lost

Finding Me Series
I NOT David
I NOT Buddy
I Joey
I Daddy (Download free from KameoMonson.com)

About Little Bird's Lullaby

The West Clear Creek Wilderness is 13,600 acres of marginally maintained wilderness (as dictated by the Wilderness Act of 1964). The rugged terrain, made up of steep cliffs, unmaintained trails, and several deep-water crossings, runs twenty miles from east to west, with Bull Pen being at the western end.

This is the once-untouched wilderness that my family was required to call "Ho-hum" throughout my teenage years. To do otherwise meant mock-correction from my father. He was convinced that if we referred to it by its correct name, everyone would rush in and ruin it, much like what has happened at Water Wheel Falls, which my family lovingly calls "Crystal Clears" because the pools were crystal clear into nineties.

As a teenager, I spent one night in West Clear Creek. That was it. I remember it was beautiful and green and the trail in was steep. We'd barely entered the canyon before we set up camp. Maybe we set up camp so soon because of how young my brother and sister were at the time. They would have been under ten. But I doubt that was the reason. Every one of us could set up a tent by ourselves by the time we were twelve. Regardless, after a night, the rain chased us out. Considering the various hikes my dad took us on, including a couple that followed deer trails instead of actual trails, in my mind, West Clear Creek remains the hardest.

So imagine my surprise when I learned that my son's scout troop planned to hike West Clear Creek as their varsity activity in 2014. Unfortunately, after a medical emergency struck one of my son's leaders, his scout troop added to the statistics of those who required rescue from the canyon.

As my writing ability increased, I itched to write a fictional version of their rescue. This book is what won the negotiation with my son. I could write about a rescue from West Clear Creek; it just couldn't resemble his. That seemed fair enough.

But what happened on his trip?

- One leader had a medical emergency.
- The troop fell behind schedule, with most of the troop coming out of the canyon several hours late.
- By choice, one leader and his two sons stayed in the canyon for an extra night and hiked to the top the next morning.
- The sick leader, his adult son, and one boy who chose to stay with them were rescued via helicopter the morning following the late arrival of the others.
- Detailed paperwork was on file with the Boy Scouts of America.
- Search and rescue was contacted shortly after the troop missed its arrival deadline.
- Coordinates of where to find those left behind were immediately available to rescuers.
- It was deemed that leaders had "done everything right."
- Everyone lived.

What about the flash floods?

I have no experience with flooding in West Clear Creek. And I've (thankfully) never experienced a flash flood. Instead, I spent many afternoons and evenings researching various aspects of flooding and hope to have set that scene well. I have a lot of gratitude for the US Forest Service, who took the time to forward my questions to the right person, Danielle. She answered the questions about flooding in the West Clear Creek Wilderness that I couldn't otherwise find answers to.

The US Forest Service website states that flash floods can occur any time of year within West Clear Creek. This is mirrored in the story line. The canyon has no warning devises, and no rescue will begin without search and rescue being notified of a missing hiker. In a personal email, Danielle, who works with the Verde Ranger District, told me that the roads in and out of the West Clear Creek area are extremely difficult to travel in wet conditions, and that they normally do not travel them for a day or two after a storm.

If you can't tell, some of my childhood has made it into this book. That said, none of the characters are based off any one family member, though Blake shares a couple of characteristics that I love about my dad. For instance, while camping in East Clear Creek, Dad once dashed down a hill at break-neck speeds to rescue his girls. Little did he know that he was running to rescue me from hikers who were about to discover my not-hidden-well-enough potty spot. Mom and my sisters were yelling out warnings. Also, like Blake, Dad always took his time to quiz us on first aid and our surroundings.

One other situation influenced this book, but it was completely accidental. My daughter was seventeen when I started writing *Little Bird's Lullaby*. It was shortly before dropping her off at Northern Arizona University that I wrote the tale that Jen and Sydney share at the beginning of the book. Sydney and my daughter have very little in common, but watching my daughter mature into the young lady she is definitely influenced that story line, and subsequently, the book's.

Acknowledgments

Little Bird's Lullaby required a lot of research, and I would be remiss if I didn't say thank you to those who helped me with it. My dad, Russ, who spent much of his life on various trails, listened to me work through how my characters would survive all that I would put them through. My sister Tanna, who is a wonderful nurse, checked my medical research, including conditions and their treatments. My amazing husband, McKay, helped me with coordinates (which were chosen specifically for their locations within the West Clear Creek Wilderness). He will always be better than me with anything number-related. Danielle Boulais with the US Forest Service not only answered questions, but also supplied me with links and maps. The information she provided was invaluable, especially when it came to the Marksam family's rescue.

Of course, more than research goes into writing a book. Author Jessica Marie Holt helped me work through the best way to write the children's story at the beginning of *Little Bird's Lullaby*. I also had a healthy number of beta readers help me locate those areas in the story that required a little more developmental oomph. Even though I edit professionally, I would be nowhere without my editor, Craig D. Barton. He understands that everyone needs another set of eyes, regardless of their abilities, and he never gives me a hard time about my ridiculous errors. Lara, owner of Wynter Book Cover Designs does incredible work. I am always thrilled to see what she comes up with. Somehow, she always knows what I'm thinking.

Thank you to each and every one of you. You have helped make *Little Bird's Lullaby* what it is.

About the Author

Kameo Monson grew up in Glendale, Arizona, where she picked cotton on the way to school through her kindergarten year and smelled orange blossoms on the way to church through junior high. The first time her husband, McKay, drove an hour across the Phoenix Valley to pick her up for a date, he thought she'd be surrounded by farmland. Unfortunately, most of that had been built up a decade previous.

When Kameo was still young, her parents allowed one family dog at a time, despite her begging. McKay has a harder time saying no. That's why they house three dogs, a cat, two guinea pigs, and four lovable rats. The fish is his. Kameo and her husband reached twenty-seven years of wedded bliss in June of 2022. They have four children, who range in age from adult to mid-teen.

Though Kameo studied music for two years at the local community college (before meeting McKay), she found her place within the literary arts. With a certificate in editing, she owns and operates KMonson Editing Services, where she helps others reach their literary dreams.

Pine and aspen trees regularly call to Kameo from the Mogollon Rim, and whenever possible, she escapes to the mountains with dreams of becoming a reverse snowbird.

Stay Connected:

Follow Me on Facebook: @KMonson.author
Follow me on Instagram: @KameoMonson
Visit my website at KameoMonson.com
Email me at KMonson.author@gmail.com

www.ingramcontent.com/pod-product-compliance
Lightning Source LLC
Chambersburg PA
CBHW020051180626
46812CB00006B/2273